To Sister R

You dear friend
Virginia purchased this
book for you!

Where
DID WE GO
Wrong?

Happy Reading!

MMS

MONICA MATHIS-STOWE

Copyright © 2011 Monica Mathis-Stowe

Cover designed by: Dzine By Kellie

Cover photos by: Roy Cox Photography

All rights reserved

Printed in the United States of America

The Literary Publishing Group

P.O. Box 1370

Temple Hills, MD 20757

www.MonicaMathisStowe.com

13 Digit: 978-0-9852209-0-7

10 Digit: 0985220902

What people are saying about Where Did We Go Wrong?...

Where Did We Go Wrong? is an honest portrait of modern relationships. It is part soap-opera, part daytime talk show and part late-night Cinemax movie. Brisk pacing, memorable players and snappy dialogue that will pique readers' interest as the characters struggle to balance their need for love and fulfillment with a desire to live an independent life. An enjoyable, lightweight read for anyone craving a mix of chick-lit drama and spicy romance. ~Kirkus Reviews

I've been an editor for more than 40 years and about 15 years of them were as a free-lancer. This story is excellent, one of the Top 2 I've encountered...great plotting, clearly drawn, sympathetic (or hateful) characters, crisp, realistic dialogue. I'm really impressed. I loved every minute of it. ~Noël Higgins, Editor, Durham, Connecticut

Where Did We Go Wrong? keeps readers in suspense until the very last page and leaves you wanting more. ~Tiphani Montgomery, Essence Bestselling Author of the *Millionaire Mistress Series*

A steamy, sexy and fun read with lots of page turning drama. ~K. Lowery Moore, Author of *When I'm Loving You*

This book is amazing! I found it hard to put my laptop down to stop reading it! Surprise after surprise! I'm pretty sure I went through every human emotion while reading it! ~Shatorra Alexander, African-American Fiction Book Lover

Dedication

In loving memory of DeShawn Antoinette Mallory.
My best friend forever. I miss you every day.

Acknowledgements

First, I would like to thank God. Without You, none of this would be possible. To my wonderful husband, Reggie, thanks for the love and support while I chased this dream of becoming a published author. I'm so proud to call you my husband. To my loving son, Shane, thanks for understanding when you had to give up time with Mommy so she could work on her book. I thank God every day for you. To the best mother in the world, Jean Miller, thank you for your unconditional love and talking me out of quitting this dream. You are a phenomenal woman and your three children are blessed to have you as our Ma. Special thanks to all my relatives in the Mathis, Stowe, Miller and Battle families. I love each and every one of you.

Kudos to my good friends and test readers Andrea Price-Lippitt and LaWanne Thomas for reading the first draft of this novel and telling me I had a story to tell. My pal Renee Latimore-Brown, I am forever in debt to you for not only reading and proofing this novel more times than I care to say, but also for talking me through my episodes of writer's block and keeping me on track when I took these characters off course. And last, but not least, hugs and kisses to Marlo Culver who listened to my dreams about writing a book and put me in contact with the right person to make it happen. My sincere thanks and gratitude to you four ladies for helping me make this happen.

To put this novel together, it took a network of talented people to make it happen. Starting with Azarel, CEO of Life

Changing Books, thank you for taking time out of your busy life to help this stranger who wanted to publish her book. It says a lot about your character and every ounce of advice you have given me is greatly appreciated. Thank you to editor Tina Nance of Perfect Prose Editing for working your magic on this novel and making it better than I ever could. I'm looking forward to working with you on my future novels. Kellie of Dzine by Kellie your talent is inspiring. Thank you for using your creativity to design my website, book cover and trailer. Thank you all for your hard work.

Special acknowledgments go to my beautiful and hard working cover models: Jasmin Burman, Lauren Dillard and Wendy Mackall. It was a long and trying road for this cover shot but you ladies stuck by my side when most others would've given up on me and I thank you so very much. Hugs and kisses to each of you. Erin and Roy of Roy Cox Photography, thank you for the beautiful photos. You are my official book cover photographer. Make-up Artist, Monica Cook, thanks for using your skills to enhance the cover models' beauty.

Although I try my best to remember everything all the time, I'm not perfect and I do forget. I apologize in advance if you have helped me during this journey and I forgot to mention you. Thanks to everyone for the love and support and I can't wait to hear your feedback.

Life is good!
www.MonicaMathisStowe.com
www.twitter.com/MMathisStowe
http://www.facebook.com/authormonicamathisstowe

Chapter 1

The bond between girlfriends, best friends, is unbreakable, Joy thought as she zigzagged and weaved through the Beltway traffic. She drove as fast and as calmly as she could with Gabby huffing and puffing through her labor pains in the passenger seat. Her normally light-skinned complexion turned a pale shade of red with each contraction, but she still managed to look beautiful through all her pain.

Joy glanced through her rear-view mirror at Maxine, who had decided to follow Joy and Gabby to the hospital in her mini-van, in case she needed to leave to tend to her family. She had already let three cars jump between her minivan and Joy's car. Since her friend didn't know how to get to the hospital, Joy thought Maxine would have attempted to follow her more closely. Drivers were definitely taking advantage of her careful driving, with the many "Caution-Baby on Board" stickers plastered to her bumper. She was so far behind, Joy couldn't see her anymore.

When Joy arrived at the hospital's emergency room entrance, she jumped out of her Toyota Corolla and ran inside the hospital to get help. Within seconds, she returned to the car with a nurse and an orderly pushing a wheelchair. She assisted Gabby into the hospital and left to find Maxine.

Back in her car, Joy pulled out her cell phone, and called Maxine. "Girl, where are you?" Joy asked, trying to sound calm. She didn't want to make timid Maxine more nervous than she already was.

"I'm lost. You were driving so fast, I couldn't keep up," Maxine whined.

Joy shook her head. "What exit are you near?"

"I see a hospital sign. Should I take that exit?" Maxine asked anxiously.

Joy sighed in frustration. "Yeah, follow the signs to the hospital. I'm gonna park my car in the garage and meet you in the lobby."

"Okay. Bye." Maxine hit the End Call button on her steering wheel as she took the exit.

Joy hung up and sped toward the parking garage. She turned into the first available spot and ran back to the hospital. She didn't want Gabby to be alone when she delivered.

Joy, Maxine, and Gabby had met at Morgan State University in Baltimore, Maryland. Maxine and Joy were roommates. Gabby stayed alone in the dorm room across the hall because her roommate never showed up. Most nights, Gabby didn't like being in her room alone, so she bunked with Maxine and Joy. By the end of their first semester, Gabby's mattress, clothes, and personal belongings were stuffed in Maxine and Joy's already overcrowded dorm room.

They got along well and became the best of friends. The following semester, they petitioned the Dean of Housing for a larger dorm room so they could stay together. They wouldn't have it any other way. They became the friends to each other that every woman should have in her life. No matter what they went through, they dealt with it together. They had no idea where they would be without each other.

Back in the hospital, after an exam revealed that Gabby had dilated nine centimeters, she was rushed into a delivery room. She grabbed the rails on the bed and squeezed her eyes shut during another contraction. "Ouch! Ouch! It hurts!" Gabby screamed between deep breaths.

After she was prepped for delivery, the private nurse assigned to her used a white cloth to dab at the sweat beads forming on Gabby's forehead. She smacked the nurse's hand away. The nurse stepped back and glared at Gabby as she crossed her arms over her chest.

Gabby's obstetrician, Dr. Fields, entered the delivery room with a comforting smile on his handsome face. He looked like he was fresh out of medical school.

"Hello, Gabrielle."

"Hi," Gabby moaned.

After Dr. Fields examined her, he removed his gloves and went to her bedside. "It looks like you're ready to deliver. Are you ready to meet your beautiful daughter?"

"I'm ready to get this over with!" Gabby looked around the delivery room. "Where are my birth coaches?" She grabbed the doctor's arm and squeezed so hard, her nails went through his skin.

"Oh, God! Ouch!"

Dr. Fields removed Gabby's hand and frowned at the nail imprint she left on his arm. He motioned for the private nurse to come help Gabby while he sat on a stool and rolled himself between Gabby's open legs. He looked at the door when he heard Joy and Maxine walk in. "Looks like your coaches finally arrived."

"Where have you been? It's time for me to push!" Gabby barked.

"I'm sorry. Maxine got lost, but we're here now so calm down," Joy said as she walked to Gabby's bed side. "Have you been doing your breathing exercises?"

"Oh, no! I need to go to the bathroom," Gabby cried.

Maxine brushed Gabby's long hair from her face before she took her place beside Gabby's leg. "Gabby, it just feels like that because it's time for you to deliver."

"Gabrielle, your coach knows what she's talking about," Dr. Fields said. "I need you to give me one good push."

"C'mon, Gabby, push!" Joy put her hand behind Gabby's back the way she had learned in Lamaze class.

Maxine pulled Gabby's left leg back while the nurse pulled the right leg. "Don't forget to breathe, Gabby," Maxine said in a cheery tone.

Gabby fell back after one push. "How much longer? I'm exhausted! Can't you just pull her out!"

"Unfortunately, I can't, Gabrielle. Come on now. It's time for another push." Dr. Fields looked up at Gabby from between her legs. "I need you to do your part."

"No! I can't!" Gabby shook her head like a defiant child refusing to obey a parent.

Joy got as close to Gabby's face as she could and screamed, "Get it together, Gabby! Your daughter needs you to push her out! Sit your ass up and push! Now!"

Gabby took a deep breath and pushed as hard and as long as she could.

"That was a good one, Gabby. Your daughter's head is almost crowning." Dr. Fields looked at the monitor for another contraction.

Maxine turned around to smile at Gabby. "See, Gabby. I knew you could do it."

"Shut up!" Gabby snapped.

Maxine's smile disappeared.

"Gabrielle, I need another good push from you," Dr. Fields said.

Gabby used all her strength to push again. "It's burning! Why is my vajayjay burning?"

"That's normal, Gabrielle. Don't worry, she's almost out. One more good push and you can meet your daughter."

Joy helped Gabby push while Maxine and the nurse pulled Gabby's legs back as far as they could.

"Oh, my God! She's here!" Maxine whispered.

"Is she all right?" Gabby asked as she fell back exhausted.

The delivery room was so quiet. The sound of the nurses suctioning the baby's nose and mouth echoed in the room. Gabby grabbed Joy's hand and squeezed it. Maxine rushed to Gabby's side when she saw the worried look on her friend's face. She took her other hand and brought it to her chest as she prayed silently.

"Why isn't she crying?" Gabby asked while trying to stretch her neck to see her baby.

"Give her a minute, Gabrielle," Dr. Fields said in a calming voice as he pushed the nurses aside to work on the baby.

Seconds later, they looked at each other with tears in their eyes when they heard Gabby's baby let out her first whimper.

"That's my girl!" Gabby shouted.

An hour later, Gabby was resting comfortably in her private maternity suite. She pushed the button on the remote to raise her bed and adjusted her pillow behind her back. "I can't believe I'm a mother!"

"I can't believe you get a room like this after giving birth. I had to share a room when I delivered both my boys and it didn't look anything like this," Maxine said. She walked around the room touching the draperies, flat-screen television, and fully stocked refrigerator to make sure her eyes weren't deceiving her.

Joy was sitting in a chair near the door. She stared at Gabby with a straight face and asked, "Did you call him? Because I'm not calling him for you anymore."

Gabby avoided Joy's gaze. She took a mirror, comb, and tube of lip gloss out of her purse and began combing through her shoulder-length, chestnut-brown hair. "We worked everything out through our lawyers. He doesn't want to be her father because of his wife and children. I respect that as long as he takes care of my little girl financially," Gabby replied.

"What is William's role in all of this?" Maxine asked.

William had been Gabby's boyfriend until she broke up with him to start dating Rayshawn Robinson, a quarterback for the Baltimore Ravens. He was better known as R&R in the NFL and to his fans. Gabby knew she hit the jackpot after R&R signed a $75 million-dollar contract with the Ravens. She had one obstacle standing between her and Rayshawn's millions: his family. She stopped using birth control the day R&R signed his new contract. Gabby knew that the best way to get part of his millions was to have his child. She seduced Rayshawn night and day. He didn't complain when she told him to stop using condoms because they felt uncomfortable. He enjoyed spending time with her because she was beautiful and she often left him in tears after they had sex. He enjoyed every bit of what she gave him, so now he needed to pay up.

Gabby looked at Joy and Maxine with a serious expression. "William will be her father. He believes she's his child and that's how we're going to keep it." Gabby placed the mirror, comb, and lip gloss on the tray attached to her bed. She then shook her head in their direction, waiting for them to agree with her.

"This lie is going to come back and bite you in the ass," Joy snapped and frowned.

"This is not a good idea, Gabby. This one lie can hurt so many people," Maxine reasoned.

The nurse entered the room with Gabby's newborn baby girl in a white bassinet. She was tightly wrapped in a pink blanket with a pink cap over her head. After the nurse placed the baby in Gabby's arms and left, Maxine and Joy stood on each side of the bed to get a closer look at their new goddaughter.

"She's beautiful, Gabby," Maxine whispered with tears in her eyes.

"Of course she is, Maxine. I wouldn't make an ugly child," Gabby declared. "Thank God she takes after my side and not Rayshawn's. I wonder why I even slept with him." Gabby let out a deep sigh and shook her head.

"Let's keep it real, Gabby. You slept with him for the money." Joy looked across the bed at Maxine who was shaking her head and smiling in agreement.

Dr. Fields entered the room. Gabby quickly passed the baby to Maxine and sat straight up in the bed, giving the doctor her full attention. Maxine stood beside the bed gently rocking the baby in her arms. Joy stepped away from the bed and walked over to the large picture window so the doctor could have access to Gabby.

Joy stared out the window overlooking the parking lot. A couple holding hands was walking across the lot kissing each other every few steps. It made her heart ache for Allen. She wasn't looking forward to calling him and cancelling their plans for the long Memorial Day weekend. She knew he wasn't going to be happy.

"Dr. Fields, are you listening to me?" Gabby shrilled as

her light complexion turned an angry shade of red.

Dr. Fields was staring at Joy's butt in a pair of tight Guess jeans. Her jet-black curly hair, inherited from her Puerto Rican father, fell down her back, stopping at her narrow waist. He was mesmerized by her caramel complexion and womanly curves. Joy turned around and caught him staring at her. She gave him a polite smile before she stepped out of the room to call Allen.

Dr. Fields kept his eyes glued to Joy's butt until she was gone. "Sorry, Gabrielle… umm, is your friend single?" he asked.

Gabby rolled her eyes at the doctor and reached for the baby. "No! She's been with her boyfriend since they were teenagers." She whined like a spoiled child who couldn't have her way.

Maxine turned her head and giggled. When the doctor left the room, he saw Joy and smiled at her again. She was having an intense phone conversation so she turned her back to him.

"Allen, baby, I know you're upset. But I promise I'll make it up to you," Joy pleaded.

"I was looking forward to a four-day weekend with you. Now we have to change our plans because Gabby had a fucking baby. Bullshit!" He hung up.

Joy swallowed hard and wiped the tears that were forming in her eyes. She hated disappointing Allen. She loved him too much to hurt him. She took a deep breath and exhaled before she walked back to Gabby's maternity suite.

"Joy, Dr. Fields couldn't keep his eyes off your behind," Maxine said, laughing.

"Most men can't," Gabby barked and rolled her eyes. She thought Dr. Fields was going to ask her out after she delivered.

Joy ignored both of them. She sat back in the chair near the front door and massaged her temples with her fingertips. Maxine and Gabby looked at each other with raised eyebrows.

"Gabby, you haven't told us our goddaughter's name. Have you decided yet?" Maxine asked.

Gabby looked at her daughter and said, "Yes, I have. Her name is Nadia Rae Roché."

Joy stopped massaging her temples and looked at Gabby

with such hatred; it made Gabby's eyes bulge. Joy jumped out of her chair with so much force, it fell back and slammed into the wall before it crashed to the floor with a loud thump.

The baby let out a soft cry as if she knew something was wrong.

Maxine gasped and shook her head. "No, Gabby! Ever since we've known each other, Joy has always said she wanted to name her daughter Nadia. What you're doing is unacceptable! Her middle name is Rae after her real father! Unbelievable! What's William going to say about that?"

Joy walked toward the bed with her index finger pointed at Gabby. "This is crossing the line even for you."

Gabby ignored her and focused her attention on Maxine. "Everybody can't have a perfect life like you, Maxine. I would love to have a husband who's a lawyer and wants me to stay home to care for our two children, but it didn't happen that way for me. I refuse to be poor and struggling all my life. I'm going to make a good life for us." She looked at Nadia and smiled.

"Are you serious, Gabby? Do you really think my life is perfect? My husband leaves at seven o'clock every morning and doesn't get home until after eight o'clock most nights. I'm stuck in the house all day with two young children watching the Disney channel while all my friends are enjoying their lives and careers." Maxine, with her mocha complexion, short pixie hair-cut, and petite frame, looked more like a high school cheerleader than a married woman with two young sons. She waved her arms in the air and smacked her lips. "While I'm eagerly waiting for my husband to come home for some adult conversation, he's too tired to talk to me. I lose a little bit of myself every day. The only difference between us, Gabby, is I don't drag anybody else into my drama. I deal with it myself." Maxine stopped herself from saying anything else. She didn't want to burden her friends with what was really happening in her household.

"If it's that bad, go get a job. You have a bachelor's and a master's degree in education. I'm sure Prince George's County Schools will hire you back."

William walked in the room with a grin as wide as the

8

door frame. "Hey, hey! How are my girls?"

Joy finally took her cold stare off Gabby and looked at William. "Hi, William, I was just leaving."

"Joy, don't leave because of me." William hugged Joy and then Maxine. "Aren't you going to congratulate me on becoming a father? Gabby wouldn't let me in the delivery room, but I'm here now and ready to meet my daughter."

Joy felt her temperature rise as she looked at the contented smirk on Gabby's face. "William, I think there is something you need to know about the baby."

Gabby cleared her throat and said, "Thanks, Joy, but we're not listening to any unsolicited advice on how to care for *our* daughter. We'll figure it out." Gabby reached her hand out for William. He ignored Joy and ran to Gabby's side.

Maxine held her breath as her eyeballs went back and forth between Joy and Gabby as if she were watching an intense tennis match.

William held Gabby's hand and said, "We're new parents, Gabby, so we need to listen to people who've already been through this. Maxine has two children; maybe she knows something that can help us out."

Joy and Gabby stared at each other uncomfortably for a few seconds. William didn't notice because he was staring at Nadia.

Joy gave in with a sigh, "Let me go so the happy family can spend some time together."

Gabby looked at Joy with a strained smile and said, "thank you for everything, Joy."

Joy snatched her Gucci handbag off the windowsill and left the room without saying another word. How was she going to pass up her plans to spend a long weekend with her man in Atlanta to play nurse maid to Gabby's selfish ass? She called Allen, but got his voice mail. "Hi, baby, change of plans, I'm on my way. I'll text you my flight details." Joy stepped onto the elevator, smiling ear to ear, knowing that in a few hours she was going to be in Allen's bed having the best make-up sex they'd ever experienced.

Chapter 2 ————————————

Later that night, Joy arrived at Hartsfield-Jackson Atlanta Airport excited about seeing Allen. After she left the hospital, she drove home, breaking all speed limits. She grabbed her packed carry-on bag and rushed to the airport. She had called Southwest Airlines and was able to change her flight for one that was leaving an hour later than the one she was booked on. She was charged a large fee, but it was worth every penny, knowing Allen was going to be waiting for her when she arrived.

When she landed, she turned on her phone, put on her Bluetooth and called Allen the minute she stepped into the terminal.

"Hi, baby. I'm here. You can pick me up at the usual gate." For the last six years, Joy had traveled to Atlanta every other weekend to visit Allen. The weekends she didn't go there, he flew into Washington National Airport or Baltimore Washington Airport to visit her.

"I'll be there," Allen said in an agitated tone.

Joy walked as fast as she could to meet Allen. She didn't like the way they left things earlier and he didn't sound like himself. He never hung up on her, no matter how angry he was and it concerned Joy. They had a terrific relationship. The sex was mind-blowing and they could talk to each other about anything for hours without getting bored.

11

She stepped out of the airport and looked around for Allen's truck but didn't see him. She decided to wait a few minutes, thinking the police made him move. He approached her while she was looking down the street for his truck.

"Hello, beautiful." Allen grabbed Joy around her waist and picked her up off the ground, causing her to drop her bag.

"Allen!" Joy wrapped her arms around his neck and kissed him hard on the lips. Every time she saw Allen, it was always like her first time. Her heart beat faster, she became warm all over, and she couldn't stop smiling no matter how hard she tried. His perfect milk-chocolate complexion and smoky black eyes blended perfectly with his bald head and neatly trimmed goatee. He was too sexy for words. Whenever she saw him after being apart, she wanted to super-glue herself to him forever because he felt so damn good.

He put her down and held her face close to his while he kissed her a few more times. "I'm sorry for hanging up on you like that. I was wrong."

"No, I should've never changed our plans for Gabby's selfish ass."

Allen stepped back and arched his eyebrows. "Uh-oh, what did she do this time?"

"I don't want to talk about it. I want to spend every second until I leave Monday night, focusing on you."

"Oh, shit! That sounds good to me. Let's go home so you can get started." Allen licked his lips playfully.

Joy smacked him on his butt. "Let's go. Where's the truck?"

"I parked in the garage so I could give you a proper greeting without the police pressing me to keep it moving."

They held hands and smiled at each other as they walked to the garage and got in his 2008 GMC Yukon Denali. Allen opened the door for Joy and helped her in, then put her luggage in the back. When he got in the truck, he leaned over and gave Joy a long, passionate kiss with tongue.

"What was that for?" Joy smiled seductively.

"Love and happiness, baby." Allen smiled at Joy as he

started his truck.

"I love you, too." She smiled back at him.

They were in the truck holding hands on the way to his apartment when Joy's phone rang. She used her free hand to answer it using her Bluetooth. When Joy heard her mother's voice, she pulled her hand away from Allen and said, "Oh, hi, Bea. What's up?"

"Gabby called me earlier and told me she had the baby."

Joy smacked her lips. "Yeah, and did she tell you the baby's name?"

"No. What is it?"

"It's Nadia. She named her daughter Nadia Rae Roché."

Bea sighed. "Joy, I'm not surprised. Don't let that end your friendship. Knowing Gabby, she probably thought stealing your baby's name was a tribute to you. What do you have planned for the holiday weekend?"

"I'm in Atlanta visiting some friends. I'll be back Monday night."

Joy glanced at Allen. He was frowning and gripping the steering wheel with both hands.

"Ummm...well, thanks for letting me know that. I'm just your mother. It would be nice to know where you are once in a while."

"Um-hum." Joy rolled her eyes.

"These must be good friends in Atlanta because you spend a lot of time there. When can I meet these friends?"

"Alright, Bea. Too many questions, time to go. I'll call you when I get home. Have a good weekend. Love you." Joy shook her head, annoyed at her mother.

"Well, since you're rushing me off the phone, love you, too. Bye."

Joy hung up then reached over to touch Allen. He pulled away.

"I'm sorry, baby."

"Why after all these years, Joy, am I still a fucking secret to your mother? I've known Bea all my life. She's best friends with my sister who practically raised me. If Tyesha doesn't have a problem with us being together, why would Bea? Huh?" Allen looked at Joy in frustration.

Joy touched Allen's thigh. "You know how controlling and nosy Bea is. If she knew about us, she'll find a way to tear us apart and I just don't want her in my business, Allen. She'll know about us when the time is right."

"Yeah, okay." Allen relaxed his grip on the steering wheel.

She half-smiled at him. "Are we good?"

Allen exhaled. "Yeah, we good. I've been meaning to tell you that I'm involved in a special project for work. If things turn out, Joy, our lives are going to change for the better. I'll get a pro-motion that would put me in another tax bracket." He held his hand out to Joy. "I just need to know if you're with me or not."

She put her hand in his and said, "I'm always with you, baby, no matter what. I'm with you. Now, tell me more about your project."

"I'll let you know everything in time." Allen smiled.

Joy squeezed Allen's hand and smiled back at him. "I'm proud of you."

"Thanks, baby." He kissed her hand.

When they arrived at his apartment, Allen's roommate Tim, was lying on the faux black leather sofa in the living room watching an NBA play-off game on their fifty-two inch flat-screen. Owen was barely over five feet tall with a pale complex-ion, buck teeth, kinky hair, and he wore thick glasses that made his eyes look like they were popping out at you in 3-D; but he was sweet as pie and had a heart of gold. Joy often wished Owen could find a woman who could get past his looks and see him for the decent man he was. She knew how shallow most women were and knew they wouldn't give him a first, let alone a second look.

"Hi, Owen," Joy said as she entered the apartment.

"Oh no! You're here! I won't get any rest this weekend," Owen joked. He couldn't count the number of times he had walked in on them over the years. He knew whenever they were in the mood for each other, nothing, not even a roommate entering the apartment, was going to stop them from fucking.

Joy put her finger on her lip, fluttered her long eye-lashes, and whispered, "I promise to be quiet when we have sex."

They all laughed.

"I know we can be loud and outrageous with our sexca-pades, but I promise to behave this Memorial Day weekend. Right, Allen?" Joy looked at Allen.

"Hell, no!" Allen picked Joy up and said, "I'm ready to do you right here, right now!"

She kissed Allen on his forehead before he put her down. "Sounds good to me, but I wanna take a shower first."

"Go ahead, I'll be back there in a minute. I want to catch some of this game," Allen replied as he sat beside Owen on the sofa.

"Good night, Owen," Joy said as she left for Allen's room.

Owen waved. "Alright, Joy."

Joy walked through the living room and turned left to-ward Allen's room. He had the master bedroom with a private bathroom and balcony. She took a long, hot shower, put lotion over her body, and put on a Betsey Johnson sheer, pink night-gown. She reached in her bag and took out her journal and pen and laid across the queen-size bed to write about her day. Within seconds, Joy was asleep with the pen in her hand.

After the game, Allen walked in the bedroom and smiled when he saw Joy stretched across the bed, snoring. He removed her journal from the bed, took the pen out of her hand, and put them back in her bag. He pulled the covers back, picked Joy up, and laid her back on the bed. She never woke up. After he took a shower, he fell asleep beside her.

The next morning, Joy woke up feeling refreshed and well rested. She brushed her teeth and washed her face then put on a pair of Daisy Dukes, a tank top and a pair of flip flops. Since Allen was still sleeping and she was hungry, she went in the kitchen to cook breakfast.

She had a pan of bacon sizzling on the stove and was standing at the sink cutting potatoes when Allen entered the kitchen. "Baby, what are you doing? You know I like to wake up inside you when you're here." He wrapped his arms around Joy and started kissing her neck.

"You have some serious morning breath going on, sweetie." Joy laughed as she pinched her nose and lips together.

"Oh yeah, well, you smell good." Allen unbuttoned her jean shorts and pulled them down to her ankles.

"Baby, I'm trying to cook breakfast." Joy stepped out of her shorts.

"I already know what I want to eat for breakfast." Allen gave Joy a wicked smile.

He got on his knees and started licking her between her legs. He raised his arm over his head, grabbed her breasts and started squeezing her nipples. She was trying to stay quiet so she wouldn't wake Owen. Her eyes were rolling back in her head as she gripped the front of the stainless steel sink with one hand and the hunter-green laminate countertop with the other. She put her foot on his shoulder and pushed his bald head further between her legs as she moved in rhythm with his licks.

Owen walked in the kitchen, jumped, and covered his eyes when he saw them. Joy could hear him yelling, "Jeez, boundaries, dude! Come on!"

Joy's legs buckled as she climaxed. Allen carried her to the couch, laid her on her stomach, and entered her from the back. Within minutes, they were both screaming in ecstasy.

Allen sat up. Joy turned on her back and said, "Owen walked in on us again."

"Shit, he should be used to us by now," Allen said and started laughing. "Babe, I need to work on this project for a couple of hours today so if you want to go out for a while..."

"Trying to get rid of me, are you?" Joy rolled her eyes at Allen.

He kissed her. "Never, babe. I'll only be there for a couple of hours. Is that alright?"

Joy sat up and stared at Allen but didn't say anything.

Allen pulled on one of her curls. "I don't have to go."

Joy frowned. "I thought this holiday was *our* weekend. We don't get long weekends too often."

"You're right. I won't go. What would you like to do today?" Allen put his hand to his ear to show Joy he was listening

16

to her.

Joy looked at Allen and tilted her head. "I'm fine with you going to work. I'll call my friend Celeste from grad school to see if she wants to have lunch and do some shopping."

"Sound like a plan. I'll give you some money before I leave." He rubbed her leg.

"Thanks! I'll buy something real sexy for you." She winked at him.

Allen smiled. "Yeah, that's what I thought."

They walked to the bedroom. Joy got in the shower while Allen stood at the sink brushing his teeth. Her cell phone rang.

Joy peeked through the shower curtain. "Baby, can you get that for me. It might be Gabby or Maxine calling about Nadia."

Allen wiped his mouth and ran to get Joy's phone off the dresser. He looked at the caller ID to make sure it wasn't Bea calling. It read PRIVATE CALLER.

"Hello?" Allen wondered who was calling Joy from a private line.

"Who this?" Rayshawn asked, expecting Joy to answer her cell phone.

"Oh, you must have the wrong number," Allen reasoned.

"I'm looking for Joy," Rayshawn barked into the phone.

"Who is this?" Allen felt heat shoot through his body as he gripped the phone tighter.

"None of your fucking business. Put Joy on the phone. I need to talk to her. Now!" Rayshawn demanded.

"I don't know who the fuck you are but you don't call my girl's phone and tell me to put her on the fucking phone," Allen screamed.

"Oh, I see. I can respect that. This Rayshawn. She know me." Rayshawn backed down when he realized he was talking to Joy's man.

"But, I don't know you, mother-fucker!" Allen paced around his bedroom with his chest heaving up and down, while trying to control his breathing.

"Everybody know me, man. I'm Rayshawn Robinson, better known as R&R, the best fucking quarterback in the NFL. Now put your bitch on the phone!" Rayshawn yelled to show his impatience with Allen.

"Fuck you!" Allen pushed the End button and threw the phone across the room.

Joy stood in the bathroom dripping wet with a towel wrapped around her. She stared at Allen with wide eyes while biting her bottom lip.

Allen stared at Joy with narrowed eyes. "You better have a good explanation as to why an NFL quarterback is calling your cell phone and questioning me about where you are!"

Joy stood in the bathroom looking like a deer caught in headlights. "Ummm...I can explain."

Chapter 3

Gabby was released from the hospital on Memorial Day and the hospital staff was happy to see her go. She mistook staying in a maternity suite at Holy Cross Hospital for a stay at the Four Seasons in Georgetown with a full-service staff. When William wasn't at the hospital catering to her every need, she expected the hospital staff to fill in for him.

When Gabby and Nadia arrived at William's home in Bowie, Maryland, she saw all her belongings neatly stacked in his living room and became instantly irritated.

She glared at him. "William, why are my things thrown around the living room like trash waiting for pickup? My designer clothes and handbags need to be hung in the closet. What were you thinking, William?"

William shrugged and ran his hand through his thick, curly hair. His vanilla skin turned pink from shame. "Sorry. I didn't have time to put it away. I had to move your things from Joy's apartment and then rush back to the hospital to be with you and Nadia. I planned to do it today, but you were released and I had to pick y'all up."

Gabby snapped her fingers twice. "Excuses, excuses. Did you get Nadia's nursery together?"

"Yep, it's ready. Moms came over last night and helped me." William smiled, eager for Gabby to see their hard work on the nursery.

"Whatever," Gabby whispered under her breath. She knew William's family didn't like her and questioned if he was Nadia's father since he and Gabby weren't together when she conceived. She had a plan to deal with them later.

William took Nadia out of her carrier and followed Gabby upstairs to the nursery. "I think you'll like it."

Gabby smacked her lips and rolled her eyes. "We'll see. Let's get her settled, then you can unpack my things while I get some rest. Oh, I need to return a few calls, too."

They entered the nursery and Gabby walked around the room, shaking her head side to side. "No, no, no," she began chanting. William's and his mother's idea of decorating the nursery was to tape tacky pink rabbits on the plain white walls. The only thing that stood out in the room was the custom-made, cherry wood crib Gabby had ordered when she was in her second trimester. Nadia's nursery proved to Gabby what she always suspected. William's family had no taste, class, or style.

She opened the nursery's closet and was glad to see all of Nadia's clothes neatly hung and arranged by their sizes. "The closet looks nice, William. We have to work on the nursery later. I don't want our daughter to get used to living in tackiness."

William looked at her with a straight face. "You do know this was my first time decorating a nursery and I know it's been years for my Moms."

Gabby shook her head. "Whatever. Just put Nadia in her crib so I can get some rest."

After they left the nursery, William said in a low voice. "I made the bed with the sheets you wanted. You can lie down while I unpack your clothes." He opened his bedroom door for her.

"Good idea." She smiled and kissed him on the cheek before she entered the bedroom. "Thank you for taking care of me."

William's face lit up like a Christmas tree. "You're welcome, Gabby."

On her way to the bed, she glanced at herself in the mirror hanging over his dresser and was glad to see that her stomach was going down. That's the one gene she could thank her lazy mother, Dee Dee, for. After giving birth to seven children, Dee Dee would be back to her normal weight by her six-week checkup. Gabby's size 36B breast had grown a full cup size since she had Nadia. She had cleavage she never had before without wearing a pushup bra. She hoped they stayed this size after she stopped breast feeding.

She called out to William before he left the bedroom. "While you're putting my things away, I need to call Joy. Can I have some privacy, please?"

William looked at Gabby with arched eyebrows. She had never needed to talk to Joy in private before. Since she just moved in, he thought it was best to not question her so he left the room and closed the door behind him.

Gabby waited a few minutes, then opened the bedroom door to make sure William wasn't within earshot. She really needed to call Rayshawn. He had been burning her phone up with nonstop calls since Nadia was born. She hoped he wasn't trying to change their plans. She didn't want to think about all the problems that would cause.

After she settled back on the bed, she took her cell phone out of her purse. It rang before she could dial Rayshawn. She answered it quickly so it wouldn't wake Nadia.

"Hello," Gabby snapped.

"Gabby, I have something to tell you!" Joy screamed into the phone.

"Joy? Are you over your juvenile temper tantrum?" Gabby placed the phone between her ear and shoulder so she could inspect her manicure.

"Be quiet, Gabby! I need you to listen to me!"

"Uhhh...Does this have to do with me using your baby's name? It's been four days now. Get over it." Gabby lay back on a pillow and closed her eyes, bored with Joy's conversation.

"Goddamn it, Gabby! Rayshawn called me Saturday morning!"

Gabby sat straight up, snatched the phone from her shoulder, and pushed it to her ear. "Why does he have your number?" Gabby asked accusingly.

"He must've saved it when I called him for you," Joy said

defensively.

Gabby smacked her lips and shook her head. "What did he say? And it's Monday; why did it take you so long to call me with this?"

"Because I didn't talk to him, Allen did, and he's been pissed off about it the whole weekend!"

Gabby tried to catch her breath. "Oh...this is not good."

"You got that right. This is the first time all weekend Allen hasn't been stuck to my side waiting for Rayshawn to call back." Joy sighed. "Whatever he said to Allen on the phone threw him for a loop. He's ready to kill Rayshawn."

"I should give him Rayshawn's address so Allen and his thug brothers can go over there and kill him." Gabby laughed out loud at the thought.

"Gabby, this shit is not funny! Allen actually accused me of having something with Rayshawn."

Gabby giggled. "Yeah, right. Allen knows you'll never cheat on him. He's the only man you ever had sex with. Another ding-dong in your stuff will probably send off all kinds of alarms in Allen's head. He's just feeling a little threatened because another man called you. Give him a blow job or do something kinky you've never done before and he'll forget about it."

"Girl, please. He *didn't* forget about it and those games don't work on Allen. He was so mad, I had to tell him the truth."

"What truth?" Gabby asked through clenched teeth.

"Your truth about Nadia. There was no way I could get around it. I tried, but he knew I was lying." She held her breath and waited for Gabby's reaction.

"Some kind of friend you are, Joy!"

"Excuse me, Gabby! EXCUSE ME! I'm the *kind of friend* who let you live with me rent free when you quit your job at Nordstrom after you found out you were pregnant. I'm the *kind of friend* who took hundreds of messages from your baby's daddy when you were trying to avoid him. I'm the *kind of friend* who missed my evening classes so I could go with you to Lamaze class. I'm the *kind of friend* who didn't kick your ass for taking a name I picked for my daughter when I found out it was what my father wanted to name me when I was born. Should I go on about the *kind of friend* I am?"

"Girl, you are soooo dramatic." Gabby exhaled and rolled her eyes. "What's Allen gonna do?"

"Well, he's still a little upset about Rayshawn's call..."

"Forget about Allen being upset! What is he going to do now that he knows William is not Nadia's father?"

"Nothing. He said he wanted no part of it and doesn't want Rayshawn to ever call me again. If he does, then you'll have something to worry about."

Gabby's body relaxed. "Good to know. I'll take care of it. Oh, I thought it best to move in with William so you wouldn't have to worry about Nadia keeping you up. You know with you working, going to school, and flying to Atlanta all the time. I didn't want your goddaughter to be a burden. Wasn't that considerate of me? Now, see what *kind of friend* I am."

Joy couldn't help but laugh at Gabby's twisted way of thinking. "Bye, girl."

Gabby threw the phone on the bed and jumped up. She paced around the bedroom while trying to think of a way to handle the situation. She felt confident that Allen wouldn't say anything because he worshipped Joy and didn't want to break her trust. Rayshawn, on the other hand, was starting to be a problem and she needed to deal with him before he showed up at her front door demanding to see Nadia.

She peeked out of the room again to make sure William wasn't nearby. She closed the door quietly and walked back to the bed, picked up her cell phone, and dialed Rayshawn's private cell number.

She knew he had used his caller ID to see it was her because he just starting yelling, "Why haven't you returned my fucking calls? My lawyer told me you had the baby."

"Yep, sure did," Gabby said in a nonchalant tone.

"Well, what's her fucking name, bitch?"

"Rayshawn, I don't respond well to ignorance. In case you forgot, I don't curse, drink, or smoke because it doesn't fit the image I want to portray. I also don't allow others to talk down to me, so if you want to continue this conversation, use some self-control."

"How's my daughter?" Rayshawn barked into the phone.

"Fine."

"Give me some goddamn details!"

"Bye, Rayshawn." Gabby was ready to push the End button but changed her mind when she remembered that Rayshawn called Joy.

"Wait! I'm sorry. I'll try not to curse. What's my daughter's name?" Rayshawn asked nicely.

"Ask your lawyers." Gabby was playing coy to get Rayshawn agitated.

"Why you playing games, Gabby?" Rayshawn asked, trying to remain calm.

"All of this has been worked out through our lawyers. You get to keep your perfect life with your wife and two sons while I get $15,000 a month to take care of our daughter and keep my mouth shut."

"I'm starting to have doubts about that. I love my sons, but I always wanted a daughter. Damn, I don't even know her name or how much she weighed when she was born." Rayshawn sounded hurt.

"Contact your lawyers for that information. I'm keeping my end of the deal and you need to do the same."

"Oh, now you keeping it professional after you set me up and blackmailed me." Rayshawn was breathing heavily on the phone.

"It takes two." Gabby frowned and shook at the thought of having sex with Rayshawn.

"I'm thinking about telling my wife the truth." Rayshawn's tone became more serious.

"Did I ever tell you about the time I met your wife at your ranch in Alpharetta, Georgia?"

"What the fuck you talking about?"

"Oh, it was easy to do using my experience from my previous job as a personal stylist at Nordstrom. I flew to Atlanta with a friend one weekend and stayed in a nice hotel you paid for, thank you. I told your wife I was a personal stylist and wanted to work with her like I did with some of the other NFL wives. She invited me over for lunch."

"What?" Rayshawn could tell Gabby was telling the truth. "You been to my ranch?"

"Yep. I showed her some pictures of clothes that could conceal her thickness and make her look more womanly. She was looking forward to working with me, but then changed her mind after realizing she's more of a jeans and T-shirt chick who lives on a ranch and runs her two sons to their sports practices all the time."

"She told me about a pregnant personal stylist visiting her at the ranch while I was at the gym a few months back."

"Yep. That was me. I was about five months pregnant then. She had a lot of motherly advice for me. I can't wait until my daughter gets a little older so I can use some of that informa-tion."

"That's fucked up! You got me just where you want me, but I'll get your ass back one day!"

"No, you won't! You have more to lose than I do. I'm smarter than you. My lawyer is smarter than your lawyers. And I know your thick, country bumpkin wife calls the shots and if she ever found out what you did, she would kill you and your sons would be devastated because they love and adore their daddy. And let's not talk about your image with the NFL. Mr. Help the Needy Children in Baltimore."

"One day, Gabby. I'm going to hang you by the same rope I'm hanging on right now."

"Ah ah ah. No threats. But I do need you to do one more thing for me before I hang up. You called my friend, Joy, Saturday and upset her boyfriend. Delete her number or I'll give him and his hoodlum brothers over there in the D.C. projects your address so they can pay you a little visit. I know you're not as hard as you think you are. Any grown man who calls his wife Momma, rather than her given name, is a joke."

Gabby heard Rayshawn gasp on the phone.

"Yep, your wife told me that, too. Goodbye and never call

me again."

Gabby pushed the End button on her cell, erased the call, and lay back on William's bed with a satisfied smile on her face.

"What was that about, Gabby?" William was standing in the doorway with bulging eyes and a handful of Gabby's clothes on the floor in front of him.

She felt her heart stop.

Chapter 4

I hate my life.

"I hate it. I hate it. I hate it," Maxine mumbled as she stood alone in her kitchen loading the dishwasher while her husband and two sons watched television in the nearby family room.

"You have nobody to blame for that but yourself," Trent said as he entered the kitchen.

Maxine jumped when she heard her husband's voice. The glass baking dish she had just spent ten minutes scrubbing burned macaroni and cheese out of slipped from her hand and hit the ceramic tile floor. The sound of breaking glass echoed throughout the kitchen and family room. Maxine froze in place, looking at Trent for a reaction to what he heard her say. The last thing she needed was for her husband to know how miserable she was. He thought he provided her with everything she needed to be a happy wife and mother.

Trent backed out of the kitchen. "Maxi, you alright?"

She looked at her favorite baking dish in pieces spread across the kitchen floor and sighed. "Yeah, I'm fine."

Trent shook his head side to side. "Don't worry about it, I'll get it. It's been a long day and you look tired. Why don't you take the boys upstairs and give them their baths while I clean the kitchen and put the leftovers away." Trent reached in the closet between the kitchen and family room and pulled out a broom and dustpan.

27

"Daddy, what happened?" TJ asked as he ran from the family room to peek inside the kitchen.

"Wha hap?" Two-year-old Maxwell asked, trying to copy his big brother.

Trent put the broom and dustpan down and picked up TJ and Maxwell before they got any closer to the broken glass in the kitchen. "Oh no, you don't. Bedtime for you guys." Trent looked at Maxine who was still standing in the same spot. "Maxi, snap out of it and take the boys upstairs."

"Oh...okay." Maxine maneuvered through the broken glass and started up the stairs with her boys.

Trent picked up the broom again and then stared at the dishwasher. "By the way, what exactly is it that you hate about the dishwasher?"

"What?" Maxine looked back at Trent with squinted eyes, not sure what he was talking about.

"When I walked in the kitchen, you were talking about how much you hate the dishwasher." Trent started sweeping the kitchen floor. "When we built this house, I told you to pick out all the kitchen appliances because you were the only one who was going to use them."

"Oh, yeah. I, um, I just wish it was bigger since I had more dishes to clean than normal because of the cookout." Maxine swallowed hard, hoping her response was enough to stop Trent's questions.

Trent bent down to pick up the bigger pieces of glass. "Alright, after I finish this, I'm going to check my e-mail and then I'll be up."

"Okay." Maxine turned around and continued up the stairs with her sons.

A few minutes later, while she was bathing her boys, a feeling of despair swept over Maxine. She was tired and wanted to go to bed, but she knew she had more to do, thanks to Trent volunteering to clean the kitchen. His idea of cleaning the kitchen was stacking the dishes in the sink and on the countertop until she was ready to deal with them. And no matter how many times she asked him to do it, he never covered the leftovers with foil or plastic wrap, which meant after she gave the boys their baths, read them a story, and tucked them in bed, she would have to go back downstairs to clean the dishes and take all the leftovers out, cover them, and put them back in the refrigerator.

Usually when they had company, there were little to no leftovers, thanks to their friends and family. There was no shame in their game when it came to making plates to go. That wasn't the case with the guests they had today. This Memorial Day, Trent decided to host a cookout for the lawyers in his department and their families. Maxine couldn't wait for them to leave. All of their bragging about what they had, their upcoming summer plans, and how they volunteer and donate to the underprivileged because they are so fortunate made Maxine want to run out of her own house, screaming for them to shut up. She knew they were all a bunch of phonies trying to outdo each other.

And the biggest phony of all was her husband, Trent Anderson. She almost didn't recognize the man she saw today. He looked the same, medium height with a slim physique, dark-chocolate complexion, short wavy hair, and a smile to die for, but everything else about him was different. Almost every word that came out of his mouth was a bold-faced lie and he knew what he was doing was wrong because he avoided eye contact with Maxine every time she stared at him with accusing eyes.

Maxine's legs wouldn't stop shaking when Trent bragged about how he was going to invest in some stock one of his wealthy clients told him about. *What a bunch of crap*, she thought. Their guests looked at her sideways when she laughed out loud thinking about how funny it would be to go in his home office to retrieve all the past due bills sitting on his desk and pass them around for his co-workers to see.

When they started discussing vacation plans, Trent refused to be outdone. He stuck his chest out and boasted about how he was going to spend two weeks on Martha's Vineyard this summer, around the same time as the Obamas. He forgot to tell them that the only reason they were going to Martha's Vineyard for two weeks in August was that her parents had rented a house and invited them because they wanted to spend time with their grandsons.

Lie after lie, Maxine wanted to pull Trent to the side and talk to him, but she couldn't bring herself to do it. She hated being confrontational. So instead she smiled, nodded, and played the perfect hostess while praying silently for Trent's colleagues to get out of her house and as far away from her as possible.

Watching Trent made her wonder what happened to the caring and generous man she married five years ago? The man she met her sophomore year in college who wanted to become a lawyer to help people who were unable to help themselves? The one who wanted to become a lawyer to make a difference. Unfortunately, that man was long gone and was now replaced by a money-hungry snob who spent most of his time trying to keep up with his associates' lifestyles while falling deeper and deeper in debt.

Once Maxine was sure the boys were asleep, she went back downstairs. She looked down the hall and saw the light on in Trent's office. She knew he was doing more than reading his e-mails. He was more than likely trying to get a jump-start on his work week, which meant he would probably be in there for a couple of hours.

She entered the kitchen and just as she had suspected, the sink and countertop were covered with dirty dishes. As she went through the mundane routine of loading the dishwasher and running dishwater for the extra pans and bowls that didn't fit, she thought about her life and what she really wanted. She loved her sons and enjoyed staying home with them, but she was starting to feel guilty.

Bills were piling up and Trent was the only one working. Since they left the mortgage-free townhouse her parents bought them as a wedding present and moved into this custom-built home a little over a year ago, their bills had tripled. Although Trent wouldn't admit it, he was struggling to pay them. She knew if she went back to work, it would take some of the pressure off him. She had been trying to think of reasons to make Trent think she wanted to go back to work. He would never agree to the idea if he knew she wanted to help him pay the bills. Although he was a young man, he thought old-school and believed it was his responsibility alone to provide for his family.

Maxine was shocked when she heard Trent's footsteps coming down the hallway as she pulled the aluminum foil and plastic wrap out of the cabinet. She thought he would be in his office longer than an hour.

Trent walked in the kitchen and laughed. "I knew you were coming back in here to inspect my work." He squeezed her butt playfully. "I'm going up. Don't be long, okay?" He winked at her as he walked upstairs.

She winked back and smiled. "I'll be up shortly." Maxine knew what Trent wanted. He had been rubbing, smacking, and pinching her breasts and butt all day. She smiled to herself thinking about sex with her husband and how much she still enjoyed it.

Twenty minutes later, Maxine went upstairs to their master bedroom. Trent was sitting up on his side of the bed, looking fresh and reading something related to law. The room smelled like his favorite soap, cologne, and mouthwash. He looked at Maxine and smiled when she entered the room.

Maxine smiled back. She went to her lingerie drawer and pulled out a nightgown and sat it on the bed while she got undressed.

Trent looked at the nightgown and then at Maxine. "You won't need that. Come here."

"Trent, can I at least take a shower first?" Maxine didn't wait for him to answer as she rushed in the bathroom to shower.

When she walked back in the bedroom minutes later, Trent put the book he was reading on his nightstand and looked at Maxine. She stood beside the bed with a towel wrapped around her body and another around her head.

She sat on the bed. "Can we talk first?"

Trent looked at her with a slight frown. "Wassup?"

Maxine stared at Trent with a serious face. "I've been thinking about this for a while and it's what I really want to do. I hope you'll support me with this."

"Maxi, I already know you want us to have a little girl." He reached out and pulled Maxine's towel down enough to expose her small breasts. "We can't make it happen by talking about it. Come here." Trent tried to pull her closer to him.

"No, Trent. That's not what I want." Maxine shook her head to reinforce what she was saying.

He frowned deeper to show his frustration. "Then what is it?"

Maxine took a deep breath and exhaled. "I want to go back to work. I miss teaching and I need to do something for me," Maxine lied.

"Absolutely not!" Trent jumped up from the bed and walked around the bedroom.

"You're not even going to talk this over with me?" Maxine pleaded.

Trent didn't say anything as he sat back down on his side of the bed.

"Trent?" Maxine moved closer to him on the bed. "Will you listen to me?"

"Not about you going back to work. Do you realize how good you have it, Maxi? Most of the women I work with would love to be in your place, and what about our plan to have another child? Are you going to start working and then quit when you find out you're pregnant again."

Maxine rubbed his back while she thought about what he said. In a way, he was right. Staying home with her children and taking care of her family was what she loved and all she ever wanted to do, but now she needed to push what she wanted aside to step up and help her husband with the bills. "I thought we could put that on hold for a year. I still want more children, but I want to work, too." Maxine turned Trent's face to look at her. "What do you think?"

"What do I think?" Trent glared at Maxine. "This isn't what we planned for our children, Maxi. Remember, we didn't want our children stuck in daycare for twelve hours a day while we both work. I thought we settled this years ago when we decided to start having children. Why the change now?"

"Because we were both raised by working parents and we turned out fine," Maxine reasoned.

Trent stood up again. "Come on, Maxi. How can you say that? My mother worked two jobs to take care of me and my two brothers after she left my abusive ass father. I barely saw her and I hated it. I want my children to know that their mother will always be home when they need her and their father will provide for them."

Maxine hunched her shoulders. "Both my parents worked while they raised me and I never felt like I missed anything."

Trent stared at Maxine with a smirk. "Be for real, Maxi! Your father is a pediatrician and your mother is a college professor. They arranged their schedules to pick you up every day after school. You either went back to the college with your mother or to your father's practice with him. Don't make it seem like your situation was anything like mine."

Maxine's eyes started burning from trying to hold back her tears. "What about what I want? Why can't we find a way to make this work for all of us?"

"The way things are now works for all of us. You just need to realize that. I'm not going to agree to anything that will change our lives so drastically." Trent walked over to Maxine and kissed her. "Forget about going back to work and focus on your family's needs. And I need you to focus on my needs tonight."

Maxine frowned. "Sure, Trent." She knew by the way he was looking her body up and down and licking his lips that she wasn't going to get through to him tonight.

Trent removed her towel and stared at her naked body. "Uhm...you look so damn sexy! Come here!" Trent laid Maxine on the bed and started kissing her all over her body. "Now, can we stop talking and start having some fun?"

"I'm ready." Maxine smiled seductively as she reached in his shorts and touched his penis. It was warm and expanding from her touch. "This is all the fun I need."

They looked at each other, anticipating what was going to happen between them. Trent moaned as Maxine kissed him on his neck. She knew what he liked. He rubbed his hands over her soft skin and pulled her close to him. He started kissing her lips. She instantly felt warm and wet between her legs and she responded by sticking her tongue in and out of his mouth with a pulsating rhythm. Trent raised her arms over her head and began sucking her breasts and biting her nipples. He stuck his fingers inside her to see if she was ready for him. When his fingers slid out, dripping with her juices, he entered her while continuing to suck her breast. After a few minutes, he pulled out. He wanted this to last as long as possible.

He lay on his back and Maxine sat on him. He held her small waist as she moved up and down on top of him. Her tiny breasts bounced, turning Trent on even more. Maxine's body trembled as the juices she released dripped down Trent's penis. She fell beside him on the bed, completely spent. Trent raised both of her legs in the air, pulled her body close to him, and entered her again. He pushed himself deep inside Maxine until his body shook. "Ahhhh, I'm coming," he groaned and fell on the bed panting.

Trent reached out to rub Maxine's stomach. "I think we just made another little boy tonight."

That's not going to happen, Maxine thought with a smile. She had started taking birth control pills last month to make sure she didn't get pregnant. Although he didn't know it yet, Trent needed her to work more than he needed her to have another child and she already had a plan in mind for how she was going to get him to see that.

Chapter 5

Joy lay in her bed Saturday morning sleeping peacefully until she felt a hand on her breast. She opened one eye and then the other to see Allen staring at her with a goofy smile on his face. "What are you up to?" Joy asked as she pulled the covers over her head.

"Oh, it's like that. Then go back to sleep." Allen got out of the bed, naked as the day his mother pushed him out, and went to the bathroom across from Joy's bed.

She pulled the covers from over her head and watched Allen as he stood in front of the toilet urinating. He washed his hands, brushed his teeth, and washed his face before he got back in the bed.

"Can I see it again?" he asked like an eager child.

Joy giggled. "You can see it as much as you want, but every time I show it to you, you lose control. I'm still sore and tired from what you did to me yesterday." She picked him up from BWI Airport last night and presented him with a special gift when they arrived at her apartment in Greenbelt, Maryland.

Allen laughed and covered his face in shame. "Last night was my first time seeing it so you should understand why a brother lost control." Allen's face became serious. "I promise to control myself if you let me see it again."

"As long as you promise," Joy laughed.

Allen put his right hand in the air and looked at her with a serious expression. "Oh...I promise. Scout's honor."

Joy shook her head and smiled. "But you were never a Scout."

They both laughed.

Joy pushed the covers off her naked body and turned over on her stomach. "Here it is."

Allen quickly sat up and stared at the new tattoo on Joy's lower back. Just above her butt crack was a lotus flower with wings on each side and a ribbon under the flower with Allen's name written on it.

"Damn, baby! It's beautiful!" Allen used his index finger to trace it. "Did it hurt?"

Joy frowned. "Hell, yeah! It felt like my skin was burning, but after a couple of days it felt better."

"When did you get it done?" Allen was too excited last night to get any details.

"Monday night after I flew home. One of the teachers at my school had a tattoo party at her house and I made an appointment to have it done before I left last weekend." Joy knew Allen would be excited but she didn't expect this level of enthusiasm.

"So this had nothing to do with that football player calling you last weekend." Allen frowned because he got mad every time he thought about it.

Joy smacked her lips. "No, baby, I had this planned before Rayshawn called me. Where is the trust, Allen?"

He bent down and kissed the tattoo on her lower back. "I trust you. It's him and Gabby I don't trust."

Joy didn't respond because she knew Allen had never liked Gabby. And since he found out the truth about Nadia and how Gabby was basically blackmailing Rayshawn, she could tell his dislike for Gabby had increased tenfold.

Joy stared at Allen's erection and pointed at it. "What's up with that?"

He pointed at his penis and laughed. "I'm losing control again, baby."

Joy laughed out loud as Allen lay on her backside and started kissing her from the side of her forehead down to her neck. He stretched beside her and pulled her body close to his. They started moaning and breathing heavily as their naked bodies connected and started rubbing against each other. Allen turned Joy over and pulled her up on her knees. He wanted to see the tattoo as he prepared to enter her from the back.

They froze when they heard a loud knock on the apartment door.

Allen looked at Joy suspiciously. "You expecting somebody?"

Joy rolled her eyes at Allen. "No, are you?" She grabbed her robe and left to answer the door.

Joy closed and tightened her robe as she ran to the front door. She looked out the peephole and saw Bea standing there. She mouthed, "Oh, shit!" Her heart started beating fast and her hands started shaking. "Hi, Bea. Give me a minute to put my robe on. I just woke up." She made sure to speak loudly enough for Allen to hear.

When she heard him close the bedroom door, she opened the door for Bea. Joy hugged her mother and looked at her as she walked into the apartment. Bea's youthful looks, even-toned caramel complexion, and voluptuous shape made her look more like Joy's sister than mother. "Hey, Bea. This is a surprise. I thought we were meeting at the mall later?"

"Since I was already out, I decided to stop by for a visit. Is that okay? I'm not interrupting anything, am I?" Bea asked as she sat on the brown, faux-suede sofa and craned her neck toward Joy's bedroom.

Joy shifted her weight from one leg to the other. "Uh-uh. No, not at all. Make yourself comfortable while I go get dressed." Joy tried to sound calm but her heart was pounding through her chest.

Bea patted the seat beside her on the sofa. "Sit down for a minute. I wanna talk to you before we leave," Bea said in a very serious tone.

Joy's pulse started racing and her legs were shaking as she sat beside her mother on the couch. "What's wrong, Bea?"

"You! I'm worried about you spending all this time in Atlanta." Bea stared at Joy with poked-out lips. "Is it interfering with you finishing school?"

"No." Joy rolled her eyes. It wasn't enough that she was spending all these years in school because of her mother; now she wanted to know every detail of her life, too.

"Aren't we close enough to talk about things?" Bea asked.

"Sure," Joy lied.

"Then why won't you tell me why you spend more time in Atlanta than here? Who are you going to Atlanta to see?" Bea pried.

Joy looked down at the carpeted floor trying to come up with an answer that would satisfy her nosy ass mother. "Why do you need to know that? I don't ask you questions about who you see." Joy decided turning the tables on her mother would end the conversation because Bea hated discussing her sex life with her daughter.

Bea sighed. "Who is it, Joy? Why is it such a secret?"

"I just wanna keep what I have with him between us. It's no secret. It's no big deal. Can I go get dressed now?" Joy stood up from the couch.

"So it's a him? I mean, a man?" Bea looked up at Joy with a puzzled expression.

"Of course it's a man, Bea! Did you think I was gay?" Joy shook her head and said, "Oh, my goodness!"

"I didn't know what to think." She pulled Joy's arm to make her sit back down on the couch and gave her daughter a bright smile. "It's a man! Thank God for small miracles. Now, why the big secret? You know I didn't raise you to be a side chick."

"I'm not. When I'm ready, I'll let you know." Joy stood up from the sofa again, ready to go back to the bedroom to check on Allen.

Bea stared at her daughter with narrowed eyes. "If I don't know who this person is soon, we have private investigators who work for the law firm. I schedule meetings with them all the time for the attorneys I work for and I'll hire one of them myself to find out everything there is to know about him."

Joy glared at her mother. "And you would seriously do that, wouldn't you?"

"Hell, yeah! Anything to protect my daughter from getting stuck with a sorry-ass man. He'll only bring you down. You have too much going for you to get attached to a no-good man just because he makes you feel good between your legs." Bea crossed her arms over her chest and sat back on the couch with an angry smirk on her face.

"Bea!" Joy let out a deep, loud sigh. She fell back on the sofa and tried to process what her mother had just said.

"You know I'm telling the truth." Bea stood up and walked to the kitchen. She looked in the refrigerator and cabinets and then stopped at the dining room table where she looked through Joy's mail. Bea turned her back, opened Joy's Visa bill, and looked it over before she put it back in the envelope and returned it to the table. She walked back in the living room like she did nothing wrong.

Joy saw her mother snooping around her apartment and reading her mail but knew complaining about it would do no good. Her only concern was to keep Bea and Allen away from each other, so she decided to save her protests for when and if Bea attempted to go in her bedroom.

Bea sat beside Joy on the couch. "Since Gabby moved out, have you been able to keep up with the rent on your own? Do you need me to help you with it? Or, are you planning to move to Atlanta?"

Joy covered her face and shook her head. "No, Bea. I don't need your help with my rent. I do have a full-time job, you know. Besides, Gabby wasn't paying rent when she lived here anyway. And to answer the last question you stuck in there about me moving to Atlanta, I haven't thought about it."

Bea looked at Joy with tears flowing. "Please give me enough notice if you decide to move because it'll kill me. It'll break my heart to have my only child move ten hours away from me. I'll hate him, whoever he is, just because he took you so far away from me." She wiped the tears from her eyes.

Although Bea was controlling and drove Joy crazy more

times than not, she still loved her mother. She couldn't imagine being far away from her. Bea had given birth to Joy when she was sixteen. Bea and Joy's father, Juan, had raised Joy together. After her parents broke up when she was four years old, they had remained friends and Juan was very active in his daughter's life. Joy loved both her parents, but because she lived with Bea, she saw how her mother put her daughter's needs before her own and for that she would be forever grateful.

Joy rubbed her mother's shoulder. "You'll be the first to know if I decide anything."

"I guess I should be thankful for that." Bea's face became serious again. "One more question before you get dressed. Are you still on the pill?" Bea stared at Joy, eagerly waiting for an answer.

Joy frowned at Bea. "Of course, Bea. I haven't stopped taking them since you gave me my first one after I started my period when I was twelve years old. Remember? You told me it was a vitamin I needed to take every day or I would get sick and die."

Bea rolled her eyes and used her hand to brush imaginary lint off her tight jeans. "I see you still have issues with that. One day when you have your own children, which I hope is at least ten years from now, you'll do the same thing. Whatever it takes to keep your child from ruining her life."

Bea's cell phone started ringing. She reached in her Coach bag, pulled out her phone, looked at the screen, and then answered it. "Hey, Tyesha. Wassup with you, girl?"

Joy stood up and waved to Bea as she walked away to her bedroom. She knew Allen called his sister and had her call Bea so she could escape from Bea's interrogation. When Joy reached her bedroom door, she heard footsteps quickly approaching her from behind. She turned around and saw Bea standing there talking on her phone.

"Where are you going!" Joy snapped.

Bea ignored her and reached past Joy to open the bedroom door. Joy moved her body to block Bea from trying to open the door. She started to protest, but stopped when she saw Bea look at her phone, frown and roll her eyes.

"Tyesha, mind your business! I know she's grown and I'm not trying to dress her like she's a damn baby. Just hurry up, Joy!" Bea sighed and threw her hand in the air as she walked back toward the living room.

Joy waited until Bea disappeared then lightly tapped on her bedroom door. Allen opened the door wearing a pair of shorts and T-shirt. The erection he had earlier was long gone. His face was tense with anger. Joy closed the door behind her, locked it, and turned the radio up so Bea couldn't hear her and Allen talking.

She hugged Allen. "Thanks for calling Tyesha."

Allen nodded but didn't say anything.

Joy ran to her closet and started pulling out clothes. "I'm sorry. I didn't know she was coming here. I need to get her out of here ASAP."

Allen sat on the bed and watched Joy in panic mode rushing to get dressed so she could get her mother out of the apartment and away from him.

Joy noticed him staring at her with a blank look. "What's wrong?" Joy whispered.

"I think we should go out there and tell her about us," Allen said in a low tone.

Joy frowned as she threw a sundress on the bed. "Are you crazy? No! She's not ready for that." Joy shook her head.

Allen held his bald head with both hands and looked at Joy angrily. "I'm tired of this, Joy. I'm a twenty-six-year-old man hiding in my girlfriend's bedroom because she doesn't want her mother to know about us. This is what we did when we were teenagers. Ain't shit changed."

"It's because I don't want her to ruin what we have. Trust me on this, Allen," Joy whispered.

They heard Bea laughing loudly on the phone with Tyesha.

"We need to talk about this, Joy," Allen insisted.

"Not now, Allen! Let me get her out of here! We'll talk about it when I get back!" Joy whispered through clenched teeth. She was becoming irritated because he knew she was already under a lot of pressure, so why was he trying to have a serious conversation now.

Allen grabbed Joy's arm, pulled her into the bathroom, and closed the door. He put the toilet seat down and sat Joy on it, then he sat across from her on the edge of the tub. "We need to stop this. We're grown, baby. Too old to keep hiding from your mother. We're going in there, hand in hand, and let her know we love each other and we plan to spend the rest of our lives together."

Joy was almost in tears. "No. Now is not the time. I have one more year of school and then I'm done. We can tell her then." Ever since Joy was a little girl, Bea made her promise that she wouldn't get serious with any man until she completed her doctoral degree. She had Joy's life mapped out for her from day one and would make life a living hell for anyone who knocked her off track.

Allen punched his hand with his fist and exhaled. "Is it because she's paying for school? Don't worry about it; I'll pay for your classes myself. Now, what's stopping us?"

Joy bit her bottom lip. "It's not that. She sacrificed so much of her life for me, Allen. I don't want to disappoint her. Let me just finish school like I promised her and then we can tell her."

Allen stared at Joy with a hurt expression. He grabbed her hands and held them. "What about me, Joy? Do you love me enough to stop hiding me from your mother?"

Tears started falling down Joy's face. "That's not fair, baby. You know I love you."

Allen tore off some toilet paper and wiped Joy's tears. "I don't want to upset you anymore. If you want me to hide in here, then that's what I'll do." Allen put his hands up to show his surrender.

"Thank you, baby. It won't be long." Joy half-smiled. "As soon as I get dressed, we're out of here." She jumped up and turned on the shower.

Allen went back to the bedroom and sat on the bed. He was thinking about going in the living room and telling Bea how much he loved her daughter and how much her support would mean to them. When Joy came out of the bathroom looking more nervous than when she went in, he decided against it. He loved her and didn't want to add more stress to her life.

After she got dressed, she looked at Allen sitting on the bed in deep thought. She sat down beside him and whispered in his ear. "I know you don't like this and I'm sorry. I love you."

Allen turned to face her. "I love you more than anything in this world. I would actually give my life to protect you, but I don't know if I can keep doing this."

Joy swallowed hard and stared at Allen with a frightened expression. There was a hardness to what he just said that she'd never heard before. She didn't think Allen would ever leave her over this, but the way he looked at her and spoke to her sent chills down her spine. She just hoped her last year in school went by quickly so she could live her life with Allen on her terms.

Chapter 6

Gabby walked in the T.G.I.Friday's in Bowie wearing a sexy, purple sundress with a wide belt to hide her small stomach pouch and a pair of three-inch, silver Kate Spade sandals and matching handbag. Her lean silhouette, beautiful features, and perfect runway walk had heads turning in her direction as she moved through the restaurant to join Maxine and Joy at their table. Gabby smiled to herself when she heard several men giving her compliments. *Not bad for a women who pushed out a six-pound baby ten days ago*, she thought to herself.

Earlier in the day, Gabby had sent Joy and Maxine text messages asking them to meet her at the restaurant because she had something important to tell them. They agreed to meet at eight-thirty to give Joy enough time to say goodbye to Allen and drop him off at BWI Airport. Maxine wanted to make sure her boys were fed, bathed, and ready for bed before she left them alone with their father for a couple of hours.

When Gabby reached their table, she smiled and hugged Maxine and Joy. She sat in a chair across from her friends smiling ear to ear, then waited a few seconds before she put up her left hand to show her two carat emerald-cut engagement ring. "Guess who's getting married?" She wiggled her ring finger.

Joy and Maxine were speechless as they turned and looked at each other before focusing their eyes back on Gabby.

"Gabby?" Maxine didn't know what else to say.

"Who are you marrying, Gabby?" Joy asked as she shook her head.

Gabby put her hand over her chest and gasped. "William, of course."

"Why?" Joy's tone was full of accusation.

Gabby pointed at Joy with a scowl. "Because of you."

"Me?" Joy couldn't wait to hear how she made this happen.

"Yes, you. All because of that incident with Rayshawn calling you in Atlanta and you discussing my business with Allen." Gabby gave Joy the evil eye.

"That was wrong, Gabby! Rayshawn should've never called Joy. Thank God I never called him for you because Trent would've been just as upset as Allen, probably more." Maxine closed her eyes and shook her head at the thought of it.

"Okay, so tell me how I'm the reason behind you marrying William." Joy put her hand under her chin and leaned in closer to hear what Gabby had to say.

Gabby cleared her throat and said dramatically, "William walked in on my conversation with Rayshawn."

Maxine gasped.

Joy nodded and said, "I told you the truth was going to come out eventually."

Gabby grinned. "It didn't. When William questioned me about it, I told him that I didn't want to upset him when I was pregnant because he was always so worried about me and the baby. Then I told him that my former supervisor at Nordstrom called me before I went into labor and tried to get me to drop my sexual harassment complaint against him."

"What are you talking about?" Maxine looked at Joy and Gabby, thinking she must have missed something during one of their many weekly phone conversations.

Joy tilted her head toward Maxine with a smirk on her face. "She's lying."

Gabby continued. "It took me most of my first night home to convince William that what he heard was only part of the conversation and that he only thought he heard me say Nadia's name.

I finally gave him some and he didn't ask any more questions that night."

"Gabby!" Maxine screamed. People at nearby tables looked at them. "You're not supposed to have sex that soon after giving birth; it's dangerous," Maxine whispered.

"Calm down, Maxine. I didn't have sex. I just gave him a blow job," Gabby explained.

Joy frowned. "TMI. So I guess you didn't do a good enough job of blowing him so you had to propose."

"No, Joy! Remember, he proposed to me after I told him I was pregnant with his child, but I turned him down because I wasn't ready to be somebody's wife."

"Oh...And you are now?" Joy asked.

"Will you let me finish, Joy?" Gabby sighed. "He still had questions the next day so I told him I wanted to drop the sexual harassment complaint and put all that ugliness I had to deal with at Nordstrom's behind me because I wanted to plan our wedding and become Mrs. William Landon." Gabby smiled. "He got down on his knee and proposed right then and there." She snapped her fingers on both hands, tossed her hair back, and said, "My work was complete. To this day, he has never asked another question about the phone call he overheard."

Joy couldn't believe what she was hearing. "Either he's the dumbest man I ever met or you have some magic powers you're not telling us about."

Gabby twirled a long strand of her hair around her finger. "I wouldn't say William is dumb. He's smart enough to hold down a job that pays him six figures. He's just a trusting person who takes people at their word. That's why we're a good fit. He trusts me and everything I say."

Joy stared at Gabby with her mouth wide open.

"Don't marry him if you don't love him, Gabby." Maxine touched Gabby's arm. "Marriage is hard enough as it is. Marrying somebody you don't love or care about is going to make it harder."

Gabby folded her arms across her chest, rolled her eyes upward, and fell back in her seat. "Oh, c'mon. I do care about

William. He's an excellent father to Nadia and he takes better care of me than I take care of myself." Gabby smiled. "And don't get me started on the sex. He knows my spots and how to work them to get me there, so I know marrying William will give me everything I ever wanted-a handsome and successful husband, a beautiful daughter, and money in the bank."

"Gabby, have you forgotten that the beautiful daughter and the money in the bank have nothing to do with William! They are courtesy of Rayshawn Robinson!" Joy couldn't believe her friend's reasoning sometimes.

Gabby waved Joy off. "Oh, please. That's a little glitch that nobody has to know about except everyone at this table." Gabby glared at Joy. "And Allen."

Joy looked around for the waitress. Gabby was starting to work her nerves and she was ready to leave. "Where's the waitress?"

"You're really going to do this, huh?" Maxine asked with concern.

Gabby held out her hand to show off her ring. "Oh, it's happening."

"Have you set a date yet?" Maxine asked.

Gabby looked at Maxine like she was irritated by her questions. "Of course I have. My wedding coordinator made me do that during our first meeting. I'm getting married on Saturday, July fourth, and I expect you both at my house early to help me get dressed."

Joy stopped looking for the waitress and looked at Gabby. "I won't be able to attend, Gabby. I hope you and William have a nice wedding. Take plenty of pictures so I can see them when I get back."

Gabby whipped her neck in Joy's direction. "Why not? I want you both at my wedding!"

Maxine saw the anger in Gabby's eyes and grabbed her hand and held it tightly, trying to prevent the argument that was sure to come. "Don't worry. I'll be there, Gabby. I promise."

Joy stared at Gabby without blinking. "Allen's company picnic is every Fourth of July weekend. This is our fourth year going and he looks forward to it so I'm not gonna miss it."

Gabby smacked her lips. "That's just an excuse, Joy. If you really wanted to be there, you would. I can't believe you're putting Allen and his company picnic before me and my wedding."

"I don't need an excuse not to attend your wedding. I already have plans and that's it." Joy refused to get into an argument with Gabby over a wedding that shouldn't even happen.

Gabby pulled her hand away from Maxine and gave Joy a phony smile. "Ah, I see. After I marry William, your two best friends will be married women and you'll still be flying back and forth to Atlanta for booty calls with your ex-con boyfriend while hiding him from your mother."

"Gabby, stop it! That's a terrible thing to say!" Maxine barked.

Joy's chest began heaving up and down as she clenched her fists with every intention of punching Gabby in the face. Then she realized a restaurant full of witnesses would probably land her in jail, so she took her Coach bag off the back of her chair and stood up. She hugged Maxine and said, "Bye, girl. Love you and I'll talk to you later in the week."

Maxine hugged Joy back. "Don't leave like this, Joy. Are you alright? You know she didn't mean it." Maxine hated it when Joy and Gabby argued because she was always stuck in the middle.

Joy didn't respond to Maxine as she leaned across the table and got in Gabby's face. "I wouldn't attend your wedding if my life depended on it, but I will be front and center when every goddamn lie you ever told comes out and buries your ass. Don't call me or come to my place unless you're on all fours begging me, like a bitch in heat, for forgiveness."

Gabby turned beet-red as she watched Joy sashay out the door without looking back.

Chapter 7

Maxine stood at the stove stirring her homemade spaghetti sauce thinking about Trent. Anytime she tried to talk to him about going back to work, he changed the subject or locked himself in his home office. She refused to back down. Last week, she went to the Prince George's County Public School's human resources office and started the paperwork to get reinstated as a teacher for the county. If Trent refused to talk to her about it, he'll know she means business when she walks out the door with him in the mornings headed to work.

The sound of Trent coming through the front door brought her back to the moment. He looked fatigued, carrying his suit jacket over his shoulders with his necktie hanging loosely around his neck and sweat stains soaking the arm-pits of his white button-down shirt. He smiled when he smelled dinner. Maxine had cooked his favorite meal, spaghetti and meatballs with a fresh garden salad, garlic bread, and freshly squeezed lemonade.

TJ and Maxwell ran to the foyer and hugged their father. "Daddy, Daddy," they yelled.

Trent dropped his briefcase on the floor and picked up both his sons. He walked in the kitchen where Maxine was finishing dinner and gave her a gentle kiss on her lips.

"How was your day, Trent?" Maxine moved to the kitchen sink to drain the pasta.

Trent put the boys down and they ran into the family

room. He stood behind Maxine at the kitchen sink and started kissing her neck. She was purring like a cat.

"It was a hectic and crazy day. Do you remember why I wanted to become a lawyer?"

"I don't remember, but dinner will be ready in ten minutes." Maxine smiled.

"Forget dinner. I missed you today." Trent turned Maxine around to face him.

She dropped the empty pot in the sink and kissed Trent passionately. She did love her husband more than anything in the world and believed that once she started working and he got promoted to partner, things would get better for them financially.

Before long, they sat down and enjoyed dinner together. Afterward, instead of closing himself off in his office as he normally did every night, Trent lay on the carpeted floor in the family room and played with his sons while Maxine cleaned the kitchen. It made her feel good to hear her sons laughing and playing with their father.

Around eight o'clock, the boys starting crying and whining, a sign that they were tired and ready for bed. Trent put each son under an arm and carried them upstairs. He gave them their baths and put them to bed so Maxine could finish her chores.

Twenty minutes later, she went upstairs to her room. She stopped dead in her tracks when she saw Trent sitting on their bed staring at the pack of birth control pills she had hidden in her nightstand. He looked up at her with so much anger, chills shot down her spine.

"I don't even know you anymore!" Trent yelled. "I'm looking in your nightstand for a pen and I find this shit!" He pointed at the pack of pills. "What? You forgot to tell me you didn't want to have any more children with me?"

She swallowed hard as she sat beside him on the edge of the bed. "That's not true, Trent. You know I want more children with you." She cleared her throat. "Ummm...I started taking them because I didn't want to get pregnant my first year back at work. I'll stop taking them now. It's no big deal; pregnant women work every day," Maxine rambled nervously.

He turned his head and looked at her. "Why do you insist on abandoning our children for work? What? I don't provide enough for you and the boys? What is it?" His eyes were narrow and the veins on his temples were enlarged and twitching.

Maxine took Trent's hand and put it to her chest. "Yes, you do." Maxine released Trent's hand and took the pills off the bed. "I'll throw these away."

Trent frowned and grabbed his head. "I can't believe you!" He leaped up from the bed, snatched the pills out of Maxine's hand, and threw them in her face.

She cringed when they hit her nose and landed on the carpeted floor. "What's wrong with you? Why did you do that?"

He put his index finger close to her face. "Do you know what I go through at work for you to have all this and you sneak behind my back to take birth control pills and then you want to disrupt our family and ruin our children by going back to work. This is some bullshit!"

Maxine started crying. "I'm sorry, Trent. I appreciate everything you do for us. I just don't agree with you. I think my going back to work will help us, not hurt us, and I'm going to do it."

He stared at her with an angry gaze and his fists clenched tight. "You're not going back to work and that's final!"

Maxine stood up and looked at Trent like a rebellious teenager and screamed, "I said, I'm going back to work! It's what I want!"

Trent raised his open hand and smacked Maxine hard across her face. She turned three hundred and sixty degrees before she fell to the bed. He stood over her body with his hand still raised, ready to strike her again. "Don't ever mention going back to work to me again!"

Maxine's mouth filled with blood. She started coughing as it drained down her throat. She rolled to the opposite side of the bed to get as far away from Trent as possible.

Trent walked over to the lounge in the corner of their bedroom and motioned for Maxine to sit. "Come here so we can talk."

Maxine got off the bed trembling. She walked over to the lounge and sat down. As soon as her butt touched the chair, Trent pulled her up by her hair, giving her an instant headache. He dragged her over to their bed and threw her on it.

Maxine was screaming, "No, Trent, please don't hit me! No! Think about what you're doing! I love you, Trent!"

"You didn't think about me when you took those goddamn pills! You didn't think about your family when you decided to leave us to go back to work!" Trent looked so different. He was biting his bottom lip so hard, it was bleeding, and his eyes were bulging out of his head. No matter how mad he got, she never thought he would treat her like this.

Trent pulled Maxine off the bed and dragged her by her hair to their walk-in closet. He grabbed the thickest belt he could find and started beating her like she was a misbehaved child.

After he finished, Trent dropped the belt to the floor. "Don't you ever let me hear you say anything else about going back to work and get those goddamn pills out of my house!" He went in their master bathroom and slammed the door.

Maxine crawled to the lounge and leaned against it to get herself together. Her body ached all over and she was full of bruises and welts from the belt buckle. She pulled her knees to her chest and wrapped her arms around her bruised legs. She felt alone and afraid, unable to believe what Trent had just done to her.

A few minutes later, she looked up when she heard noises. TJ and Maxwell were standing in her doorway holding each other, shaking and crying. She could tell by the fearful expressions on their faces and the way they just stood there scared to move that they had seen everything their father did to her.

She shook her head and cried. "No, no, no! I'm sorry babies! Oh, my God! What did you see?" she sobbed as she collapsed to the floor.

Chapter 8

Gabby walked around the crib in the newly decorated lavender and white nursery with Nadia in her arms trying to console her. "Don't do this today, Nadia. I'm getting married. Please stop crying."

William walked in and extended his arms. "I'll take her so you can get ready."

Gabby happily handed Nadia over to William. As she left the room, she heard William singing a lullaby. His horrible singing stopped the baby's crying instantly. Gabby smiled because she knew marrying William today was the best thing she could do for her daughter. William loved Nadia and gave her the love every little girl deserves from her daddy, unlike Nadia's real father.

The doorbell rang. Gabby ran to the door and yanked it open. Joy and Maxine were standing carrying their bags and dresses.

"Are you just going to stand there and stare at us or let us in?" Joy asked. She fussed with Gabby all the time, but she loved her and had to be there for her special day, even if it meant changing her plans with Allen...again.

"Are you nervous, Gabby? You look nervous," Maxine commented.

"No, I'm not. Come in. We can go up to my room and get dressed." She looked back at Maxine and Joy as they followed her upstairs. "I moved to the guest bedroom a couple of weeks ago because of William's loud snoring."

Maxine and Joy looked at each other and shook their heads. Only Gabby could pull off having a baby by a professional football player, make him pay her huge monthly child support, then tell her ex-boyfriend that the baby was his, move in with him, and arrange to marry him six weeks later. And then decide a couple of weeks before the wedding that separate bedrooms would work better for them.

"What time is Bea coming, Joy? She's keeping Nadia during the ceremony. Maxine, does Dr. Jim know to be here by one o'clock?" Gabby stared at both her friends, waiting for them to answer her.

"Calm down, Gabby. Bea knows when to be here." Joy hugged Gabby.

"Dad knows what time to be here, too, Gabby. Don't worry. He's done this before." Maxine smiled.

They entered Gabby's room and gasped. She had made over the guest bedroom into an inviting and tranquil space decorated in pastel colors, silk, and lace. The king-size bed was the focal point with three rows of different-sized pillows arranged neatly at the head of the bed like sirens inviting you to join them for a peaceful sleep.

"Wow, Gabby! When did you do this? It's beautiful," Joy said as she looked around.

"Gabby, you're so talented. I would've never been able to make my room look like this. Thank God for comforter sets in the bag for people like me." Maxine laughed.

"Thank you. I'm glad you like it. I invite William in two or three times a week so he can enjoy it with me and when we're finished, I send him back to his room." Gabby giggled and rubbed her hands together like an evil villain.

"So I'm guessing you're in love with William again," Joy reasoned.

"Of course she is, Joy, that's why we're here. You do love him, don't you, Gabby?"

Gabby rolled her eyes and said, "Of course I do, in my

own way."

Joy and Maxine looked at each other again and shook their heads.

"Don't judge me." She stared at Joy and said, "At least I'm not a grown woman hiding my boyfriend from my mother." Then she looked at Maxine and said, "And when I'm ready to go back to work, I will because I want to, not because my husband won't let me."

Joy looked around the room to avoid eye contact with her girlfriends, while Maxine looked at the floor to hide her look of shame.

"Okay. Ladies, let's get started. Let's transform me from beautiful to perfect so I am worthy to wear this." Gabby reached in her closet and pulled out an ivory, one-shouldered, crinkle-silk gown with a matching grosgrain sash decorated with tiny pearls and an asymmetrical hem that stopped mid-thigh.

Joy and Maxine ran toward Gabby and gushed over the gown.

Gabby loved every bit of the attention she was getting from her best friends. She knew when the rest of the guests arrived, she would be the center of attention. "It's a Vera Wang," Gabby bragged.

"Sounds expensive," Maxine said.

"Well, you only do this once so you might as well splurge," Gabby said.

"How much did you splurge?" Joy looked at Gabby with an attitude because Gabby had lived with Joy during her entire pregnancy without paying a penny in rent or even offering to buy a loaf of bread, knowing Rayshawn was dropping a load of cash into her account every month.

Gabby caught on to what Joy was thinking and said, "That's not important. Let's get started. The ceremony starts in two hours."

Gabby sat at her vanity while Joy styled her hair around a two-hundred-and-fifty dollar-crystal and pearl tiara. Maxine did her make-up using only MAC cosmetics, Gabby's favorite. When they finished, Gabby put on her wedding dress and sat patiently while Joy and Maxine got dressed, then immediately started giving orders.

"Maxine, I need you to go see if the guests have arrived."
Maxine left immediately.

"Joy, here is the program. This is exactly how I want the ceremony to go. The wedding planner's name is Stephon. You'll know him when you see him. He's probably the biggest man in the room and dressed in as many colors as his big behind could find, but he's good at what he does."

Joy left.

Gabby sat in her room alone and closed her eyes to calm her nerves and center herself. A loud knock on the door startled her. *Who is this and it better be an emergency, knocking like they lost their mind.* She stood up, walked to the door and snatched it open.

It was two of William's family members. Before Gabby could say anything, William's youngest sister, Denise, and her cousin, Tanya, walked into Gabby's room. They were on summer break for Hampton University.

"What's up with this?" Denise snapped, waving the wedding program in her hand.

"Yeah, why isn't my *aunt* on the program to be escorted down the aisle?" Tanya asked with her hands on her hips and her neck rolling.

"I'm the bride. I'm the only person walking down the aisle on my wedding day," Gabby said very calmly.

"And she is the groom's mother, show her some respect. If my sister, Phyllis, was here, she would put you in your place!" Denise screamed, then looked at Tanya and said, "Phyllis might fly back from Germany when she hears about this."

Tanya got in Gabby's face and said, "I can't believe your stuck-up ass. If it wasn't my cousin's wedding day, I would wipe the floor with you."

Gabby snatched the crystal tiara out of her hair causing her long curls to drop in and around her face, kicked off her shoes and started removing her dress. She stood in front of Denise and Tanya with nothing but a matching strapless bra and bikini set decorated with tiny jewels in the pubic area. Gabby's lips smiled, but her eyes shot daggers as she said, "There will be no wedding today. You'll regret coming in my room on my wedding day, dressed like poster children for the Dollar Store and Wal-Mart. I'll change my clothes and meet you outside so you can attempt to wipe the floor with me. Are you going to leave while I remove my underwear or are you going to continue to stand there and wish you looked as good as I do after giving birth six weeks ago?"

Denise and Tanya looked at each other with terrified expressions. They weren't prepared for Gabby's reaction. They thought they could intimidate her into letting William's mother be walked down the aisle. Little did they know, Gabby refused to be intimidated by anyone.

Gabby removed her bra and then her jewel-encrusted panties with Denise and Tanya still in the room.

They left quickly.

Seconds later, Joy and Maxine returned with Bea.

"What's going on? We heard someone arguing. Why are you naked?" Joy asked.

Gabby waved her hands in the air. "William's sister and cousin came in here and threatened me. I changed my mind. I'm not marrying William. I'm moving back in with you, Joy, and I will pay my share of the rent until I find my own place."

"Why did they threaten you?" Bea asked with her back to Gabby to avoid her naked body.

"Something about William's mother not being walked down the aisle. They think I'm disrespecting her." Gabby shook her head.

Maxine and Joy weren't fazed by Gabby's naked body. They lived with her in college and were used to her carefree attitude when it came to her exposing what she called her perfect body. Maxine reached in Gabby's closet, pulled out a robe, and put it around Gabby's body. "Do they understand that you have no bridesmaids? Did you explain that to them?"

"I'm not explaining anything to them! They want to wipe the floor with me, so I told them to meet me outside! Let William know it's over!"

"Well, you're not going out there by yourself, that's for sure. Let me take off my dress and put my street clothes back on," Joy said.

"I don't think so. You two are not going out there to fight anybody. Sit still and let's figure this out. Gabby, if you don't want to get married, that's fine. I don't believe anybody should be forced to do anything she doesn't want to do, but I think you need to let William know yourself. Maxine, go get William while I keep Mike Tyson and Oscar de la Hoya in their corners," Bea said.

Minutes later, William entered the room. Everybody, except Gabby, left.

"What's wrong, Gabby? The ceremony was supposed to start fifteen minutes ago. I know you wanted to start on time."

"I changed my mind, William." Gabby walked to her dresser and pulled two tissues out of her tissue box and said, "Your family came in here and threatened my life. I will *not* marry into a family where people want to harm me." She dabbed at her eyes, but there wasn't a tear in sight. "What about Nadia? What if she's injured while they're trying to attack me?" She dabbed at her eyes again with the tissue.

"Who threatened you, Gabby? What did they say?" William's face was full of concern.

She dramatically laid her head on his chest and said, "Denise and Tanya burst in here just as I was about to leave and meet you downstairs. They think I'm disrespecting your mother because she's not walking down the aisle. You know I said that I wanted to be the only one walking down the aisle on my wedding day! That's why I have no bridesmaids. This is too much for me, William! I'm moving back in with Joy until I can find Nadia and me another place."

William's eyes widened at the thought of losing Gabby and Nadia. "No, Gabby. Don't do that. I'll take care of Denise and Tanya. Their asses are out of here."

"What about the rest of your family, William? They don't like me. I can't marry you with them looking at me cross-eyed," Gabby whined.

William looked at Gabby with raised eyebrows and asked, "You want all of my family to leave, Gabby?"

"No, William. They can stay; I'm leaving. We can arrange visitation for you and Nadia. She loves you. I wouldn't dare keep you away from her. She needs her daddy," Gabby whimpered and dabbed at her eyes again.

"Why don't I get rid of Denise and Tanya and have a talk with the rest of my family," William reasoned.

Gabby pulled a suitcase out of her closet and opened it on her bed. As she walked to the dresser, she loosened the belt on her robe, grabbed a handful of lingerie from her drawer, and walked back to the suitcase with her robe wide open, revealing her naked body.

William put both of his hands inside of Gabby's robe and hugged her close to him. "I don't want you and our daughter to leave me. What can we do to make everybody happy?"

Gabby kissed William gently on his lips and said, "Nothing. I'll have Stephon make an announcement. The guests can stay and eat and drink as much as they like if that's alright with you. Everything's already paid for." She stepped back from William and returned to packing.

"Gabby, I'm sorry. I'm caught in the middle, between you and my family," William complained.

Gabby didn't respond as she continued packing. When the suitcase was half full, she removed her robe and walked back to her dresser, knowing her drawers were all empty. She turned around and saw William's erect penis bulging under his white tuxedo pants. "William, will you make love to me one last time before I leave? I know within months, probably weeks, we'll both be with someone else." She walked closer to him and started kissing him using her tongue. "One last time William, please."

William swiftly removed the suitcase from the bed while Gabby locked her bedroom door. She laid in the middle of her king-size bed with her legs and arms stretched out and whispered, "Make love to me, William."

He removed his shoes, pants, and underwear and jumped on top of Gabby. He tried to enter her, but she wouldn't let him.

"I thought you wanted to do this," William said.

"I do. Since this is our last time together, I thought we could try something different and make it memorable." She reached into the nightstand beside her bed and pulled out a tube of KY Jelly. She handed it to William and said, "Use this before you go in." She turned over on her knees and used her fingers to spread her butt cheeks open.

William's eyes and mouth were wide open as he squeezed a generous amount of K-Y Jelly on his hands and rubbed it all over his penis. "Are you ready for this?"

"I'm ready, William. Be gentle." It had been a while since she had anal sex, but she played along and moaned like it was her first time. William didn't last a full minute before he released his juices inside of her.

He collapsed on the bed, completely spent.

Gabby rubbed his back and kissed him on the cheek. "I'll miss you, William."

William shook his head no. "I don't want you to go. I'll talk to my family and make them leave. I'll show them the video and pictures when they come back."

"You would do that for me, William?" Gabby put her hand over her breast and smiled.

He sat up and leaned on his elbow. "I'll do anything for you and Nadia. I love you."

"We care about you, too, William." Gabby smiled. "You better go talk to your family so we can get married. I need to shower and get my dress back on. Let me know when they're gone and I'll come down." Gabby jumped up and started gathering her things.

"Okay. I'll have them leave after I take a shower." William picked his clothes off the floor and kissed Gabby before he peeked out Gabby's bedroom door and left for his room.

Gabby showered and dressed again, but this time with no help. She waited for William to come back to the room.

Fifteen minutes later, William knocked on the door and said, "Gabby, they're gone. I'll meet you downstairs."

"Thank you, William. I'm on my way."

She walked downstairs and made her way to the backyard. Stephon decorated it just the way he promised. Tiny Christmas lights spread from one end of the yard to the other. Potted plants and small trees framed the guests' seats. Fifty white chairs elegantly decorated in coral taffeta bows were neatly arranged under an awning that prevented the hot July sun from beaming on their guests. William stood under a beautiful canopy decorated with white calla lilies, Gabby's favorite flower. She looked to the left and smiled when she saw her friends and their families. She made sure not to invite any of her poor and tacky relatives because she didn't want to be embarrassed by them on her wedding day. She looked to the right and smiled an even wider smile when she saw all the groom's guests' seats empty.

Gabby slid her arm around Maxine's dad's waiting arm and proceeded down the aisle using the model walk she had been practicing all her life. She knew she was making the right choice marrying William. He proved his loyalty when he kicked his parents and the rest of his family out of his own wedding just to please his new wife.

Chapter 9 —————

"Did you hear me, Maxine?" Her mother, Pat, asked.

Maxine turned to look at her parents sitting on the sofa in her family room. They had followed Maxine and Trent home for a short visit after Gabby's wedding. "I'm sorry, Momma. I didn't hear you."

"I said, when is Gabby ever going to learn to behave herself? Kicking her husband's family out like that! I was so embarrassed for William's mother. She seemed like such a nice lady." Pat sighed as she looked at her daughter with a disappointed expression.

"Momma, don't try to figure Gabby out. She's my best friend and I love her, but I'll never understand her," Maxine explained.

"And what happened to Joy? She left right after the bride and groom said their vows." Pat frowned. "Um, um, um...Bea wasn't happy about that at all."

Maxine ignored her mother as she went in the kitchen to get them some drinks. She wasn't going to discuss her best friends' business with her mother. Pat Crawford had no shame in spreading other people's business around like it was her own.

Trent joined Maxine in the kitchen after changing into a pair of shorts and a T-shirt. He made sure to kiss her on the lips while her parents looked on, then took the tray she prepared to the family room. "Mom, Dad, here are your drinks."

Maxine felt her temperature rise as she followed Trent into the family room. *How dare he kiss me after the way he's been beating my ass lately?* She thought back to three weeks ago when Trent beat her with his belt. He lied to their sons and told them that Mommy and Daddy were playing and Mommy fell down. TJ didn't question it because he was still young and tended to believe everything his father said, and Maxwell was asleep before Trent finished talking to them. Trent even slept in their room that night to ease their fears.

That night opened something in Trent Maxine thought she would never see. Almost every night since then, he had been violent toward her. She felt as if he kept all the stress from his workday bottled up and released it on her every couple of nights after their sons went to sleep.

She had a gut feeling that her sons weren't always asleep when Trent hit her because she noticed TJ pulling away from his father and Maxwell following his big brother's lead. Long gone were the days when they ran to the front door excited to see their father come home. Now, when they heard Trent arrive, they ran to Maxine's side and wrapped themselves around her legs.

"Can I get you anything else?" Trent asked with a phony smile.

"This water is all I need, Trent. Thank you, baby." Pat rubbed her stomach. "I'm still full from the wedding."

"Okay." He put the tray in front of his father-in-law, Dr. Jim.

"Thanks, son," Dr. Jim said as he took a glass of soda from the tray.

Trent put the tray on the coffee table and sat beside Maxine on the loveseat.

Maxine watched TJ and Maxwell play while her parents and Trent discussed the wedding. She noticed how aggressively TJ was playing with Maxwell.

TJ screamed, "Be quiet, Maxwell, or you're going to get it! Now, Maxwell, scream like Mommy and say, 'Stop, Trent... '"

Maxine looked at her parents to see if they were listening, but they were deep in conversation about something else. She walked over to her children, picked TJ up and whispered, "Stop baby. Don't play that game. Somebody might hear you."

TJ looked at his mother's worried face and knew it was time for him to play another game.

Maxine joined Trent back on the loveseat and kept a watchful eye on her sons.

Trent put his arms around Maxine's shoulder and pulled her close to him. "Did my wife tell you we're trying for our third child?"

Pat shrieked. "Congratulations you two! I know you want a daughter, Maxine."

"Thanks, Momma." Maxine wondered if she should've sounded more excited.

"Well, let me know when it happens," Dr. Jim said nonchalantly. As a pediatrician, he's seen enough babies to not get excited over someone announcing she's trying to have one.

Trent kissed Maxine on her cheek and said, "Yes, sir. We sure will."

Everybody's heads turned toward the children when they heard Maxwell scream and start crying. TJ had pushed Maxwell down and was punching his little brother with his fists.

Maxine looked at Trent with a terrified expression.

Dr. Jim picked up TJ while Pat consoled Maxwell.

"What was that about, young man? I've never seen you hit your brother before," Dr. Jim said in a stern voice.

TJ bent his head down and started crying.

Trent got up and took his son off his father-in-law's lap while Maxine sat beside her mother and rubbed Maxwell's back.

"I've never seen them fight. TJ, don't let Grandma see you hit your brother like that again. Do you hear me?"

Trent looked at TJ. "That's what brothers do. I know I fought with my brothers all the time when I was younger."

TJ shook his head no. "No, Daddy! I hit Maxwell like you hit Mommy."

Maxine gasped.

"What?!" Pat shrieked and looked at Maxine with bulging eyes.

Dr. Jim sat on the edge of the sofa and glared at Trent. "What the hell is my grandson talking about?" He turned his gaze on his daughter. "Maxine?"

There was an uncomfortable silence for a few seconds. Maxine didn't know whether to tell the truth and leave with her parents or lie and work things out with Trent. Trent decided for her.

"Um, unfortunately, our boys walked in our bedroom a few nights ago when we were in the midst of something." Trent looked around the family room to avoid eye contact with his in-laws. "They thought what they saw was Daddy hurting Mommy. I tried to explain that we were just playing, but maybe I didn't do a good job."

Maxine looked at her father as he relaxed and leaned back on the sofa. Her mother kept patting Maxwell's back as if she didn't hear a thing.

"I know you're trying to have another child, but maybe you should consider locking your door." Dr. Jim gave Trent the evil eye. "Children are very impressionable at this age and I don't want my grandsons confusing sex and violence."

Trent nodded. "Yes, sir. I agree."

"Jim, I think it's time for us to go. The boys look tired." Pat gave Maxwell to Maxine and stood up. She deliberately avoided eye contact with her daughter and son-in-law. The conversation about her grandchildren seeing their parents have sex was too much for her to handle.

After her parents left, they carried their exhausted sons upstairs and put them to bed. It had been a long day and they fell asleep without a single complaint. There was an uncomfortable silence between them as they entered their bedroom, sat on their side of the bed, and thought about what happened earlier.

"I want to talk about what's been happening between us." Trent looked down at the carpeted floor as he spoke.

Maxine turned to look at him. "For what? You promised me when we were in college that you would never hit me again; now it's happening almost every day." Tears fell down her face. "I don't want to live like this anymore, Trent. Today, you made me lie to my parents."

Trent turned around, grabbed Maxine's arm, and squeezed it. "How did *I* make you *lie* to your parents?

Maxine pulled her arm from Trent's grip, stood up, and spoke through clenched teeth. "What are you going to do, Trent? How are you going to beat me up tonight? Is it with your fist? Or your open hand? Should I go in the closet and get the belt or are you going to throw everything on the dresser at my head while I curl up in a ball in the corner?" Maxine pulled her hair. "Or maybe you should just kill me now and get it over with!"

Trent stared at her with tears in his eyes.

Maxine stood on top of their bed and started removing her clothes. "Look at my body, Trent."

Trent looked at her face instead.

"No, Trent! I need you to look at my body!" After she removed all her clothes, she turned around so Trent could see every inch of her body. "Do you see all the bruises you put on me in the last three weeks? Look at my skin, it's still scarred and bruised from the belt buckle ripping into my flesh."

Tears rolled down Trent's face.

"It's affecting our children and I hate it!" Maxine continued to turn around on the bed in front of Trent so he could see her bruised body.

He closed his eyes and bent his head down in shame.

Maxine raised her voice slightly as she said, "You need to get help, Trent. You're destroying our family."

Trent had a frightened look on his face and she knew he was thinking about what he saw growing up with his father abusing his mother.

"Do you want our boys to grow up the same way you and your brothers did, watching your mother get beaten over and over by your father?" Maxine stared at Trent, waiting for an answer.

Trent shook his head and covered his face with his hands. "I'm sorry, Maxi. I don't know why I do it. I hate myself for doing that to you, but I lose control and can't stop myself."

She held back her tears and yelled, "If you ever do this to me again, I'll take the boys and leave you. If you want to stay married to me and be a father to our sons, you need to get some counseling to learn how to control your temper. From this day on, I will not lie to my family and friends about any of this. Do you understand Trent?"

Trent looked at Maxine's bruised body and started crying again. "Yes. I'm sorry, Maxi. I didn't realize I did that to you. It'll never happen again. I promise."

Chapter 10

Later that night, Allen was parked outside waiting for Joy when she stepped out of the airport terminal later that evening. She jumped in the truck and kissed him. "Hey, baby, it's so good to see you," Joy said as she hugged him.

She felt guilty for breaking their plans and not going to his company's picnic, but Gabby needed her more than Allen did today. She was glad to be at the wedding to have her girl's back when William's family started acting up. Joy and Gabby got into their squabbles more than they should, but no matter what, they always had each other's back.

"Hey, you! Got all your luggage?" Allen asked then regretted it.

"I have my carry-on bag. What's wrong with you? You know I never check my luggage. Is everything alright?" She was concerned because Allen usually had his tongue down her throat as soon as she got in the truck.

"I'm good. Owen left for the evening to give us some privacy." Allen rubbed her thigh.

Joy laughed. "You know he left because he didn't want to hear me screaming and moaning from what you're going to do to me tonight." She blew him a kiss.

"You might have a point there, babe." Allen half-smiled.

Joy tried not to stare at Allen as he drove them to his apartment, but she had a terrible feeling that something was wrong. Whenever she touched him, he would give her a half smile or not look at her like he normally did. There was tension between them and she didn't like it.

As soon as they walked in the apartment, all of Joy's concerns melted away. Allen had moved the living room furniture against the wall and placed the dining room table in the middle of the floor. It was covered with a white table-cloth and decorated with a crystal vase full of red roses and two candles. It took Joy's breath away and brought tears to her eyes.

"Ahhh, you did this for us?" Joy wiped the tears from her eyes.

Allen held her in his arms and kissed her forehead. "I did this for you. I love you, baby."

"Oh, Allen! This is wonderful! Thank you baby. I love you, too." She looked Allen in the eye to let him know she meant every word.

He pulled Joy's chair out for her, lit the candles then dimmed the overhead lights. They ate shrimp scampi in a lemon butter sauce over angel hair pasta, with garden salad and cheese toast from Joy's favorite Italian restaurant.

After they finished dinner, Allen picked Joy up and carried her to his bed. He gently put her down and turned her over to unzip her dress. When he saw Joy's tattoo, he kissed it and stared at it until he saw Joy trying to wiggle out of her dress.

Allen turned Joy around to face him. "Joy, I wanna make love to you tonight."

Joy giggled and looked at Allen. "I wanna make love to you, too, baby." She kissed him and their tongues danced in each other's mouths.

He whispered in her ear. "I love you so much, baby. I want you to know that."

Her body shivered from his breath in her ear. "I do and I love you, too."

Allen lay beside Joy. She turned her body to face his and they stared at each other, smiling. Allen touched her face lovingly before he removed his clothes and moved on top of her. Joy closed her eyes, anticipating what he was going to do to her.

"Open your eyes, baby. I want all of you tonight. Keep your eyes on mine."

Joy opened her eyes and stared at Allen as he requested. When he entered her, it took her breath away. They looked in each other's eyes as their bodies moved as one. Joy could feel the tears rolling down her face. Allen stopped and wiped her tears. When she looked at him, he was crying too. She touched his wet face before she wrapped her legs around his back and squeezed her internal muscles while Allen moved inside her as if he were in a race. Their bodies quivered as their juices released and their bodies melted into one. They fell asleep wrapped in each other's arms.

The next morning, Joy woke up and smiled at Allen who was already dressed and sitting at his computer desk in the corner.

Joy stretched her naked body and yawned. "Good morning."

"Hey, beautiful." He got up from his desk and kissed her. "Can you get dressed? I have something special planned for us today."

Joy propped herself up on her elbow. "Wow! You're on a romantic role this weekend." She smiled. "I love it. I'll be dressed in twenty."

"Cool." Allen watched Joy as she swished her naked body to the bathroom. While she was in the shower, he closed his eyes and prayed for what he had planned to go his way.

After Joy was dressed, they opened his bedroom door and walked into the living room where the furniture was back in place and dozens of beautiful red roses were everywhere.

Joy gasped. "Oh, my God! These are beautiful, Allen. Are these for me? What are these for?" Joy had a big smile on her face as she ran around the living room smelling and touching the roses. "How did you do this?"

Allen chuckled as he leaned against the wall and watched Joy running around and smelling the roses. "Owen helped me last night when he came home. I need to talk to you about something. Come here and sit down with me," Allen instructed in a serious tone.

Joy held his hand as they sat on the couch, then released it when she saw the perturbed look on his face. She had a bad feeling something was wrong so she folded her hands in prayer position under her chin to prepare herself for what Allen had to say.

"Baby, something very good, very important has happened to my career. Remember the project I've been working on for the past couple of months?" Allen asked nervously.

"Yes." Joy stared at him with big eyes and nodded, anxious to hear what he had to say.

"I was put in charge of a project for a client in Shanghai, China. It was my first solo project and I did an outstanding job!" Allen smiled.

"Congratulations! We should go out and celebrate tonight!" She hugged Allen, but he pulled away.

"I need to finish telling you, Joy. I completed the first half of the project here in our corporate office. Now I need to go away to complete the second half of the project, which is estimated to take about two years."

Joy's body tensed as she asked, "Go away where?"

Allen held her hand. "I love you baby and I want you to go with me."

"Go where, Allen?" Joy could hear her pulse thumping in her ear.

"Shanghai," Allen answered nervously.

She pulled her hand back. "China! Why China, Allen? Why did you make such a huge decision without discussing it with me first?" Joy snapped.

"Because this is my career and it's what I really want. Do you understand that?" Allen asked in a raised tone. He was starting to get upset with Joy, but he decided to calm down and finish what he had to say. "The reason the room is covered with roses is because I love you." He grabbed Joy's hand and knelt down on one knee. "Joy, everything is coming to fruition for me. I love my job and just got promoted to lead a project in China. The only thing missing is you. I want to marry you." Allen pulled out a ring box and opened it. "Will you marry me, Joy? I love you and I need you. I can't be thousands of miles away from you. I need you by my side and in my life in China every day. Will you marry me and go with me to China?"

Joy knew he was going to propose one day, but she thought she would be able to finish her doctorate first. And what about Bea? She couldn't leave her and go half way around the world.

"Allen, what about our plans? I have another year in school. I love you and of course I want to be your wife." Her whole body was shaking.

Allen took the ring out of the box and started putting it in on her finger. "That's all that matters. There are on-line graduate classes everywhere. You don't have to physically sit in a class-room anymore, Joy. Half my graduate classes were on-line."

"I know, but we planned things differently, Allen," Joy said sadly.

"Plans change, damn it, Joy!" Allen was getting upset. He had a feeling things would turn out this way, but he knew he had to do what he needed to do. Go to China with or without Joy.

"I'm ready to marry you, but..." Joy said.

Allen shouted. "But what, Joy? Say it! But what?" He was furious. He knew exactly whom she was thinking about.

"What about Bea?" Joy whispered.

"What about her?" Allen spat the words at her.

"Who will she have if I go with you to China?" Joy asked in tears.

"She's a grown woman, Joy. She's your mother, not your man. She'll figure shit out." Allen couldn't take her need to please her mother any more.

"I'm not gonna ask you again. This is it, Joy. Please, baby, say yes. I picked this ring out just for you and the roses, too. Will you marry me and come with me to Shanghai?" Allen begged. He thought giving her an explanation on how much energy he put into the proposal would make her say yes.

"I want to but..."

"That's it, Joy. I can't do this anymore." Allen stood up, put the ring back in the box, and closed it. He knew it would end this way but it didn't make it hurt any less.

"What do you mean you can't do this anymore?" Joy asked, surprised to hear those words come out of Allen's mouth. "Are you ending our relationship because I won't run off to China with you?"

"No! I'm ending it because you never put me first. I bend over backwards to love you and support you. I would give you anything. You have one hundred percent of me. But what do I get in return? At best, forty percent, maybe forty-five at the most. But you have never loved me completely."

Joy jumped up and got in Allen's face. "Bullshit, Allen! You know what you're saying is bullshit. I have loved you since I was fifteen years old. Since we danced together at your sixteenth birthday party."

Allen stared back at her with nostrils flaring. "Wrong! You never loved me. We started sneaking around when you were fifteen and I was sixteen. I'm almost twenty-seven years old and we're still sneaking. If you can't understand that, I know it's time to end this."

"You know what I mean Allen. Don't twist my words. We're not ending our relationship over a job offer in China. Our love is stronger than this. Think about our connection last night," Joy said, trying to hold back her tears.

"I have waited and waited for you to love me back with your whole being, Joy. Instead, you put Bea, school, your friends, everybody in front of me. I feel like I'm an afterthought sometimes. Somebody you have sex with. Where is the love, Joy?"

She turned away from Allen and cried, "How can you say that I don't love you! I have loved nobody but you! I've never been with another man, Allen!"

"Maybe not, but listen to this. I have been arrested for you, didn't go to my prom because you were afraid of Bea finding out, was stood up by you because Bea found somebody else to take you to your senior prom. To this day, you haven't told Bea that you've been in a relationship with me since you were fifteen years old. How do you think that makes me feel? Ten years with you. Am I an embarrassment to you? I know I'm a poor boy from the projects and my brothers are in and out of jail, but damn, am I such a horrible human being that you can't let your fucking mother know about me? What kind of love is that, Joy?"

"Don't say that, baby. What do you want me to do? I'll call her now and tell her about us. Just don't leave me and go to China. I can't handle it." Joy started sobbing uncontrollably.

"Well, you're going to have to learn how to handle it because I'm going. It's over, Joy. Let's break free from each other now and never look back." Allen was hurt and angry, but he knew this was something he needed to do. It was time to have all of Joy or none of her.

"Please, Allen! Stop it! Don't say this! Don't leave me! I love you! You're a part of me! I can't go a day without talking to you! We love each other! You're my best friend, my lover, my future! Don't end my future! Don't end what we have! I need you in my life, baby!"

"You made your choice and I made mine." Allen looked at Joy with pure hatred.

"I'm not going to do this. Let's stay in and spend the day talking it over," Joy pleaded.

"No! I want you to leave, now," Allen spat.

"How could you invite me here, make love to me, and then kick me out. Is there somebody else? Is this why you're hurting me like this, Allen?" Joy could barely speak. Her heart was pounding, her head was swimming, and her stomach was queasy.

"Yeah, there is somebody else. Her name is Bea. Your loving, controlling-ass mother. Because of her, you can't begin your life with me. You're worried about her being alone here. What about me being alone in China? Did that cross your fucking mind? I should've done this shit years ago. Do you know how many women I've met since I've been with you who really wanted to be with me? I turned down all kinds of pussy because I love Joy. But you didn't love me back. What a fucking waste! You were a goddamn waste of my time! Two years in high school, four years in college, two years in graduate school, and the past two years turning down women and pussy left and right. Why? Because I love Joy. Not anymore. Get out! I'm through with you! Get out!"

"No! I'm not leaving you like this. Our love is stronger than this." Joy tried to hug Allen but he pushed her away and turned his back on her.

"Allen, please! Please, baby! I love you! I need you! I'll go with you to China! Let's do it. Let's go. When do we leave? I'll call Bea. Where is the phone? I'll call her and tell her everything. I just can't lose you, baby," Joy was sobbing and out of control.

"It's over. I leave for China in a week. Alone. I never want to hear from you again. It's time for me to find a woman who will love me back with no strings attached," Allen said, fighting back tears.

"No! No! No!" Joy screamed.

"It's time for you to go. I'll call you a cab. You can wait outside for the cab. Here is some money, my treat," Allen said in a cold voice as he handed Joy a fifty dollar bill.

Joy took the money from Allen then ran to the bathroom and vomited. She couldn't believe she was losing the only man she had ever loved. Why didn't she tell Bea about them years ago and just let her have her say? Why did she mess up both their proms when they wanted to go together? Why did she cancel her trips to visit him when her friends were having a crisis? Why did she do homework during their short visits together? She knew she screwed up sometimes but she thought their love could overcome anything. She thought she had more time to make things up to him.

Allen called Joy a cab. He was sitting on his coffee table, holding onto it like it was the only thing keeping him grounded. He was trying to be strong. He was fighting the urge to run in the bathroom and hold her. He loved her so much. He didn't want to lose her, but he knew it would be hard on both of them if he went to China alone for two years. He struggled to stay faithful every day when they were in college and living in different states, but he did it. He never cheated on Joy. China was a different story. He had his needs. Why didn't she fucking say yes. His face was wet. He didn't realize he was crying. He wiped his face and eyes when he heard Joy coming.

When she came out of the bathroom, her eyes were swollen and her skin looked pale. Her eyes were bloodshot red from crying. She looked at him, waiting for him to change his mind.

"I'm not changing my mind, Joy," he said as if he was reading hers.

"What do you want me to do, Allen? I'll do it. I promise you. I'll do it. Just tell me," Joy pleaded.

"Get out. That's what I want you to do. Leave," Allen demanded.

Joy didn't say anything. She just stood and stared at Allen for what seemed like an eternity but was actually two minutes.

Allen didn't show any emotion. It hurt him to see Joy staring at him with pleading eyes. He felt like his heart was going to jump out of his chest.

"Okay. If that's what you want, I'll leave. Allen, I'm coming over there because I want to give you a hug. I want to hug you one more time. Please don't push me away."

Allen didn't say a word. Joy walked slowly as if each step hurt her. She wrapped her arms around him. He didn't hug her back. He didn't respond at all. He stood as still as a cold statue and let her hug him as he used all his strength to fight the urge to hug her back. He knew he had to do this. One way or the other, she was going to be hurt, breaking up with her here or infidelity in China.

Owen walked out of his bedroom, saw the tension between them and turned around.

Joy squeezed Allen's hand and said, "Okay. I get it. I understand. I'll leave. Please be careful in China. If you ever want to talk..." Joy said, her words trailing off because she knew she was defeated. She knew Allen was serious and it was over. She just lost her soul-mate and there was nothing she could do about it. "Just remember I still love you and always will, baby."

Joy grabbed her purse and carry-on and walked out the door. A cab was waiting outside for her. She got in crying and shaking. "Southwest Airlines," was all she could say.

Allen watched from his living room window as Joy got in

the cab. He picked up one of the vases full of red roses and threw it across the room. The vase shattered into pieces before it fell to the floor with the roses and water falling on top of it.

Owen ran out of his bedroom to see what had happened.

Allen sat on the couch with tears dripping down his face.

"You alright, man?" Owen couldn't believe they were over.

"No! I just lost a big part of me today," Allen said, turning to walk to his bedroom. With tears streaming, he slammed his bedroom door shut so hard it almost broke at the hinges.

Chapter 11

Gabby returned home after taking Nadia for a walk around the block. As she took the baby out of her stroller, the blinking light on the answering machine caught Gabby's eye. She frowned and rolled her eyes, thinking it was Joy calling again to cry over Allen dumping her a month ago. *Get over it already.* She pressed the button on the phone's base and listened to the message. It was CVS Pharmacy calling William to let him know that his prescription was ready for pickup. *What prescription?* William didn't tell her he was taking medicine. If he slept with somebody else and got a disease, she was going to kill him. She listened to the message again, wrote down the phone number, then she called to get the address.

Gabby was furious. This was not what she expected to deal with on her one month wedding anniversary. Maxine agreed to let Nadia stay over so the newlyweds could go out for a romantic dinner. Gabby was planning to reward William with some loud and freaky sex for being the perfect husband so far, but now she was having doubts. She loved being Mrs. William Landon, but she wasn't going to let her husband betray her in any way.

Within minutes, she had Nadia in her car seat and was heading to the CVS in the strip mall around the corner to get William's prescription. She was going to find out for herself what kind of medicine he was taking and why. When she arrived at the drug store, she sat in the car for a few minutes to compose herself.

She didn't want to go in looking upset.

 She touched up her make-up and lip gloss before she exited the car and placed Nadia in her stroller. She walked in the CVS, headed straight to the pharmacy counter, and said, "Good afternoon. I'm here to pick up my husband's prescription. His name is William Landon."

 "Just a minute." The cashier left and returned to the counter a few minutes later holding a prescription bag. "Can you verify his date of birth?"

 Gabby rolled her eyes and tried to remember William's birthday. "August 21, 1975."

 The cashier poked out her lips and said, "It's fifty dollars."

 Gabby slid the credit card William gave her into the machine and then signed her name before she took the prescription bag and left. After she put Nadia back in her car seat, she jumped in her car and barely closed the door before she ripped open the bag and read the prescription bottle. It was for Zoloft. She snatched off the information sheet attached to the bag and started reading every word.

 After she finished, she couldn't believe William was taking medicine for depression. If she had known this about him, she would've never married him. *William was depressed? About what? Was she in danger? Was Nadia in danger?* She looked at the clock on the dashboard of her Lexus. It was 4:45. William would be home in less than an hour. *He'd better be prepared to tell me what's going on with him.* She stuffed the prescription bag in her purse and drove off.

 As she pulled out of the parking lot, she saw William turning in, driving his black Cadillac Escalade. She decided to turn back around and greet William. She wanted to see his expression when he stepped out of the pharmacy knowing she had his prescription.

 She watched him walk in, then parked her Lexus in front of the store, ignoring the fire lane signs, and waited for him to exit. Her phone was ringing, but she ignored it. William came out with his phone to his ear and nearly jumped out of his skin when he saw Gabby parked there with the passenger window rolled down.

"Hey, Gabby. I just called you," William said. He leaned over and looked in the car through the passenger window.

"We need to talk now!" Gabby barked.

William shrugged his shoulders. "Okay. Cool. Can we talk at home? I'll meet you there."

Gabby rolled her eyes and glared at William. "And you'd better come straight home!" she ordered.

William put up his hands in defeat and said, "I'll follow you there."

Twenty minutes later, Gabby walked in the house and sat on the sofa with Nadia in her arms waiting for William. When he walked in a few minutes later, she pointed upstairs to William and then followed him up the steps. She put Nadia in her crib, then met William in his bedroom. He sat on the bed and waited for Gabby to say something. She paced back and forth for two minutes before she spoke. William sat patiently on the bed rubbing his forehead.

Gabby opened her purse, pulled out the prescription bag and threw it at William. He blocked it just before it hit him in his chest. "What is this about, William? Are you sick? Why didn't you tell me about this before I married you? I would've never married you if I knew you were dealing with depression."

William took a deep breath and shook his head to show his disappointment in what Gabby said. "My doctor put me back on medication after I told him I've been feeling sad lately."

Gabby gasped. "Put you *back on medicine*? How long have you been taking this medicine and what are you sad about lately? We just got married and have a beautiful daughter. Is this too much for you to handle? We can leave if it is."

William leaned over, placed his elbows on his thighs, and said, "When I was sixteen, I got real sad, didn't eat, stopped playing sports, and basically didn't feel like living anymore."

Gabby's eyes nearly popped out of her head and her mouth shot open involuntarily from the shock of William's words. "Oh, my God! You mean I married someone who actually thought about committing suicide! Who else knows? How is this going to make me look, William?"

William sighed. "Just listen for a minute, Gabby. My parents took me to our family doctor and he admitted me to the hospital. I stayed in a mental hospital for two months while the doctors tried to figure out what kind of medicine would work to treat the chemical imbalance that caused my depression. I stayed on the medicine until I was eighteen and didn't have any more problems until I turned twenty-two. The stress of graduating from college and not being able to find a job right away caused another episode of depression. I took the medicine again for about a year and I felt better until recently."

Gabby clutched her chest. "Is being married to me and a father to Nadia too stressful for you? Is that why you're back on this medicine?"

William stood up from the bed and tried to hug Gabby but she pushed him away. "It's not you or Nadia, Gabby. My family has been giving me a hard time since I asked them to leave our wedding. My mother was crushed and my father said he's disappointed in me for treating our family the way I did. I can't talk to you about them or them about you, so it's caused me some stress."

"You don't seem stressed or act sad to me." Gabby looked William up and down like he was wearing his depression for everyone to see.

"That's because every time I see you and Nadia, you make me happy. I love coming home to my family every day. I love holding my daughter. I look forward to making love to you and holding you in my arms, Gabby. I live for you two. I take the medicine to help me cope with all the negative feedback I'm getting from my family."

"Just cut them off, William. If they're making you so miserable, that you need to take antidepressants, which is affecting our family by the way, you need to stop talking to them. I did the same thing with my family years ago."

"Gabby, that's my family. We're..."

"William, we're your family, me and Nadia. I'm afraid you might want to hurt yourself again if they keep causing you all

84

this stress. Then what will happen to me and Nadia?" Gabby walked close to William and leaned her head on his chest. "I don't want anybody to hurt you so take a break from your family for a while and then you can stop taking this medicine. I'll make sure you're happy. Didn't I make us a beautiful home? Don't I satisfy your needs? Trust me, William. Nadia and me, we're all you need." She stroked his face lovingly.

"I do trust you, Gabby, and I'll seriously think about it." William took a deep breath and lowered his head.

Gabby kissed William on his lips and said, "Let's go get our daughter and spend some time together as a family."

William hugged Gabby and kissed her back. "Thank you, Gabby. I don't know what I would do without you and Nadia."

Gabby smiled and said, "You'll never have to worry about losing either of us."

Chapter 12 ⎯⎯⎯⎯⎯⎯

The next day, Maxine stood on the front steps of the Prince George's County Public School System's office building feeling guilty. When she dropped Nadia off to Gabby this morning, she left her sons with Gabby so she could interview for a position that became available at one of the schools where she was interested in teaching. After the interview, Maxine was offered the job and accepted it immediately. She stood on the steps wondering how she was going to explain this to Trent.

"Maxine? Maxine Anderson?" A tall, muscular man with a dark brown complexion and a shiny bald head, fine enough to stop women dead in their tracks looked at Maxine with the sexiest smile she had ever seen.

Maxine almost dropped her bag when she looked up at him and said, "Yes?"

He smiled again, showing Maxine a perfect set of straight, white teeth. "How are you?" Maxine looked at the man with a confused expression. He looked familiar, but she couldn't remember where she met him.

"I'm sorry. You don't remember me. I'm Kevin Bradley. We used to teach together at Capitol Heights Elementary School."

"Oh, yeah." Maxine remembered him. He was the only male teacher and all the other teachers, married and single, wanted him, except Maxine because she was so in love with Trent.

Kevin touched her shoulder and laughed. "I'm glad you remember."

As soon as he touched her shoulder, she felt a lightning bolt shoot between her legs and her nipples got so hard, they felt like they were trying to drill a hole through her lace bra. "Yes, I remember you now. I'm fine. How are you? Are you still at Capitol Heights?"

"No. I went back to school, finished a dual master's and doctorate degree program at the University of Maryland then got promoted to principal." He moved beside Maxine as a group of people walked by.

Maxine tried to control her breathing after Kevin brushed up against her. "I, um, I'm very familiar with that program at the University of Maryland. One of my closest friends, Joy Marshall, is finishing her last year in that same program while teaching full-time for the county. So I know how hard it is. Congratulations!"

Kevin smiled and rubbed Maxine's arm. "Thank you. I hope you're here because you're thinking about teaching again."

She crossed her leg, fearing the moisture between her legs was going to soak through her underwear and stockings and Kevin was going to look down and see a puddle there. She nodded nervously. "Uh-huh."

"The county could use a good teacher like you."

"Oh, thanks! Yes, um, I, um, just got offered a position at Allenwood Elementary." She was so nervous, she could barely speak.

A group of people walked by and Kevin moved closer to Maxine so they could get by. "Do you have a few minutes to catch up? There's a picnic table over there."

Maxine nodded eagerly. "Oh, yeah, sure."

Kevin put his hand on Maxine's lower back and held her arm as they walked through the patchy, uneven grass. As they approached the picnic table, Maxine had a vision of Kevin laying her on the table and fucking her. She giggled.

"Are you alright?" Kevin asked as he helped Maxine sit down.

She nodded and smiled. "Um, hum."

"So, you're coming back to teaching." He touched Maxine's hand. "I see it all the time. Women leave teaching after they get married and then when the marriage ends, they come back. Sorry, it didn't work out for you."

"Oh, but..." Maxine was about to tell him she was still married, but changed her mind. She enjoyed looking at him and would probably never see him again after today.

"I know it's hard. I'm in the middle of a divorce myself." He looked at his watch. "Maxine, I didn't realize it was this late. Can we exchange numbers? I would love to go out with you sometimes." He showed Maxine a devious grin. "You didn't know this, but I had a crush on you when we worked together at Capitol Heights."

Maxine's eyes almost jumped out of her head. She could feel her stomach doing back flips. "Really?"

"Sure did." Kevin took out his wallet, pulled out a business card, and gave it to Maxine. "Call me later this evening if you can." He helped Maxine off the bench and walked her to the parking lot before they went their separate ways.

She buried Kevin's business card deep in her wallet. She didn't know it felt this good being so bad. She had no business interviewing and accepting a job after Trent told her not to. She should've definitely told Kevin she was still married, but she didn't because she was having fun looking at that fine ass brother. Trent better watch out. If he didn't get his act together, he might push her into Kevin's muscular arms.

Chapter 13

Gabby rolled her eyes, shook her head, and crossed her arms over her chest. "I bet she's on the phone begging Allen to take her back." Gabby pointed at the boxes stacked in Joy's living and dining rooms. "She'll be in China by the end of the week."

Maxine smiled. "I hope so. They love each other and they should be together."

"Whatever." Gabby looked at Maxine with a confused expression. "Girl, it's a hundred degrees outside. Why do you have on a long-sleeved shirt in August?"

"I get cold from the air conditioner when I'm inside and in the car," Maxine lied as she pulled on her sleeves unconsciously.

"Shoot, you got me sweating like a menopausal woman during a hot flash." Gabby fanned her face with her hand and laughed.

Maxine frowned at Gabby as Joy walked in the living room and hugged them. "This is a nice surprise. What brings you guys over this late?"

Maxine looked at Joy and shook her head. "Joy, don't act like you don't know why we're here. We wanted to come earlier but didn't want to bring the children in case you were upset again."

Joy winced and thought back to a month ago when Maxine and Gabby picked her up from the airport with their children in Maxine's minivan. Joy was crying and hysterical the entire ride home over Allen breaking up with her. Maxine had to pull over twice because her children started crying and questioning her about what was wrong with Aunt Joy. Even baby Nadia, who didn't know what was going on, started crying.

Gabby looked Joy up and down. "You look better, but you can still look a whole lot better." She frowned. "When we picked you up from the airport after losing the so-called love of your life, I thought you were at death's door. I have to admit, I was expecting the same thing today."

Joy fell back on her loveseat and threw her hands up. "Fuck Allen Todd Johnson! I may still love his black ass, but I'm sure as hell trying not to."

Gabby and Maxine stared at each other with concern, shocked by Joy's words.

Gabby clapped her hands. "Thank God! I knew you would pull it together. Weeping over a man for the past month is weak and that's not you, girlfriend. There are too many ding-dongs in the world to cry over one."

Maxine bumped Gabby with her shoulder. "Why the change, Joy? I thought today would be hard for you."

Joy pointed at the boxes and said, "Sunday morning I woke up and realized I couldn't live another day without Allen so I packed everything I owned and called Tyesha to come over. When she got here, I had her call Allen for me." Joy stood up and started pacing around the living room. "When I heard his voice, I knew I made the right decision. I apologized and told him I loved him and was ready to come to China."

Gabby sat up straight and leaned over to hear Joy better. "What happened?"

Maxine stared at Joy with a huge smile on her face. "When do you leave?"

Joy shook her head side to side. "He told me we needed this time apart. He didn't want me to come, then I heard a woman with a British accent ask him if he was ready to go." Joy closed her eyes. "Why was he with a woman on a Sunday?"

Gabby fell back on the sofa and snapped her fingers. "I *knew* he had somebody else! I pray every day for him to catch the worst kind of swine flu they have in China!"

Maxine was almost in tears. "Joy, I'm sorry."

"Don't be! I will *not* shed another tear over that black, bastard mother-fucker!" Joy turned her back to her friends as tears streamed down her face.

Maxine went to her friend and hugged her. "But you're crying now, sweetie. It's okay, let it out."

Joy pulled away from Maxine, wiped her face, and screamed, "I hate him!"

Gabby nodded. "I heard there was a thin line between love and hate."

Joy reached into her pocketbook on the dining room table and pulled out an envelope. She handed it to Maxine as they walked back to the living room to sit down. "I got this from him the next day."

Before Maxine could look at it, Gabby snatched it out of her hand. "What is it?"

Maxine looked at Joy and shrugged her shoulders.

"It's a certified check for $27,000," Joy explained.

"What?" Maxine asked as her eyes bulged. "Where did he get that much money and why did he send it to you?"

"When we first started working, we opened a joint savings account for our wedding and the down payment on our first home. I forgot all about it because I had the money come out of my pay-check automatically." Joy sighed. "Why would he send me all the money in the account?" Joy looked at her friends for the answer.

"Oh, one word, guilt. He thinks giving you this money will ease his guilt over leaving you for another woman in China." Gabby put the check back in the envelope and handed it to Joy. "Ummm, all I can say is good riddance."

Joy looked at Gabby with an angry gaze. "It doesn't make it hurt any less!"

"I know, Joy, but school starts soon, so that'll help you," Maxine advised.

"A classroom full of spoiled third graders will not help me, Maxine." Joy smiled.

Maxine stood up and looked down at Joy. "At least you

have a job!" she spat.

"Calm down, woman!" Joy wiped some of Maxine's spit off her face and looked at her with a frown. "And by the way, Allen is not the only one who can find somebody else!"

"Um hum...They say watch out for a woman scorned." Gabby surveyed Maxine with squinted eyes.

Maxine sat down after she saw Gabby looking at her like she was crazy. "That money isn't going to last long."

"I know that," Joy replied.

Gabby looked at Joy with a devilish smirk. "So what are you going to do with all that money? Wanna go shopping this weekend?"

"I'm not going to waste it on shopping, Gabby. I asked my father to sell me one of his investment properties in Fort Washington. I'm going to use that money as the down payment and to fix it up. I'm planning to move next month. I can't stay in this apartment, too many memories." Joy looked down at the carpet.

"I understand and congratulations on buying a house." Maxine beamed.

"Hmmm...I can relate to you not wanting to stay here. All that screwing y'all used to do up in here, it got on my nerves. I couldn't wait to move out," Gabby complained.

Joy laughed and tossed one of her throw pillows at Gabby.

"Gabby, look at Joy now. She's better and will get better with time. Your strength inspires me." Maxine smiled and felt stronger than she had in a long while.

Joy sighed. "I'm glad somebody got something positive from my broken heart." Joy wondered if Maxine would think she was so inspiring if she knew how she cried herself to sleep every night holding Allen's T-shirt or how she threw up every time she ate.

"Now, on to serious business. I believe the best way to get over one man is to get under another one." Gabby tapped Maxine's leg. "Tell her Maxine."

Maxine cringed when Gabby touched the bruise Trent put on her thigh last night. "I gave one of Trent's co-workers your phone number." She smiled. "He saw you last year at one of the parties we had and he's never stopped asking about you."

Joy gasped. "Oh, no! Maxine, I'm not ready to start dating yet."

Gabby snapped her finger in Joy's face. "Stop it! You don't have to date him, just have some fun with him. I met him and he's fine."

Joy frowned because she knew she and Gabby had different opinions of what *fine* was. Joy liked her men tall, chocolate, and masculine while Gabby liked light-skinned pretty boys she could run over. The last thing Joy wanted was a henpecked, high-yellow man who spent more time at the mirror than she did. "I can't promise you that I'll go out with him, Maxine."

Maxine pulled a piece of paper out of her wallet with Dean Bennett's name and phone numbers on it and gave it to Joy. "Just take his information, you never know."

Gabby smiled. "Did she mention that he's a lawyer with plenty of money?"

Joy took the paper from Maxine and stared at it. Although she was an emotional wreck right now, the thought of being with a man other than Allen had her aroused and surprisingly horny. Maybe Dean Bennett was just what she needed to get Allen off her mind and out of her heart.

Chapter 14

Gabby sat at her vanity in her bedroom with the door closed staring at her cell phone. Rayshawn's number was bouncing around angrily on the screen. It was the end of August and she knew he was calling her because he was back in the area for the Baltimore Ravens' training camp. She needed to talk to him and make him understand once and for all that his trying to see Nadia could end both their marriages and she wasn't going to let that happen because she was happy right where she was.

She didn't want to risk William overhearing her conversation with him again, so she turned off her cell phone and walked to her closet. Her hands shook as she moved hangers, trying to find the perfect outfit for today. She had so much going on at once and her nerves were on edge with Rayshawn calling to see Nadia, Joy's calls and mood swings over losing Allen, and now dinner with William's family.

William's mother called her last week and apologized for her family's behavior at their wedding. She wanted Gabby, William and Nadia to come to her house today for a family dinner to welcome William's oldest sister, Phyllis and her husband, Sam back home after Sam's job had kept them in Germany for three years. She should've declined but felt she needed to show William that by her going and trying to extend an olive branch, she wouldn't look like the bad person in his eyes.

She sat on her bed, massaged her temples, and took a few

deep breaths. She didn't drink but felt as if she needed a glass of wine to take the edge off.

There was a knock on her bedroom door. *What now?* She snatched the door open and saw William standing there looking as needy as ever. "What is it William? I'm trying to decide what to wear," she snapped.

William tilted his head and stared at her with sad, puppy dog eyes. "You asked me to come to your room after I put Nadia down for her nap."

She smiled when she remembered. She thought sex with her husband would calm her nerves. "Oh, I forgot." She pulled William into her room and started kissing him.

As usual, he responded on cue. He untied the belt on her robe and began caressing her naked body as he whispered in her ear, "Gabby, you're so beautiful."

"Um-hum, thanks." Gabby let her silk robe fall to the floor. "William, this dinner with your family is making me a nervous wreck. I need you to calm me down. Make my body feel good and relaxed. Can you handle that?"

William's eyes popped out of his head as he looked at Gabby's naked body. "Of course, Gabby."

William picked her up and carried her to the bed,. laid her on her stomach, and started kissing the back of her neck, then moved down her back all the way to her buttocks. He used both his hands to squeeze her butt cheeks as hard as he could. Gabby let out a soft moan. Sometimes, she liked pain during sex. She turned around and held her head back for William to kiss her neck. Instead, he licked her neck, then her collarbone, and worked his way down to her breasts and nipples before he stopped at her pubic hair. Gabby moaned louder. He jumped off the bed and took his pants off. He wasn't wearing underwear and his erection stood straight out with a slight curve, pointing at Gabby on the bed.

He laid on top of her and started kissing her lips, teasing her with his tongue. Gabby was ready. She arched her back and begged William to make love to her. William obliged, but took his time. He sat up and used his fingers to play with her clitoris. She was moaning and breathing heavily. William took his fingers away and started using his tongue. He was teasing Gabby, going in and out of her vagina, licking her clitoris, alternating between his tongue and his fingers. She was almost screaming. William whispered, "I love you, Gabby." She didn't respond. Instead, she grabbed him and pulled him on top of her. He pushed his penis inside her moist vagina. She started moving back and forth with her hips. William didn't move. She was begging him to give it to her. He made one hard thrust with his penis inside of her. She grabbed William's butt to get him deeper inside her, begging him for more. He was making her work for her orgasm. She moved her hips faster and faster. When William felt her body tense, he started moving in tempo with her. They both came on each other within minutes. William kept his penis inside Gabby as it got softer. He loved her and wanted the closeness between them to last forever. Unfortunately, it only took a few seconds for the real Gabby to surface.

"Get up, William, I'm done. I want to soak in my bathtub before I get dressed." She stood up, retrieved her robe from the floor, and put it on.

William looked at her, noticeably perturbed. "We don't have to rush, Gabby. Can't I just hold you for a while?" William pleaded as he lay on the bed.

Gabby pointed to the door with a phony smile. "Next time."

After William left her bedroom, she ran her bath water and soaked for twenty minutes while her husband dressed Nadia in the pastel sundress she picked out. She laid William's outfit out before she got in the bathtub and her dress was hanging on her closet door. She wanted her family color-coordinated in stylish designer outfits to show William's relatives that no matter how they felt about her, he was her husband and they were a family.

Two hours later, they pulled up at William's parents' house, fashionably late. Gabby's idea. Thanks to William, she was relaxed and ready to take on whatever his family threw her way.

William's mother opened the door. "Thank the Lord! Y'all made it just in time. We ready to sit down and eat." She hugged Gabby and William and kissed Nadia who was sleeping in her carrier. "I got a beautiful granddaughter right there. Come on in. William, take your wife to the dining room where everybody is."

Gabby followed him, ready for the animosity she knew was coming her way. When she entered the dining room, everybody stopped talking and all eyes were on her. She tossed her long hair over her shoulders and gave them a phony smile. "Good afternoon, everyone. I hope we're not too late."

William's father and brother-in-law, Sam were the only ones who spoke. Phyllis jumped up from the table with her younger sister, Denise, on her heels and headed toward Gabby, full of attitude.

William stopped Phyllis before she reached Gabby. "Hey, sis! I haven't seen you in three years and you walk right pass me." William hugged Phyllis.

"Hey!" Phyllis half hugged William back as she stared at Gabby standing behind him. She could tell already that everything her younger sister and cousin had said about Gabby was true. She was a stuck-up bitch who thought the world revolved around her and had William pussy-whipped.

William turned to face Gabby. "Let me introduce you to my beautiful wife..."

Phyllis cut him off. She looked Gabby up and down with her fist on her right hip. "I heard all I need to know about your wife. So you're the one who kicked my family out of my parents' only son's wedding?" Phyllis asked with her neck rolling full of attitude.

Gabby looked at William with a sad and vulnerable expression. "William, I told you this wasn't a good idea. Maybe we should leave."

William looked angrily at Phyllis. "I think you're right."

Mrs. Landon stopped them dead in their tracks. "No! You're here now and we're going to have a nice family dinner. Leave all the tension at the door." Mrs. Landon glared at Phyllis and Denise and shook her head toward their seats for them to sit down. "William, you and Gabby sit right here. Here is an empty seat for you to put the baby's carrier on."

William and Gabby took their seats across from Phyllis,

Sam, and Denise. Mr. and Mrs. Landon sat at the end of the table. After Mr. Landon prayed, everyone fixed a dinner plate.

Sam picked up a platter full of fried chicken. "It's about time." He looked at William. "Boy, we been waiting over two hours for you. I was ready to eat."

Gabby squeezed William's thigh playfully. She smiled at Sam as she fluttered her eyelashes. "It's not William's fault. I'm sorry, but we're newlyweds and still in that honeymoon phase." Gabby nibbled on William's ear. "Forgive me, but I can't get enough of my sexy husband."

Phyllis growled.

"Ewwwww," Denise whispered.

Mrs. Landon looked at her husband and rolled her eyes to the heavens. "William, Gabby, fix your plates."

Gabby whispered something in William's ear. He smiled, took the empty plate in front of her, put a small amount of food on it, and placed it back in front of Gabby, then he fixed his plate with the same amount of food.

"So you a slave now, William? You gotta fix your wife's plate every day?" Phyllis inquired looking William in his eyes.

William ignored her and ate his food.

"Mind your business, Phyllis." Sam looked at his wife with a frown. "Huh, they were two hours late and he hasn't stopped smiling since he walked in that door, so she's doing something worthy of him fixing her plate."

William laughed. "Go ahead with that, Sam."

Gabby smiled. She liked Sam's personality and she could tell he liked her because he couldn't take his eyes off her. Phyllis had better be thankful Gabby's married to William now because if she were single, Gabby would've screwed Sam and made Phyllis listen to the whole thing with a call to her cell phone, then she would've made Sam take care of her financially until she got bored with him. She smiled wickedly thinking about her old ways.

Mr. Landon looked at William's plate. "Son, you and the misses didn't eat much. Y'all on a diet?"

William rubbed his stomach and said, "Naw, I'm just trying to get my six-pack back."

"What about you, Gabby?" Mr. Landon asked.

Before she could answer, Sam said, "I know you not on a diet, Gabby. You look perfect to me." He stared at Gabby with a seductive grin.

Phyllis punched him in his arm. "Watch it, Sam!"

"Sam, man, are you flirting with *my* wife with your wife sitting right beside you?" William asked angrily.

"I'm just joking, William. I didn't mean no harm," Sam lied. He would leave Phyllis in a hot second if he had a chance with Gabby.

Gabby hugged William, then turned his face to hers and kissed him on the lips. "Sweetheart, don't get upset. He didn't mean anything by it." Gabby looked at Phyllis. "Look who he's married to."

Phyllis slammed her fist on the table. "What did you say?"

Gabby let out a phony laugh. "Oh, Mr. Landon, to answer your question about me being on a diet. I'm not. I just like to watch what I put in my body so I can stay attractive to my husband." She looked at Phyllis. "I wish I could feel comfortable being plus size like Phyllis and eating manly portions, but I know there are hundreds of women standing in line to take my William from me if I stop caring like some women." Gabby looked across the table at Phyllis with a devilish smirk.

Phyllis jumped up. "That's it! You think you can insult me like that and get away with it. I don't think so. I heard you were a conniving bitch, but you've met your match in me."

Gabby played innocent. "What's wrong, Phyllis? What did I say to make you so upset?"

Denise stood up. "Come on, Phyllis, let's take her outside and whip her ass!"

"That's enough!" Mrs. Landon pointed at Phyllis, Denise, and Sam and said, "Come in the kitchen. I need to talk to you."

They got up and followed her to the kitchen.

Mrs. Landon barked, "I want you three to leave your brother and his wife alone. We may not agree with his choice but he's happier because of her. Do you know how many times I got on my knees and prayed to God to stop William from feeling so sad? Do you know how many times he's been in and out of hospitals dealing with depression? Since she said that baby was his, he's been happier than ever. No suicide talk, no pills, no sadness, and no hospital stays. Whether you like her or not, or believe that Nadia is his or not, let it go. If he loves her and believes that child is his, then they are our family. That's the end of it."

"Ma, she broke up with him and then came back three months later, claiming she was pregnant by him. I tried to make him see the dates didn't match up, but he wouldn't listen. He'll listen to Phyllis, though!" Denise yelled.

"Don't raise your voice at me, Denise. For whatever reason, he wants to claim that child as his own so let him. He's happy; that's all that matters," Mrs. Landon said.

"No! That's not all that matters. She brought a lot of confusion to this family. Didn't you just hear the slick way she tried to insult me!" Phyllis barked.

"Yeah, and the way she had William kick us out of his wedding; that was just wrong." Denise poked out her lips and shook her head.

Mrs. Landon stared at her daughters and son-in-law. "You heard what I said. Let it go." She gave them all one last firm glare, then stomped out of the kitchen.

Phyllis looked at Sam and Denise with an evil expression. "Don't mention this to Ma, but Gabby is going to get a big eye-opener, courtesy of her husband's big sister. That bitch is not going to know what hit her."

Chapter 15

"I had to leave the office to call you," Trent said in a tense voice.

Maxine immediately left the family room where she was watching her sons play and went in the kitchen so they couldn't hear her. "Why? What's wrong?" she whispered, sensing something was seriously troubling from Trent's tone.

"The Jaguar was repossessed." Trent groaned. "Shit! This is the last thing I need. I told them I would send a payment tomorrow on the first."

"We'll come get you," Maxine offered.

"No! I told one of my co-workers I put the car in the shop and it wasn't ready so he offered to bring me home."

"Oh...okay."

"I just wanted to let you know." Trent ended the call.

Maxine started worrying the second Trent told her about his car. Things had been better between them lately. Since she confronted him about the abuse a month ago, he had only lost his temper once, leaving an ugly bruise on her thigh, and then spent the whole night apologizing for what he did. He even spent the past weekend with them sightseeing in D.C. and joined them for church, something he hadn't done in a long time.

She made herself stop worrying by focusing on helping her children put up an indoor play tent Trent bought them over the weekend. While she was on the phone, the boys had opened the box and were trying to assemble the tent without her. Trash from the ripped box and packing Styrofoam was everywhere. Since they were so excited, Maxine decided to finish putting up the tent before cleaning up the mess.

An hour later, Trent walked in the house with his coworker. "Maxine, where are you?" Trent asked.

"We're in the family room," Maxine yelled back.

Trent turned the corner to the family room with his colleague following close behind him. When Maxine saw the newcomer, she jumped up from the floor and went over to introduce herself. She bit her bottom lip nervously when she saw the angry look on Trent's face.

She extended her hand to the man and said, "Hello, I'm Trent's wife, Maxine. It's nice to meet you. Excuse the mess. Trent bought the boys a tent over the weekend and they started putting it up without me."

"I'm Jack Collins, and believe me, it's no problem. You have a beautiful home. If you don't mind, I just need to use the bathroom and get home. I know my wife is waiting for me," he said.

"It's right behind you," Trent said. He stared at Maxine when Collins went into the bathroom. "What the hell, Maxi? I told you I was bringing a coworker with me," Trent whispered through clenched teeth.

"I'm sorry. I didn't know he was coming in and the boys..." Maxine tried to explain.

"Shut up!" Trent snapped.

Collins came out the bathroom drying his hands with a paper towel. "Thanks. I appreciate it. Do you need me to pick you up tomorrow, Trent?"

"I'll call the dealership and let you know after I talk to them," Trent said, lying through his teeth.

Both Andersons walked him to the door.

"Goodbye and nice meeting you," Maxine said. She didn't want Collins to leave because she knew Trent was in one of his moods. After he closed the door, she ran to the family room floor and tried to clean up the mess.

Trent quickly followed her. He was mad and didn't try to hide it. "Why would you do something like this, Maxi? You know I work with that man. Now he's going to go to the office and tell them that we live like slobs."

"I'm sorry, Trent. I'm cleaning it up now. Come on. boys, help Mommy get this mess up so we can wash up for dinner." She was on her hands and knees scooping up the trash from the floor.

"Leave it! You already fucked up my image!" Trent yelled.

She stayed on her knees, cleaning up the trash as fast as she could.

Maxwell shouted, "Ahhh, Daddy said bad word."

TJ could feel the tension between his parents. He was moving as fast as he could to get the trash off the floor. He knew his dad was angry because he never said bad words in front of them.

Out of the blue, Trent bent down and grabbed a handful of Maxine's hair. She started to scream but then realized her children were in the room. She didn't want to frighten them.

"I told you on the phone that I was bringing a coworker home with me! Didn't you hear me!" Trent barked.

TJ's little body shook. He didn't like the way his father was treating his mother. Maxwell ran over to TJ crying and wrapped his arms around his big brother.

Maxine turned her body and got out of Trent's grip. "Trent, you can't be upset about this. It's something you bought the boys. They were excited and wanted to put it together. Are you upset over the car being repossessed? You can take the mini-van to work. My parents have an extra car in their garage. I'll call them and ask if I can borrow it for a couple of days until we figure this out."

"Why do you always feel the need to call your parents when something happens to us? I am your husband! I take care of you and our sons. Not your fucking parents!"

Maxine looked at TJ and Maxwell. They were crying and holding each other, trembling. She didn't want them to witness their father acting like this. "TJ, take Maxwell with you upstairs to wash up for dinner. Okay?"

TJ held Maxwell's hand as they walked toward the stairs.

"Are you going to ignore me?" Trent asked Maxine as she walked past him to the kitchen.

Trent took his open hand and smacked Maxine hard across her face. She lost her balance on the kitchen's ceramic tile floor and fell backwards. The side of her head hit the kitchen countertop's granite edge. Blood gushed from her head as she landed face down on the hard floor. Immediately, a gash opened on her forehead and more blood spilled.

TJ and Maxwell stood on the steps and watched the exchange between their parents. They were crying and screaming, "Mommy! Mommy!"

Maxine's cell phone rang in her pocketbook. TJ left Maxwell on the steps and ran back downstairs to grab his mother's purse off the small table by the front door. He pulled her cell phone out and answered it as he walked back to Maxwell who was crying hysterically on the steps.

"My daddy killed my mommy!" TJ screamed. "Can you help her?"

"TJ? This is Aunt Joy. Where is your mother?"

"She's bleeding on the floor, Aunt Joy!" TJ started crying loudly. "I'm scared!"

Trent was sitting on the kitchen floor, holding Maxine, trying to get her to wake up. There was no response. He was screaming, "Maxi, wake up! What did I do to you, Maxi! Wake up!"

Joy could hear crying in the background. She knew something was horribly wrong. "TJ, I need you to calm down and tell me what happened." She bypassed the traffic she was sitting in, pulled onto the shoulder, and sped down Route 5 at top speed to get to Maxine's house as fast as she could.

"I'm scared. I want Mommy," he cried.

"TJ, I need you to be a big boy and tell me what happened," Joy said calmly.

"Daddy was mad at Mommy because we made a mess with our new tent. He pulled Mommy's hair and then hit her. She fell down and there's blood. I'm scared Aunt Joy. Can you come get us? I'm scared," TJ sobbed.

"Where are you now, TJ?" Joy asked.

"On the steps looking at them," TJ said.

"Is Maxwell with you?"

"He's beside me." TJ looked at Maxwell. "He's crying!"

"Take the phone with you, go to your room, and lock the door. I'm on my way to get you. Don't let anybody in your room. Okay?"

"Okay," TJ cried.

"Then do it while I'm on the phone." Joy waited for a few seconds, then asked, "Are you in your room now?"

Another few seconds flew by before TJ said, "I'm in my room with Maxwell now."

"Good. Lock your bedroom door and I'll be there in a few minutes. I need to make another phone call but I'll call you right back. Okay?"

"Yes, but can you come get us now?"

"Baby, I'll be there in a few minutes. I need you to hang up so I can get Mommy some help."

"Okay," TJ said in a low voice.

Joy ended the call with TJ and called 911.

"911, what's your emergency?" The operator asked.

"My friend is bleeding! There's been a domestic dispute and she needs help!"

"What's the address?"

Joy took a deep breath and tried to remember Maxine's address. "20706 Great Lake Lane, Brandywine, Maryland."

"Help is on the way. Are you there?"

"I'm five minutes away."

"The police and an ambulance have been dispatched. Do you need me to stay on the line with you until you get there?"

"No, just send help. I need to make a few calls."

Joy hung up, then called Maxine's mother, Ms. Pat, and Gabby and told them what was happening, then she called TJ back. "Hi, TJ, it's Aunt Joy. I'm pulling on to your street now. Can you open the door for me? Don't hang up; keep me on the phone and open the door."

TJ did just as Aunt Joy told him to do.

When he walked down the stairs, he saw his father still sitting on the bloody kitchen floor holding his mother. He opened the door for Joy, wrapped his arms around her legs, and started crying hysterically.

Joy picked him up and held him for a few seconds before she put him back down. "TJ, go back upstairs with Maxwell and lock the door. Don't open it for anybody but me."

TJ was pulling her arm to go upstairs with him.

She bent down, hugged him again, and said, "Please, baby. I'll be up there shortly. I need to get your mommy some help."

TJ ran upstairs and didn't look back.

An eerie feeling swept over Joy as she walked further into the house. The strong smell of baked chicken overwhelmed her and made her queasy. The kitchen looked like it had so many times before at dinner time at the Andersons. Food was simmering on the stove top with plates and utensils neatly stacked on the counter. Trent's crying brought her back to reality. As she walked further in the kitchen, she was dazed by what she saw. Sticky blood covered half the kitchen floor. Trent was sitting in a puddle of blood with his legs stretched out, holding Maxine's lifeless body with her arms flung by her side. Her entire face was covered in blood. Joy thought for sure Maxine was dead. She starting crying as she rushed over, bent down, and asked, "Trent, is she breathing?"

Just as she put her hand on Maxine's neck to feel for a pulse, two police officers entered the house. Joy screamed, "My friend needs an ambulance! She's bleeding from her head and I don't know if she's breathing!"

The paramedics were making their way through the door. They began working on Maxine immediately. Trent was sobbing as they pulled Maxine from his arms.

"What happened?" the police officer asked Joy.

Joy told the police officers exactly what TJ told her. The police tried to talk to Trent but he was in shock and didn't answer their questions. He couldn't take his eyes off the paramedics working on Maxine.

Minutes later, Ms. Pat ran in the house just as the paramedics were taking Maxine out the front door on a stretcher. "Oh, my dear God! Is my child alive?" Pat screamed. The paramedic said, "Ma'am, she's alive but we need to get her to the hospital as soon as possible."

"What happened? Where are the boys? And Trent?" Pat asked.

"Ms. Pat, you go with Maxine. I'll get the boys and meet you at the hospital." Joy touched one of the paramedic's arm. "What hospital are you taking her to?"

"She needs to go to the closest one, Southern Maryland."

"Go, Ms. Pat. I'll meet you there. I need to get the boys together," Joy said as she ran upstairs.

A few minutes later, two police officers were reading Trent his rights and handcuffing him. They were putting him in the squad car when Joy walked out of the house with the boys.

TJ and Maxwell ran to the police car with their father sitting in the backseat.

"Daddy, Daddy, don't go! Where's Mommy?" Maxwell screamed.

TJ stared at his father through the police car window with a dazed look on his face. He didn't have anything to say to him as he watched the squad car drive away.

Joy looked at the boys and couldn't believe what was happening. She took them by their hands, got Maxwell's car seat and TJ's booster seat out of Maxine's minivan, and then left for the hospital.

Twenty minutes later, Gabby caught up with Joy and the boys as they entered the hospital. Gabby's stomach started doing flips when she saw their tear-stained, worried faces. They entered the hospital and followed the signs to the emergency room.

When they entered the ER waiting area, Joy knew something was seriously wrong by the frantic look on Maxine's father's face. Dr. Jim was holding his sobbing wife in his arms. Ms Pat looked up at them and shook her head.

Joy screamed, "Oh, my God! Maxine's dead!"

Chapter 16 ———————————

Joy rang the doorbell at Maxine's parents' house while trying to juggle her new Prada bag, a Toys R Us bag full of new playthings for TJ and Maxwell, and a cake carrier with her home-made pound cake inside it. Ms. Pat opened the door and rescued the cake from Joy's hand before she dropped it.

"Hi, Ms. Pat. Thank you," Joy said as she rearranged the bags in her hand.

"You're welcome, baby. Come on in and thank you for this." Joy followed Ms. Pat in to the dining room where she moved some aluminum pans and casserole dishes around on her table to make room for Joy's cake.

"Wow! What are you going to do with all this?" Joy looked at all the food on the table and wondered who was going to eat it all. She knew people had been dropping off food, but she didn't expect to see this much.

Ms. Pat sighed and shook her head. "I'll figure something out."

"Okay. Well, let me know if you need me to help you." Joy turned around to go speak to Dr. Jim, but Ms. Pat stopped her.

Ms. Pat hugged Joy with tears in her eyes. "I'm going to tell you the same thing I told Gabby when she got here. Thank you from the bottom of my heart. I would've never made it through this without you two."

113

Joy smiled and held back her tears as she wrapped her arms tightly around Ms. Pat. "You don't have to thank me. We helped each other through it."

In a way, Joy was still in shock, unable to process all that had happened the past week. From seeing Maxine covered in blood on her kitchen floor to thinking she died after her parents saw her have a seizure in the emergency room. Watching Maxine lie in her hospital bed with tubes and wires all over her body and machines beeping all around took a toll on all of them. When Maxine was released from the hospital yesterday, five days after she was admitted, Joy felt like she was able to breathe for the first time since everything happened.

Joy spoke and hugged Dr. Jim in the den on her way to the living room where she heard Gabby yelling at William about something having to do with Nadia.

Joy walked in the living room with her mouth wide open. "Oh, my God! Look at you, Maxine!" she paused. "I'm so glad to see you out of that hospital!" Joy hugged Maxine who was sitting on the couch with her legs up.

"Me too, girl. Me too." Maxine smiled at Joy as she sank back on the sofa. "I hear you have a hot date tonight."

Joy nodded and half-smiled. She didn't want to talk about her date tonight with Trent's associate, Dean, because she wasn't looking forward to it. She felt obligated to go out with him be-cause she had stood him up twice already-once when she had a stomach virus and couldn't stop vomiting and again when Maxine was in the hospital. All she wanted to do was go back to her new house and unpack all the boxes her father and some of his em-ployees moved for her last week while she stood vigil at Maxine's bedside. Plus, she was still furious at Trent and didn't want any-thing to do with him, including Dean. But Maxine begged her to go out with him and with all she'd been through, Joy didn't want to disappoint her friend.

Joy spent the next two hours at Maxine's parents' house, laughing and talking with her girlfriends and their children, eating too much food and listening to Gabby's advice on what to expect and how to act on her date tonight. After Joy helped Ms. Pat freeze some of the food that looked and tasted good and throw away the food that didn't, she went home determined to unpack as much as she could before Dean showed up at her house at eight o'clock.

When Joy walked into her house through the garage door and saw all the boxes from her apartment stacked in the living and dining rooms, she wanted to scream. She knew she needed to unpack them because this was her last weekend of freedom before she started work and school next Tuesday.

She went upstairs to her bedroom, changed into her favorite pair of Daisy Duke shorts, a cropped T-shirt, and her fuzzy slippers then went back downstairs. She set up her portable iPod speaker, put on her party playlist and started unpacking boxes while jamming to her favorite songs. She had half the boxes unpacked when the doorbell rang.

She ran to the door wondering who it could be. She looked through the peep hole and saw a well-dressed, attractive man standing there. "Yes."

"Hi. Joy?"

"Yes?"

"I'm Dean, Dean Bennett."

Joy frowned, sighed, and punched at the air in frustration. She forgot about her date with Dean and wasn't in the mood for what they had planned. She opened the door with a fake smile plastered on her face. "Hi, Dean. I'm sorry, but I forgot. I started unpacking and didn't pay attention to the time," she explained.

Dean stood at the front door looking more like Gabby's type than hers, light-skinned with short, curly hair, light green eyes, and a slim frame. Nothing about him made her want to spend an evening with him, but she remembered her promise to Maxine.

"You're not going to tell me you want to reschedule again, are you?" Dean showed Joy a sad face, then smiled.

Joy decided to just get it over with, then she'd never have to see him again after tonight. "No, of course not. Come in." She rolled her eyes behind his back after he walked in the house. "We can talk in the living room before I go upstairs and change."

"Okay," Dean replied. He followed Joy to the living room

with his eyes glued to her butt and sat on the sofa.

Joy turned the volume down on the iPod speaker and sat beside him on the sofa. "Nice to finally meet you in person. Sorry about cancelling on you twice."

"Oh, no problem. I understand. How is Maxine doing?"

Joy smiled. "Much better, thanks for asking." She looked at Dean with a serious expression. "So, you're friends with Trent, huh?"

Dean was taken aback by her sudden change in attitude. "Um, we're co-workers, not friends. And not even that anymore since the firm fired him."

Joy gave Dean a wicked look. "Good. Now his ass needs to go to jail to pay for what he did to my girl."

Dean put his hands up defensively. "No argument from me on that. I like Maxine. Hey, she called me about going out with you, so I appreciate her for that."

Joy still wasn't feeling this guy and wasn't going to hide how she felt. "Um-hum. She told me you just got out of a relationship too. What happened?" Joy sat back with pinched lips and crossed arms, expecting to hear how he screwed up his relationship.

"After two years, she met somebody else." He shrugged his shoulders. "Nothing else to say. What happened with your relationship?" Dean stared at Joy with an evil look because he didn't like talking about his ex.

"We were together for ten years. He proposed and asked me to move to China with him. I messed up!" She pointed to the front door and said, "If he came through that door right now, I would beg him to take me back. I wouldn't make that mistake again."

"That's good to know," Dean said sarcastically. He was ready to flee after he heard that. Dean looked at the door and tried to think of an excuse to leave. He knew he didn't stand a chance with this evil bitch because she still had feelings for her ex.

Joy smacked her lips and sighed. "So, I'm just letting you know, this is my first date since my relationship ended, so if I seem a little nervous, understand this is all new to me." Joy thought she owed him an explanation because he was starting to look a little concerned.

"Cool." Dean laughed. "You're my second blind date since..."

Joy cut him off. "Oh, so this is new for you too, huh? What happened on your first date?"

Dean shook his head and closed his eyes, trying to erase it from his memory.

"That bad huh? Uh-uh, what happened? I'm new to dating so tell me what happened so I won't make the same mistake." Joy moved closer to Dean so she could hear all the details.

Dean glanced at her with an uncertain frown and narrowed eyes. "You sure?"

"I'm dying to know now. Please tell me." Joy pushed Dean's arm playfully.

Dean sighed. "Alright, you asked for it. A so-called friend set me up with a friend's cousin's roommate's sister. I should've never made a date with her after she asked me to call her Shaniqua Boo during our first phone conversation."

Joy fell back on the sofa laughing.

Dean continued. "We met at the Cheesecake Factory in White Flint. She came in with weave down her back and fake fingernails with a month's worth of dirt under them. She ordered an entrée and a drink, then asked if she could get another entrée in case she got hungry later after we fucked. I had no intention of fucking her at all, but I let her order a second entrée to go because I was ready to jet. And then...get this," he paused. "While we waited for the to-go order, she ordered three Long Island ice teas and drank them like they were water. When the entrée came and I paid the check, she asked me if we were going to my place or hers to fuck."

Joy slid off the couch onto the carpeted floor, laughing hysterically.

"I'm glad you think it's funny, because I don't." Dean couldn't help but laugh at Joy's reaction.

"All I wanna know is this, do you plan to go out with her again?" Joy couldn't stop laughing.

117

"Yeah, okay. I see you got jokes." Dean laughed.

Joy pulled herself together and sat back on the couch. Hearing Dean's story made her realize he was in the same boat as she was, newly available and trying to figure shit out. She saw him differently now. "Dean, I hate to do this to you, but instead of us going to Chinatown like we planned, do you mind if we order something to eat and stay here?" Joy leaned back on the couch and covered her face with both hands. "It's been the week from hell, I'm tired from unpacking all day, and I don't really feel like going out."

"Sure. We can grab something to eat, bring it back here, and get to know each other a little better." Dean wanted to continue his date with Joy now that he broke the ice and saw that she had a sense of humor.

"Great. Let me change my clothes and grab my purse, then we can leave." Joy stood up.

Dean looked her up and down. "You don't have to change. I like what you have on."

Joy looked at her outfit and grinned. "I bet you do. Well, let me change my shoes, grab my bag, and then we can leave." Joy could feel Dean checking her ass out as she walked away.

Two hours later, after eating an extra-large pizza with the works and drinking one of the two bottles of Ciroc Vodka Dean purchased, they sat on Joy's sofa in the living room talking and listening to music.

"Thanks for dinner. Either that was the best pizza I ever had or I was just hungry." Joy giggled, feeling loose and relaxed after drinking two cocktails Dean made her.

"I told you, it's my favorite pizza joint." Dean stood up, opened the second bottle of vodka on the dining room table, and fixed himself another drink.

When Dean sat back down, Joy turned to face him. "I'm sorry this isn't the date you had planned." She pointed at his black slacks and tan silk shirt. "You look so nice and we're eating pizza in my living room."

Dean smiled and shrugged his shoulders. "Don't worry about it. This date with you is much better than the last blind date

118

I had, so I'm not complaining." Dean frowned, thinking about his other date before he took a gulp of his vodka with cranberry juice.

"I hope so." Joy started laughing again as she stood up, turned up the volume on her portable speaker, and started dancing to a fast Mary J. Blige song. She moved her arms in Dean's direction, inviting him to join her.

"Naw, I don't like to dance." Dean's eyes followed Joy as she danced around the living room. "But you look good. I see you got moves."

Joy laughed. "Thanks! I love to dance!" She continued dancing alone to two more songs before she sat back down on the couch.

"I like watching you dance. You got the whole Beyoncé and J-Lo thing going on," Dean said with a devious smirk.

She tried to stand up to protest but fell back down."Oh, hell no! I dance better than both of those heifers!"

Dean shook his head because he knew Joy was drunk. He looked at his watch and it was almost one o'clock. "It's getting late, so I'm about ready to leave."

"No, not yet. Aren't you having fun?" Joy closed her eyes and shook her head no to protest Dean's departure.

Dean looked at her and tried not to laugh. He could tell by her behavior that she wasn't used to drinking vodka.

Joy leaned on Dean. "Can you hug me, Dean? It's been two months since a man hugged me." She pulled one of his arms around her.

Dean wrapped both his arms around Joy as she cuddled up beside him and laid her head on his chest. After a few minutes, Dean started getting an erection. He sat Joy up. "Hey, I need to go. I'll call you tomorrow."

When they stood up, Joy wrapped her arms around Dean's neck. He bent down and kissed her on her lips. At first, she pulled back, but then she realized how good it felt and leaned in for more.

"You might regret this tomorrow, " Dean protested.

"I thought we were having a good date, Dean." She hugged him around his waist.

"We are." Dean sat Joy back on the sofa.

She pulled him on top of her and started kissing him again.

Dean stood up, prepared to leave but stopped when Joy removed her shirt to reveal her perky breasts and erect nipples.

Dean stared at her chest and licked his lips. "Damn, girl! You sexy as shit!"

Joy stood up, pulled down her shorts and stepped out of them. She turned around in the living room for Dean to see all of her nakedness.

He tried to control his breathing as he took in every inch of Joy's body with his eyes bulging out of his head and his penis straining through his slacks. "Are you sure you want to do this, Joy?" Dean rubbed his erect penis, feeling like he was going to come just from looking at her naked body.

"Yes, I'm sure." Joy put her finger in her mouth and gave Dean a naughty look.

She pushed him down on her sofa and laid her naked body on top of him. She could feel the wetness between her legs drip down her inner thighs. She reached down, touched Dean's penis and frowned, disappointed that he wasn't half as large as Allen. She sat on his thighs as she unbuckled his belt and pulled down his zipper. She put her hand inside his pants and squeezed his penis as she slid her hand up and down.

"Damn, girl, you gonna make me come like that," Dean moaned.

Joy stopped, leaned over, and whispered in his ear. "I'm not ready for you to do that. I want this to last all night."

Dean was breathing so hard, he could barely say, "Okay."

Joy removed Dean's shirt and rubbed her breasts against his hairy chest. After a few minutes, she helped Dean pull his pants down, then they lay on the carpeted floor. She positioned herself on top of his naked body with her eyes closed, thinking about how she used to do this with Allen. Dean held her so tight in his arms, she thought she was going to have an orgasm just from his embrace.

She turned over on her back and motioned for him to get

on top of her.

"Okay. Let me put on a condom." He sat up, took his wallet out of his pants, and pulled out a condom.

"I hate condoms!" Joy muttered in a drunken slur.

Dean threw the open package on the floor and lay on top of her. He moaned when he entered her and started stroking her and kissing her all over her face. "Damn, girl, this pussy feels good as shit."

Joy tried to move her hips to help Dean because she couldn't feel him inside her. "Are you in yet? Put it in already!" Joy yelled.

Dean was inside of Joy, stroking her so hard, he was dripping sweat all over her. Exactly ninety seconds later, Dean shouted, "Oh shit! I'm coming!" He scrunched his face as his body quivered and went limp on top of Joy. "Damn, girl, that was good."

Joy screamed, "No! I was just getting started." She pushed Dean off her, rolled over on her side, and started crying. "That was horrible!"

Joy cried herself to sleep thinking she'd never find another man to make her feel the way Allen did. She prayed for Allen to come back and take her with him to China.

Dean watched Joy sleep for hours that night with a bizarre smile on his face. He always dreamed about settling down with a woman like Joy, smart, funny, and sexy as hell. He decided to do whatever it took to make Joy his because he had no intentions of ever letting her go.

Chapter 17

On a cool and rainy afternoon in mid-September, Gabby walked in Phillip's Seafood Restaurant at the Baltimore Harbor wearing a pair of black Marc Jacobs shades, a large floppy hat, and a black Burberry trench coat with the collar turned up to hide her face. She proceeded to the rear of the restaurant, removed her shades, and inspected the restaurant to make sure she didn't recognize any of the customers. When she knew she was safe, she proceeded to unbutton her coat and remove her hat before she sat in the booth across from Rayshawn.

"You have five minutes. Don't waste it admiring my beauty," Gabby said as she ran her fingers through her long hair and glared at Rayshawn.

Rayshawn didn't say a word as he stared at Gabby's cleavage poking through her coat. He became instantly irritated with himself because after all the trouble she caused him, whenever he saw her or heard her voice, he still wanted her. He couldn't believe he ever had a woman this beautiful. She used to do things to him that left him begging for more. Just looking at her made him want to take her across the street to his loft and let her work her magic on him.

"Oh, after all the messages you left on my cell, you can't talk now? What do you want?" Gabby rolled her eyes and folded her arms across her chest.

Rayshawn looked across the table with pleading eyes. "Why didn't you bring Nadia like I asked you to? I just finished training camp and it was the worst I played in my career. The regular season starts next Thursday and I need my head clear for the game." He reached his hand across the table and touched Gabby's folded arms. "The guilt of knowing I have a daughter in this world that I've never met or seen is fucking me up."

Gabby sighed and brushed Rayshawn's hand off her arm. Looking at his chunky physique, thick nappy hair, and unappealing features made her shiver with disgust. The denim jumper and too-small T-shirt he wore made him look like he just stepped out of the fields from picking cotton. She knew meeting him like this was a mistake the minute she saw him, but she needed to do something. Rayshawn had been calling her so much the past few weeks, whenever William was home, she had to turn her cell phone off. And now William was starting to get suspicious because he knew she couldn't live without her cell phone by her side 24/7. She hoped this meeting with Rayshawn would finally get him out of her life for good.

Gabby stared at Rayshawn with pinched lips, not at all fazed by his words. "Why do you want to see her now? Because you're back in Maryland?"

"Naw..."

Gabby put her hand up like a stop sign. "Where were all the calls during the summer when you were home with wifey and the kids? Do you think I'm going to expose my baby to you being a part-time father whenever you're in town? What if I let her spend time with you? When the season is over, then what? You go back home to your family and forget she exists until next season. You'll leave her heartbroken and I will not let you hurt my baby. My husband is the better man and he'll be the better father to her. "Gabby explained through clenched teeth.

Rayshawn's mouth dropped open. "You married? You didn't tell me you got married. Does he know I'm Nadia's father?"

"He's her father," Gabby insisted.

"No, I'm her father!" Rayshawn insisted. "Listen, Gabby, I think if I see her and know she's alright, I can get my head back in the game and everything will be better for me."

Gabby shook her head. "What kind of father would blame his four month old daughter for his poor performance on the field? Your performing badly has nothing to do with *my* daughter, but everything to do with your anxiety because the Ravens are paying you millions of dollars to take them to the Super Bowl and you realize you can't deliver. Your time is up. I have to get home to my husband and daughter." Gabby grabbed her belongings and stood up to leave.

Rayshawn grabbed Gabby's arm and pulled her back down in the booth.

"Get your hands off me!" She used her open hand and smacked Rayshawn across his face with all her strength. "Don't you ever touch me again!"

Rayshawn stroked his face from the burning smack and tried to hide his face when he saw people looking in their direction. "Sit your ass down. You got people looking over here," Rayshawn whispered as he cowered in the corner.

Gabby sat down when she saw diners in the restaurant looking at her. She glared at Rayshawn like she wanted to jump across the table and whip his ass. She could tell by the way he was trying to hide his face that he was terrified of people seeing them together because he didn't want the news to get back to his loving wife.

Rayshawn gave Gabby a deceitful grin. "I'm going to see my daughter one way or another! And let your punk-ass husband know he's not *my* daughter's father!"

Gabby pulled out her cell phone."Okay. I'll do it for you." She dialed a number on her cell phone, put the phone to her ear, and waited for an answer. "Hi, Rayshawn, Jr., this is Mrs. Landon. I'm a friend of your father's in Maryland. Is your mother around?"

Rayshawn reached across the table, snatched the phone from Gabby's hand, and put it to his ear. "Hello."

"Dad? Oh, Mom's at her tennis lesson. Who was that lady?" Rayshawn, Jr., asked.

"Ummm, nobody important. I'll call your mother on her cell. Don't tell her we called. Bye." Sweat started pouring down

Rayshawn's face as he stared at Gabby's phone.

Gabby laughed at Rayshawn's reaction. "May I have my phone back please so I can call your wife on her cell. I have that number, too," Gabby teased.

Rayshawn slid the phone across the table. "You one cold bitch!" he barked.

Gabby leaned across the table and looked Rayshawn in his eyes with an evil glare. "And don't you forget it. If you ever try to see my daughter again, I'll make sure your family crumbles just like mine. And I'll be on every talk show telling my side of how you manipulated me and tried to pay me off to keep *our* daughter a secret."

They stared at each other with angry glares until a waiter approached the table to take their order.

"Give us a minute," Rayshawn snarled without looking at the waiter.

The waiter walked away, but not too far because he wanted to hear what his favorite quarterback and this attractive woman were arguing about. He posted up a few tables away from theirs and pretended to clean the table while he listened to their conversation.

Gabby grabbed her things and stood up to leave again. "Stay away from me and forget about *my* daughter," Gabby yelled as she tossed a glass of ice water in his face.

Everybody in the restaurant turned to look in their direction again as Gabby stomped out of the restaurant full of attitude. She was so upset, she forgot to cover her face as she had when she entered the restaurant.

Neither Gabby nor Rayshawn noticed the freelance photo-journalist secretly snapping pictures of them the entire time they were at the restaurant. When Rayshawn left minutes after Gabby, the photojournalist talked to their waiter and some of the customers who sat near Rayshawn Robinson and the mystery woman. They were excited and willing to tell every detail of what they heard. The photojournalist left the restaurant an hour later feeling satisfied that he had enough information to make a killing selling this story to the highest bidder.

Chapter 18

Maxine eased behind the wheel of her minivan, started the engine, and leaned back on the headrest with her eyes closed and a big smile on her face. It had been a month since her head injury and her doctors finally released her from their care and restored her driving privileges. They were amazed that she recovered so quickly, but Maxine wasn't. She knew her faith, determination and love for her family and friends were what helped her heal, but if she had to credit one person for helping her the most, it would be her special friend, and after today, he'd become her secret lover if everything went as planned.

After she was released from the hospital, you couldn't tell it by looking at her, but Maxine was a broken woman. She hated the way everyone looked at her with pity and constantly questioned her about why she didn't leave or get help when Trent started abusing her. Everybody treated her like she wasn't smart enough to think for herself or too fragile to defend herself. Just when she was starting to sink into a depression, he called.

She wasn't expecting his phone call two days after she was released from the hospital, but she was glad to hear from him. His voice and concern put a smile on her face and his encouraging words gave her hope. He continued to call her every day and they talked for hours at a time. He was the reason Maxine started putting her life back together. He was the reason she started feeling like a woman again and not a victim.

Two weeks ago, when she walked into the Prince George's

County Courthouse to testify at Trent's pre-trial hearing, she was a nervous wreck. Although she had her parents, Gabby, and Joy by her side, the thought of seeing Trent again had every muscle in her body in knots and her stomach doing all kinds of somersaults. When she walked in the courtroom, trembling and in tears, ready to turn around and run out the door, she saw her special friend. She didn't know he was going to be there and, of course, he didn't tell her. That's just the kind of person he was, there when you needed him. When he saw her, he gave her a gentle smile and, with it, the strength she needed to stay in that courtroom.

Thankfully, she didn't have to testify because Trent took a plea deal of six months of extensive counseling in a half-way house for violent offenders. Everybody, except Maxine, was upset because they wanted Trent to serve more time. As long as he was getting help and out of their lives, Maxine was fine with it. She was ready to move on with her life.

Gabby, on the other hand, almost had to be escorted out the courthouse by the bailiff and police officers because of her actions. She wanted Trent to get the death penalty and screamed her punishment for Trent to the judge, public defender and even Maxine's court appointed prosecutor. She was so angry and belligerent about Trent's sentence she took it out on his family and blamed his mother, Gloria, for Trent's history of abuse and told her that he should die for what he did to Maxine and their sons. Trent's brothers had to help their weeping, heartbroken mother out of the courthouse. Joy finally pulled Gabby to the side and shut her up the way only Joy could do.

Maxine opened her eyes, put her minivan in drive and proceeded to her destination with a naughty look on her face. She requested they keep their new friendship a secret because she didn't want everybody all up in her business when they found out she was seeing a new man. He didn't object and that was one of the things she liked about him. He was comfortable allowing her to make the rules in their new relationship and went along with whatever she wanted.

She pulled into the parking lot at the Radisson Hotel in Largo, parked her car, and proceeded to the room he had booked for them. He suggested meeting here because he had two foreign exchange students staying with him and wanted their first time alone together to be special, without his houseguests interrupting them.

Maxine stepped off the elevator on the third floor and turned right. When she reached room 307, she knocked three times and waited impatiently for him to open the door. She took two long, deep breaths to control her jittery nerves. Her pulse was racing knowing he was on the other side of the door waiting for her. She took a step back when she heard him opening the door. She didn't want to appear too desperate.

He opened the door and looked at Maxine with a smile that made her melt. She walked in the room and threw her arms around him. He released the door, letting it close on its own, and hugged her back while he rested his head on hers. They stayed this way for a few minutes until Maxine pulled away.

"Hi, Kevin." She looked up at him with pure admiration.

"I'm so glad to finally see you. To finally be able to hold you." He touched the scar on her forehead and looked at her with concern. "How do you feel?"

"Wonderful, now that I'm with you." Maxine held his hand and walked into the room. They sat on the sofa near the window and smiled at each other.

"What did the doctor say today? Was it okay for you to drive here?" He kissed her hand. "I don't want you to rush your recovery."

"I'm fine, Kevin. He gave me the okay to drive and go to work." She sighed. "I start next Monday. Thanks for getting the county to hold my job for me. You've done so much for me this past month, I don't know how I'll ever thank you."

When Maxine didn't show up for the new-teacher orientation, Kevin got her number from human resources and called her. That's when he found out what Trent had done to her. He went to human resources, explained Maxine's situation, and practically begged them to hold her job until she was ready to return.

"You don't have to thank me. You're a beautiful woman who deserves the best and I'm going to make sure you get it." He kissed Maxine's hand again and smiled.

She leaned closer to him and kissed him on the lips. He hugged her and closed his eyes, enjoying their kiss. Maxine rubbed his chest, then moved her hand down his chest, past his six-pack, and rested on his crotch.

He touched her hand and shook his head negatively. "I want to spend time with you. I don't want you to feel like you have to do this because you owe me anything."

"I don't feel that way, Kevin." She kissed him on his lips. "I *want* to be with you." She opened her black leather purse and pulled out a pack of Magnum condoms and put them on the coffee table in front of them.

Kevin opened his eyes wide and exhaled loudly. He looked as if somebody let the air out of him as he slumped down in the couch. "Oh, um." He looked embarrassed as he stared at the condoms on the table.

Maxine regarded him with wide eyes as she swallowed hard. "What's wrong? Oh, I'm sorry. I'm moving too fast." She buried her face in her hands. "This is so embarrassing. Maybe I should go."

He grabbed her by the wrist before she stood up. "No, please don't leave. I'm the one who's embarrassed." He picked the pack of condoms off the table and stared at it. "What's the best way to say this? Well, um, Maxine, um, I'm not a Magnum-size man."

Maxine gasped and covered her mouth.

He stood up, reached in his back pocket, took out an unopened pack of Trojan condoms, and showed them to Maxine. "You see. I'm an average-size man." Kevin sighed. "Your Magnums are giving me a little performance anxiety."

Maxine was almost in tears. "I'm sorry, Kevin. I thought I was being responsible buying my own condoms and that's the only brand..." She stopped talking before she said Trent's name.

Kevin pulled Maxine into his arms and held her. "It's alright. I may not be as big as your husband, but I've been told I know how to please with what I have."

Maxine sat up and gave Kevin a seductive smirk. "Oh,

yeah, prove it."

Kevin stood up, picked Maxine off the couch, and carried her to the bed. He looked at her as he removed her clothes. When she tried to help him, he brushed her hand away. After she was completely undressed, Kevin pushed her up on the bed, spread her legs wide open, and buried his bald head between her legs. Within minutes, she was moaning from the waves of back-to-back orgasms she was having from him licking, kissing, and nibbling her clitoris. When he came up for air twenty minutes later, she was spent. Trent never ate her out like that.

Kevin removed his clothes, put on one of his average-size Trojan condoms, and joined her back on the bed. He looked at Maxine with concern. "You okay?"

Maxine nodded and smiled because she was more than okay. She couldn't talk even if she wanted to. She was breathing heavily and her body still tingled from the multiple orgasms he made her have. She lay on her side, curled up in a fetal position.

He curled beside her and whispered in her ear. "Can you handle any more of me, Maxine? I need to know."

She whispered, "Yes," and turned around to face him.

He bent his head down to her chest and started sucking her breasts, alternating between the two to give them equal attention. Her breasts hadn't had this much fun in a long time and they were grateful. Her nipples were so erect, they felt like they were going to shoot off like bullets. When Kevin entered her, she thought she was going to scream. Then she heard a strange sound and realized she *was* screaming. He kept moving his penis into different positions inside her while asking, "Is that your spot? Is this it?" He knew he found it when Maxine arched her back and grabbed the covers with both hands. Within minutes, she cried out from another orgasm. He turned her over and helped her get into the doggy-style position, then he pushed himself deep inside her as if he were trying to permanently become one with her. After what felt like an hour but was about ten minutes or so, his body shook and he collapsed on the bed, bringing Maxine down with him. They faced each other smiling.

After a few minutes, Kevin pulled Maxine close to him

and whispered in her ear, "You just turned me out, Mrs. Anderson."

Maxine's smile disappeared. Hearing Kevin call her Mrs. Anderson felt like a punch to her gut. It was a shocking reminder that she was still a married woman. She turned her back to him and started crying. *What have I done?* she wondered. Although she knew her marriage was over, she was still legally married. "Kevin, I need to go."

He propped himself up on his elbow and looked at her with questioning eyes. "Did I do something wrong? Are you sick?"

Maxine didn't say anything as she picked her clothes off the floor, ran in the bathroom, and locked the door. She turned on the shower and sink faucets and let the water run so Kevin couldn't hear her sobs. After what Trent did to her, she didn't understand why she felt so guilty. She knew her marriage was over and she wanted to be with Kevin, but it felt wrong.

Kevin knocked on the door. "Maxine, can you come out so we can talk? I need to know what's wrong."

Maxine didn't answer him. She took a shower, put on her clothes, and left the bathroom.

Kevin was sitting on the edge of the bed, half-dressed in his slacks and socks. "Maxine?"

She didn't look at him as she rushed to the door to leave. He stopped her. "Please, Maxine, tell me what's wrong. Was I too rough? Did I hurt you?"

She looked at the floor and said, "No, I need to get home to my children." She turned and walked to the door.

Kevin followed her. "Can I call you later, Maxine?"

She opened the door and stepped out of the room. "How about I call you?"

Kevin looked disappointed as he watched Maxine walk down the hallway toward the elevator.

She got off in the lobby, ran to her minivan, and drove away at top speed. The entire ride back to her parents' house, she prayed and asked God to forgive her for cheating on her husband.

Chapter 19 ——————

Joy opened her front door with her eyes bulging out of her head and a look of panic spread across her face. Her hair was matted to one side of her head while the other side was sticking straight out in a kinky, curly bush. She stood at the door wearing a matching mint-green bikini and bra set while she bounced from one foot to the other like she was going to pee on herself any second.

Maxine walked in the house and couldn't believe her eyes. "Joy?" Maxine pointed at Joy's outfit.

Joy looked down at her body and realized with all that was going on, she forgot to get dressed. She yelled, "Look at the dining room table," as she ran upstairs to put on some clothes.

Maxine casually walked to the dining room. Her mouth dropped wide open as she walked around the table. "Oh, my! Is this what I think it is? Is this yours, Joy? How? I mean, when? Who?" Maxine's stared at the table in shock.

Joy ran back downstairs to the dining room in a pair of jeans and a T-shirt. She pointed at the table with tears in her eyes. "Is this real? Can this be right?"

The doorbell rang before Maxine could answer. Joy left to answer the door. Gabby stomped in the house and looked Joy up and down with an annoyed expression. She joined Maxine when she saw her standing in the dining room.

"Hey, girl," Maxine hugged Gabby.

Gabby looked at her friends with tight lips. "I finally get William to take a Friday off so we can have a long, fun weekend and you call me hysterical. What's the emergency, Joy? Why aren't you two at work?"

"We're off for a Teacher Professional Development day and you might want to reschedule with William. I think we're going to be here for a while." Maxine pointed at the dining room table.

Gabby gasped and covered her mouth as she walked around the table. She stopped and leaned over to get a closer look at the ten pregnancy tests Joy had laid out on paper towels. All of them showed a positive sign or some other indication that Joy was definitely pregnant.

They stared at each other with shocked expressions.

Gabby walked over to Joy and said, "What the …" She stopped herself because she didn't believe any woman should curse because it demeans her.

Joy walked around the table and pointed at the pregnancy tests. "I know right. How could this be? Do you think I'm really pregnant?"

Maxine and Gabby looked at each other, then at the tests in front of them before they nodded.

"Yes, sweetie. You're definitely pregnant," Maxine said tenderly.

"Who's the father?" Gabby stared at Joy eagerly waiting to hear the answer.

"Gabby!" Maxine cried out.

Joy replied, "I only slept with one person since Allen." Tears starting streaming down her face. "It's Dean's. How did I get pregnant? The sex wasn't even good. He was finished before I even started. It's not fair."

"Oh, girl, please. Sex is overrated. Anyway, I thought you were on the pill," Gabby said.

"I stopped taking them after Allen left and never went back to the doctor to get more because I wasn't having sex and didn't plan to. I can't believe I got drunk, had unprotected sex, and got pregnant. That's not me at all. What am I going to do?"

"You need to go to your doctor and start prenatal care," Maxine suggested.

"Or, you can go to the clinic and get rid of it. The choice is yours," Gabby said nonchalantly.

"She wouldn't do that, Gabby! Would you, Joy?" Maxine asked.

Joy shook her head yes. "Uh-huh, I'm thinking about it Maxine. I finally told him last week that I just wasn't into him like that, but he still keeps calling me every day. I called him this morning after I took the first test. He's on his way over so I can tell him."

"I don't know what you're complaining about, girl. He's a cute attorney with money and a house in Rockville and he drives a Porsche. What's not to like?" Gabby sighed.

"He's too damn clingy and needy." Joy imitated Dean's voice. "I care about you, Joy. I think I'm falling in love with you, Joy. What time are you coming home tonight? I'll meet you there. Joy, sex with you is so..."

Gabby raised her hand to stop Joy. "We get it."

"Maybe you're comparing him to Allen and you can't do that. Allen was your first and you had a deep connection with him. You and Dean have to learn how to satisfy each other the way you and Allen did," Maxine reasoned.

Joy thought back to when she and Allen had sex for the first time. Since he didn't go to his prom, they met at a hotel in-stead. Allen was so excited, as soon as she walked through the door he threw her on the bed, lay on top of her, and climaxed. Then he did it again later when they took a shower together. Joy was disappointed and ready to leave, but the third time was the charm. He knocked it out of the park and had been hitting home runs ever since.

"Maybe," Joy said.

Gabby snapped her fingers. "I have plans. Which appoint-ment are we making? Clinic or private doctor's office." She held her cell phone up and rolled her eyes.

Joy looked at Maxine sadly as she said, "I'm not ready. I want to be married to the man I have children with. I don't love

Dean. I don't even think I like him. And I don't want to be some-body's baby's momma."

Maxine rubbed Joy's arm. "Joy, I'll support you with whatever decision you make. I'll be there for you."

"Thanks, girl!" Joy hugged Maxine.

"I'll call now and get you an appointment. They should be able to take you soon. When did you get pregnant?"

"It was definitely Saturday, September 5th, and my last pe-riod was August 17th, in case they ask," Joy volunteered.

Gabby looked at the calendar on her cell phone. "That should make you around four weeks. You still have plenty of time," Gabby said as she started dialing the clinic.

Joy and Maxine sat on the couch. Maxine saw the tears forming in Joy's eyes again and reached for her hand.

After a few minutes, Gabby hung up the phone and joined them in the living room. "It's all set. Tomorrow morning at ten."

"That soon?" Joy cried.

"Yes. I know somebody who works there and he owes me a favor so he squeezed you in," Gabby bragged as she sat down in the living room.

"You scare me sometimes, Gabby," Maxine said as she stared at her friend from the corner of her eye. *How does Gabby know someone who works at an abortion clinic? Why do they owe her a favor and why does she have the number to an abortion clinic in her cell phone?* Maxine wondered.

Gabby stood up to leave. "And, Joy, I'll be here at nine to-morrow morning to scoop you up. Be ready."

"I'll be ready," Joy said in a low voice, wondering if she was making the right decision.

"I'll be here, too. Although I don't agree with your choice, I said I'll be there for you no matter what decision you make," Maxine said.

"Maxine, it's not a good idea for you to go. You've been through enough already. I'll take her and let you know how every-thing went," Gabby commanded.

Maxine clenched her teeth, rolled her eyes, and grunted. She hated it when Gabby treated her like a child.

"Maxine, if you really feel that strongly about it, you can go." Joy secretly winked at Gabby to let her know Maxine would probably be too busy with her sons.

The doorbell rang.

"I'll get it on my way out. See you in the A.M." Gabby waved.

Seconds later, Dean walked in the living room looking handsome in a Gucci navy-and-red pinstripe suit. "Morning, ladies. How are you?" He hugged Joy, then Maxine. "You look good, Maxine. I don't see any evidence of you ever being in the hospital."

Maxine blushed. "Thanks, Dean. That's nice of you to say." She stood up to leave. "I'll show myself out. Bye." When she got behind Dean, she gestured for Joy to call her later.

Joy nodded.

Dean sat down and looked at Joy with a blank stare."What's up, Joy? I was surprised to hear from you after you said you didn't want to see me anymore."

Joy looked down at the carpeted floor. "Oh, yeah, well I've been pretty busy with work and school, but thanks for coming over. I have something important I need to tell you."

"You look nervous. What's wrong?" *Is she getting ready to tell me she has an STD?* he wondered.

"I'm trying to find an easy way to tell you this, but I don't think there is an easy way." Joy turned around on the couch and sat Indian style while looking at Dean. "Dean, when we had sex..."

Dean looked at Joy, noticeably perturbed. "Yes? What about it?"

"I'm pregnant." Joy sat frozen waiting for his reaction.

Dean fell back on the couch and said, "What? Are you sure? I mean, is it mine?"

Joy remained calm. She prepared herself for this sort of comment. "It's definitely yours. You're the only person I've been with since my relationship ended. I'm not asking you for anything. I just wanted to let you know that I'm planning to have an abortion tomorrow morning."

Dean's light complexion turned crimson as he covered his mouth with both hands. "I don't believe in abortions." Dean stood up and exhaled loudly. "Can you give me a few minutes to digest this?"

"Sure." Joy watched Dean as he walked away.

He went to the sliding glass door in the den, pulled the blinds back, and slid the door open. He stood on the patio for about ten minutes rubbing his head, then his chin, and then his head again. He continued to do this until he returned to the living room and sat beside Joy again.

"Joy, I'm kind of old-fashioned when it comes to children being born out of wedlock. I always wanted to have my children with my wife," Dean explained.

"I understand. I thought I would be married when I had my first child, but sometimes things don't always happen the way we plan," Joy said.

"I think this pregnancy happened for a reason and since we both don't want to have a child while we're not married, I guess, um, you know, um, what I'm asking is, um, if you'll marry me so our child can have my last name and grow up with two parents under the same roof."

What's his last name? Marriage? I can't even remember his last name! Am I ready for marriage? Oh, Lord! Bea! I do want our child to have two parents, but I'm not ready.

"Did you hear me, Joy?"

"Um, yes, I heard you, but I don't want to marry you. I already decided to have an abortion," Joy explained.

Dean stood up and pointed his finger in Joy's face. "You will not kill my baby! Have it and give it to me! I'll raise it by myself."

Joy pushed his finger away. "I can't do that. I'd worry about my child every day."

"But you can kill it?" Dean spat the words at Joy.

Joy had enough of Dean. "Get out!" She jumped off the couch and opened her front door. "Leave now!"

"I'll leave, but you forgot one thing. I'm a damn good lawyer and I'll have your ass in court to prevent you from killing my child," Dean threatened.

"I guess I'll see you in court then!" Joy shouted as she slammed the door shut behind him.

There was no doubt in her mind now that she needed to have an abortion. Having this baby would mean a long-term connection with Dean she just didn't want. She called Gabby to confirm her appointment for tomorrow. She needed to get this done as soon as possible before Dean tried to stop her with some legal action. She felt relieved knowing that after tomorrow, she would never have to see his face again.

Chapter 20 ————————

Gabby arrived at Joy's house the next day and to her surprise, Maxine was already there. Joy avoided eye and physical contact with them as she moved around the first floor of her house, trying to keep her hands busy until it was time to go to the abortion clinic. Gabby and Maxine watched Joy as she sprayed lemon-scented Pledge and polished the same table three times within minutes. They glanced at each other repeatedly with raised eyebrows in an attempt to send unspoken messages to each about their concern for Joy. The doorbell rang and broke the uncomfortable silence between them.

Fear took over Joy's face as she looked at them with questioning eyes wondering who could be at her door at this hour of the morning. The last thing she needed was Bea showing up and interrogating them until one of them broke down and told her the truth.

"Calm your nerves, Joy. I'll get it." Gabby left to answer the door.

Joy quickly wiped the polish off the table and ran to the kitchen to put the Pledge and dust towel away. On her way back to the living room, Dean's voice stopped her dead in her tracks. *What now?*

Dean actually took Joy's breath away when she saw him standing in the middle of her living room. He was wearing a gray, perfectly tailored tuxedo and vest with satin trim around the lapel and a matching satin tie and handkerchief. He was holding a bouquet of cream roses with specks of greenery tied together by a white satin bow.

"Good morning, Joy," Dean said nervously as he handed her the bouquet.

Joy took the flowers and smelled them. "Thanks. You look nice." She smiled.

"I'm sorry about how we left things yesterday." He swallowed hard and sighed. "I realized after I left that you deserved a better proposal than the one I threw at you out the blue."

Maxine and Gabby looked at each other with scrunched faces, wondering why Joy didn't tell them about this last night during one of the dozens of phone calls she made to them.

"It's okay, Dean. We were both in shock yesterday," Joy said.

Dean got down on one knee.

Maxine and Gabby gasped.

"Dean, please..." Joy started to protest.

"Just let me say what I came to say, Joy. I know men have a history of saying they're going to do one thing and making all these promises, but end up doing something else. I'm not one of those men. I care about you and I want you to have the baby. *Our* baby. I'll do whatever you want me to do, whatever you need me to do to make this work." He pulled a ring box from his inside jacket pocket and opened it. "Joy, will you honor me by becoming my wife? I promise you, I will be the best husband to you and father to our child that I can be. Joy Hope Marshall, will you marry me?" He took the platinum, one-carat baguette engagement ring out of the box and slid it on a stunned Joy's ring finger.

Joy shook her head. "Uh-uh, I can't, Dean. I have an appointment..." She started taking the ring off, but Dean stopped her.

"You don't have to answer me now, but don't take the ring off. I can't go to your appointment with you, but if you keep my ring on, it'll feel like I'm there in spirit." Dean smiled as he stood.

Joy hugged him and kissed him on his lips. "I'll keep it

on for now. That was a beautiful proposal, Dean, and you look so handsome." She straightened his tie. "If I was planning to keep the baby, I would've said yes." She kissed him again with tears in her eyes. "Thank you."

Gabby smiled as she watched them together. She knew men better than she knew anything else in this world, and she knew Dean Bennett had it bad for Joy. She knew if Joy wasn't still trying to deal with Allen leaving her, she would be more open to giving Dean a chance. But Gabby could tell by the way Joy looked at Dean that she had no feelings for him.

"If we're going, we need to leave now," Gabby announced.

Gabby and Maxine grabbed their purses and walked outside to Gabby's car to give Dean and Joy a few minutes alone before they left. When Joy got in the car, Gabby noticed the ring still on her finger, but didn't question her about it because she knew Joy better than Joy knew herself sometimes and she knew exactly how this whole scenario was going to play out, but she had to let Joy go through the motions.

Thirty minutes later, when they arrived at the clinic, Joy jumped out of the car and vomited on the sidewalk in front of the clinic. Maxine got out of the car and tried to help Joy with napkins and a bottle of water.

Gabby got out of her car and said, "When you leave here, all of your vomiting will be over."

They walked inside the clinic and saw six women and a couple of men sitting in the lobby with the same confused expressions on their faces. Joy swallowed hard as she went to the reception desk and signed her name. When she turned around to sit down, she noticed people glancing at each other for signs of approval that it was okay to be there.

Joy sat between Maxine and Gabby and attempted to look at one of the hundreds of magazines displayed on the coffee table. The room smelled sterile as if it had been rubbed down in alcohol and Clorox. The walls were bare but painted a relaxing, soft yellow tone. Joy glanced at staff members when they came out to call a patient back. Their faces showed no expression and they all wore the same royal-blue scrubs with matching caps.

Thirty minutes later, a nurse came out and called, "Joy Marshall." Joy grabbed Gabby's and Maxine's arms and squeezed them both before she stood up. Gabby ignored her and kept reading her magazine. Maxine stood up, hugged Joy, and whispered the Serenity Prayer in her ear. Joy closed her eyes and smiled as she felt a sense of calm wash over her.

She turned around and followed the nurse into the back where she was given several forms to read, fill out and sign. Then she was taken into a room full of lockers where she removed her clothes and shoes and placed them in locker number 705. She put on a gown and waited for the nurse to come back to get her. She stared at the locker with her clothes inside it and realized the number 705 was July fifth, the day Allen proposed and then left her. Tears formed in her eyes as she thought about how different her life would be now if she had said yes to Allen's proposal and moved to China. She definitely wouldn't be sitting in an abortion clinic and she would probably be happier than she was now.

When the nurse came back, she said, "Follow me, Ms. Marshall."

Joy followed her to an exam room where a tall, thin male doctor was standing near an ultrasound machine. Without looking at Joy, he pointed to the exam table and said, "I need you to lie back on the table for the ultrasound." The doctor opened her medical gown and squirted warm gel on her lower abdomen. He said, "You can turn your head if you don't want to see this."

"I want to see," Joy said eagerly as she looked at the monitor and saw a flutter on the screen. "What's that?"

"Heartbeat," he said as he turned the monitor off.

"It looked small. How does it have a heartbeat already?" Joy asked.

The doctor gave Joy a book with pictures of fetuses at different stages. "This is where the fetus is developmentally."

Joy ignored the page the doctor showed her and started at the chapter on conception and quickly read through the first trimester. She had no idea her baby had already started to develop and grow inside of her and realized she couldn't go through with the procedure. She sat up on the exam table and gave the doctor the book back. "I changed my mind, doc, I need to get my clothes. I'm sorry, I don't want to do this. I'm going to have my baby." Joy smiled and used the gown she was wearing to wipe the gel off her stomach as she stood up.

"Calm down Ms. Marshall. We don't force anybody to do anything she doesn't want to do. I'll have the nurse take you back to get your clothes and you can pay for the sonogram at the front desk." The doctor smiled at her before he left the room. "Good luck to you."

"Thank you." Joy paced around the room until the nurse came and took her to get her clothes. She was fully dressed in less than five minutes. When she started walking out, the nurse told her not to worry about the charges for the sonogram. The doctor waived the fee.

When she entered the lobby, she looked at Maxine and Gabby and said, "Let's go." She rushed outside and waited for them. After a few minutes, when they finally came out, she was surprised to see them smiling and laughing. She looked at them with her mouth open and eyebrows raised.

"Gabby was right," Maxine laughed. "She called me last night and said you'll never go through with it."

"What?" Joy asked.

"I know you, girl. It's not in you to do this. I just wanted you to make the choice so when Junior is in his terrible twos and driving you crazy, you'll know you decided to have him or her and nobody made that choice for you." Gabby hugged Joy.

Joy rubbed her stomach and screamed, "Oh, my God! I'm having a baby!" Then she looked at the ring on her finger. "And I guess I'm getting married, too."

"What!" Maxine shouted.

"I knew it! Let's go back to your house, Joy, and start planning your wedding," Gabby said with a big smile across her face.

Chapter 21

Maxine sat in P.F. Chang's China Bistro at Tyson's Galleria sipping on a soda while Gabby and Joy discussed the upcoming wedding. Gabby had already called ahead and reserved a private table for six for Joy's bridal shower. Regrettably, the other three guests didn't show. Bea refused to come because she thought her daughter was making a mistake marrying Dean. Tyesha was with Bea trying to convince her friend to attend her daughter's wedding tomorrow and Ms. Pat offered to babysit TJ and Maxwell so Maxine could go and support Joy. Unfortunately, being in the restaurant tonight with her two best friends was the last place Maxine wanted to be. She agreed with Bea and thought Joy was moving way too fast with the wedding, but Joy had her mind made up and refused to listen to anyone. As her friends continued talking, Maxine closed her eyes and thought about Kevin and how she wished she were with him right now.

Oddly, she had no intentions on seeing Kevin again after their first time together at the hotel, but he had called her later that night and talked her through her guilty feelings. He made her understand and accept that this was all part of going through a divorce. One minute you're happy and ready to move on and minutes later, you want to run back to the comfort of what you know from your previous life. He made her feel like everything he said or did was with her in mind and she loved that about him.

They'd been meeting every Monday and Wednesday at the Radisson after work. On her first day of teaching, he sent her a dozen roses to her classroom and later, when they met at the hotel, he listened attentively as she told him all the details about her first day. He did things for her to make her happy and everything was easy between them. Maxine didn't feel obligated to Kevin and she liked the way he saw her as a smart, independent woman who could handle herself.

"What do you think Maxine?" Gabby asked as she faced her with an annoyed expression.

Maxine was caught off guard. "Huh?"

"Are you even listening to us? I swear Maxine, I don't know what's going on with you these days!" Gabby complained as she slid a piece of paper in front of Maxine. "This is the seating chart for the reception. Should I put your parents with the children to keep them in order?"

"No. Everybody should watch their own children at the reception," Maxine replied with a straight face.

"I agree, girl. Let the parents watch his or her own brats," Joy said, then giggled. "So what's going on with you? You seem distracted. I know you just started working again; maybe it's too soon after your injury."

Maxine shook her head no and smiled. "No, it's not that. Joy, I'm worried about you. Why are you rushing to marry a man you barely know or like? One week ago today, you found out you were pregnant. You decided to have an abortion, but changed your mind. When Dean proposed, you turned him down, then changed your mind again. I think if you take some time and think this through, you'll change your mind about getting married so fast."

"Thank you for your concern, Maxine, but I know what I'm doing. I don't want to be a baby's mama and I'm definitely not walking down the aisle while I'm showing," Joy explained.

"Maxine, who are you to question Joy about getting married? Just because your marriage ended badly doesn't mean hers will. Joy is stronger than you. She won't make the same mistakes you did." Gabby stared at Maxine with twisted lips.

Maxine pointed her index finger in Gabby's face. "I know I made a lot of mistakes the way I handled the abuse in my marriage, but I'm stronger than you know, so stop treating me like an invalid who can't think for herself." Maxine stood up and put her purse on her shoulder.

Gabby looked up at Maxine with a frown. "What's your problem? I think you've been without sex too long. Maybe if you find yourself a man and get some ding-dong, you won't be so evil."

Maxine looked down at Gabby with a hateful stare and said, "Oh, honey, that's not my problem. I get mine, regularly. That's right, bitch, so stop trying to be my mother and be my friend again."

"Who are you sleeping with Maxine?" Gabby inquired.

"Don't worry about it. He's taking care of what I need and that's all that matters." She threw a fifty-dollar bill on the table and looked at Joy. "And, Joy, just to let you know, we make sure to use condoms so we won't be in the same situation as you are right now."

"Okay." Joy had never seen Maxine this outspoken, but she liked it.

Gabby's eyes and mouth were wide open as she watched Maxine walk away. "Who is she sleeping with and did she just call me the B word?"

Joy clapped her hands lightly and said, "I'm so proud of Maxine. Our girl finally grew a backbone today. I knew this day would come." She smiled as she looked at Gabby's shocked expression.

"Backbone my behind," Gabby snapped. "All this proves is Trent did more damage to her brain than we thought."

After finally telling her girlfriends how she felt, Maxine left the restaurant with a big smile on her face. She called Kevin when she got in her minivan. She wanted to cry when she got his voicemail. She drove to a liquor store she passed on the way to the restaurant earlier and bought a bottle of Moët Champagne. She decided to surprise Kevin with a spur-of-the-moment visit. So far, all of their time together had been pre-arranged to the last second. She thought it was time for them to do something different.

He wanted to see her yesterday, but she couldn't meet him because her father arranged an appointment for her with his financial planner to discuss paying off the debt Trent had gotten them in. She was working hard to put her past life with Trent behind her and move forward, hopefully with Kevin.

When he called and texted her today about getting together, she hurried home after work to spend some time with her boys before she drove to Virginia in rush hour traffic to meet up for Joy's bridal shower dinner. She hated turning him down twice, especially since she wasn't going to see him again until Monday.

Maxine was all smiles as she drove the forty minutes to Kevin's house. The thought of surprising him had her tingling all over with excitement. She had looked up his address weeks ago, but she had never felt comfortable visiting him because of the two exchange students he had staying with him. She had already decided to make her surprise visit short with a quick Champagne toast and maybe a quickie in his room if they could manage it.

Forty minutes later, she parked her car, walked up the steps to Kevin's single family home, and rang the doorbell.

An attractive woman answered the door dressed in a sweat suit and a pair of house slippers. She was holding a pretty little girl around two or three years old on her hip.

Maxine was caught off guard. "Hi. Oh, I must have the wrong address."

"Who are you looking for?" the woman asked with a southern accent.

"Kevin Bradley," Maxine replied.

She smiled at Maxine and said, "Oh, then you're at the right place. I'm his wife and this is our youngest daughter, Kendall. He's in the shower. Just got finished working out." Kevin's wife moved the child to her other hip and smiled. "Is he expecting you?"

Maxine felt like someone knocked the wind out of her. She tried to take a deep breath but couldn't and started coughing. She didn't know what to do. *I'm sleeping with a married man.* She looked past the woman into the house and saw three older children who didn't look like the foreign exchange students Kevin had shown her pictures of; instead, they looked like miniature versions of Kevin. She gave his wife the bottle of Champagne and said, "I just wanted to drop this off to him. Can you make sure he gets this? Thank you." She turned to leave before the woman could see how upset she was.

"What's your name?" the woman called after Maxine as she walked down the steps.

"Tell him it's from Maxine, Mrs. Anderson," Maxine yelled back.

She ran back to her car and drove away in shock. She slammed on her brakes and almost banged her head on the steering wheel when she failed to notice a stop sign and almost hit another car at the end of Kevin's block. She pulled her minivan over and took deep breaths to calm herself down. She refused to let herself shed one tear over Kevin. *How stupid am I to believe everything out of his mouth?*

Twenty minutes later when she pulled into her parent's driveway, her cell phone rang. She glanced at it and saw Kevin's name. She wanted to make sure she never heard from him or saw his face again so she answered it before she stepped in the house.

"You lying piece of shit. Don't ever dial my number again. If you do, I'll make another visit to your house and tell your wife everything." She pushed the End Call button and walked in the house, determined never to let another man make a fool out of her.

Chapter 22———————

Bea stood in the church's choir room in front of Joy with her arms crossed over her chest. She was dressed in an all-black, short-sleeved suit with black gloves up to her elbows, thick, black stockings and black shoes. She even wore a black hat with a short, lace, black veil attached to it to cover her face. She was making her point. You had to be blind if you didn't know how Bea felt about this union.

"Why are you doing this to me?" Bea asked as she lifted the black veil and threw it back over her head dramatically.

Joy sighed. "If this is going to be another don't-marry-Dean-speech, save it." Joy walked in front of the mirror and made sure her veil was straight before she walked down the aisle in fifteen minutes.

"I thought I raised you to be smarter than this. Where did I go wrong?" Bea cried out.

"Bea, please don't do this. Poppy is walking me down the aisle shortly and I don't need you playing mind games on me about how I failed you as a daughter," Joy said.

Bea grabbed Joy by the shoulders and stared in her eyes. "Tell me you love him and you want to spend the rest of your life with him and I won't say another word. But if you're only marrying him because he got you pregnant, I'm not going to let you do this."

Joy swallowed hard and looked down. "No matter what, Bea, I'm getting married today."

"Not if I can help it!" Bea stomped out of the room.

Joy sat down in a chair in the corner of the room, closed her eyes, and asked God to give her the strength to get through this day. Earlier this morning, Maxine had called and begged her not to get married. Shortly after she got Maxine off the phone, her father called to make sure this was what she wanted to do. Then Bea started calling every few minutes, alternating between crying one minute and threatening her the next. To her surprise, Gabby was the only person who didn't question her decision to marry Dean and Joy assumed that was because she was having such a good time planning the wedding with the unlimited budget Dean gave her.

Looking at Dean, thinking about Dean, and having sex with Dean did nothing for Joy. She hoped that changed soon or they were going to be one of those happily married couples living in separate homes. He started moving his things into her house and staying there the week before they were to be married. By the third night, she had enough of Dean's clinginess and his need to know where she was every second of the day. One night, she lied and told him she didn't hear the doorbell or the phone ringing because she was tired from the pregnancy. He joked about her being tired from all the sex they were having, which was bullshit because he still hadn't lasted longer than two minutes yet. The next day, he took her keys and had copies made so it wouldn't happen again. *There goes my freedom*, she thought.

Joy opened her eyes when she heard someone enter the room.

Tyesha walked in the room and looked at Joy with concern. "How is everything going, sweetie?"

When Joy saw Tyesha, she jumped out of the chair and hugged her. "Am I doing the right thing?" Joy whispered.

"I can't answer that for you, Joy. The decision is yours and yours alone. But I'll tell you this, if you have any doubts, now is the time to run out the door." Tyesha realized Bea was right. Joy didn't love Dean. She was just going through the motions because she was pregnant.

"Have you talked to Allen? How is he doing?" Joy still

loved Allen and wished she were marrying him instead of Dean.

"He's fine. It took a while, but he's dating now," Tyesha answered, then she realized she shouldn't have said that when she saw the disappointment on Joy's face.

Joy wondered why Tyesha was lying to her about Allen dating somebody else. She already knew Allen was dating a woman with a British accent from the time she called him and practically begged him to let her come to China. Joy swallowed hard and patted her hair.

"Well, I'd better get ready to do this. It's my wedding day," Joy said with a fake smile plastered on her cute face. She was more determined than ever to get married now that she knew Allen had moved on without her.

"Joy, are you sure? Tyrese is in town and he came with me so we can kidnap you and get you out of here if you have any doubts." Tyesha knew from the look on Joy's face that she didn't want to get married.

Tyesha and her twin brother, Tyrese, raised Allen after their mother died when Allen was twelve and they were twenty-eight. Tyrese joined the Navy but stayed very active in his younger brother's life as a positive role model, unlike their other brothers. For the first time, Joy could see the family resemblance between Allen and Tyesha. They both possessed the same smooth complexion, dimples, and smoky eyes. Looking at Tyesha made Joy realize how much she still loved and missed Allen.

"Thanks, Tyesha, but I'm getting married. Thanks for coming and getting Bea to come, too. I know that wasn't easy." Joy walked Tyesha to the door.

"Girl, you got that right." Tyesha hugged Joy again. "I love you, sweetie, and you know I'm here for you if you need me."

Joy held back her tears, smiled, and nodded as she watched Tyesha leave.

Minutes later, Gabby made the wedding party line up in the foyer. Neither Joy or Dean wanted a large ceremony. Fewer than fifty people were invited. Gabby and Maxine were Joy's bridesmaids. They wore matching lilac organza, three-quarter-length gowns that Gabby ordered. Two of Dean's friends from law school were his groomsmen. They wore black suits with white shirts and matching lilac ties and handkerchiefs peeking out of their suit jackets.

Gabby took Juan to the choir room so he could walk Joy down the aisle. She looked the bride up and down with a disapproving glare. Joy wore a short, ivory dress with a jeweled neckline she'd found on the clearance rack at David's Bridal during her lunch hour one day. Gabby was horrified when she found out and was prepared to buy Joy another dress herself. When she saw how little interest Joy had in her own wedding, she decided that the original choice would do for the ceremony.

Juan was dressed like the rest of the men in the wedding party. He was more nervous than Joy. He knew his daughter didn't love Dean, but he had to let her make her own decisions. She was a grown woman now. He whispered in Joy's ear, "You'll always be my baby girl. I love you."

Joy kissed her father on the cheek and they left the room for the sanctuary. Joy stood with her father between the first pews and waited for Gabby's nod to start down the aisle.

Joy smiled at Juan and said, "I love you, too, Poppy."

Gabby gave the nod. Joy slid her hand under her father's arm, and he kissed her on her cheek before they began their march down the aisle. Joy smiled at her guest.

Juan patted her hand and whispered, "Look at Bea sitting over there."

Joy started laughing. Her mother should've been an actress. Bea's black head-to-toe ensemble stood out starkly among the autumnal shades of the other guests. Before Juan presented Joy to Dean, Joy made a detour to Bea. She bent down, removed her mother's hat and veil, and gave her a kiss. "I love you. Thank you for coming." Then she returned to Juan and took his arm as he led her to her future husband.

When Juan let go of her hand to take his seat, Joy almost turned around to follow him, but she stopped herself. She felt empty inside and knew this wasn't the way she was supposed to feel on her wedding day. She didn't love Dean, but she assumed that with time, she would grow to love him. When the minister made them face each other and hold hands, Joy looked around at her bridesmaids and guests in confusion. She felt like something was missing. As she listened to the minister, she started to relax.

"It is a time of celebration when two people have come together and found mutual joy." The minister looked at Joy and smiled. "They have shared their lives and decided to create a covenant between themselves, a partnership guided by spirit and supported by our community. Joy Hope Marshall and Dean Caleb Bennett ask all you in attendance in body and spirit to pledge your support and encouragement for them to keep true to their vows."

"I don't support or encourage this marriage in any way!" Bea yelled from her seat.

Joy covered her face with her hands. "This is not happening," she whispered to herself.

"Your objection has been noted," the minister stated.

"I want more than my objection to be noted; I want this wedding to stop! NOW!" Bea screamed.

The minister stepped closer to Dean and Joy and whispered. "Would you like to continue?"

"Yes," Dean said quickly before Joy could respond.

"The bride and groom have decided to continue with the ceremony. I ask that all guests refrain from anymore outbursts and respect their wishes," the minister said firmly while staring at Bea.

"Joy, don't do this! There isn't a drug in this world that will kill me quicker than you marrying him. Please think about what you're doing, honey," Bea begged.

"Bea, please don't do this. Sit down and let us get married," Joy pleaded.

"If you do, you'll gain a husband and lose a mother! I promise you that." Bea tried to walk over to Joy but Juan stopped her. "Don't you want your mother by your side when you have that baby in a few months?"

Dean held Joy's hand. "She won't be alone, Bea. I'll be there when our child is born."

Joy shook her head to agree with Dean. She knew if she

let Bea stop her wedding, the woman would never stop trying to control her life. "Please sit down, Bea."

Bea sat and started sobbing in Juan's arms.

"Let us continue." The minister said and gave a reassuring smile to everyone.

Joy and Dean turned to face each other again. Dean looked at Joy with love, but Joy was peeking out the corner of her eye at Bea who was still sobbing loudly. Dean gently touched Joy's face so she could turn and look at him.

She looked at Dean with no emotion on her face. She kept feeling that something was missing. No matter how hard she tried, she couldn't look directly at Dean. She closed her eyes and saw Allen's face clear as day. She opened them and imagined Dean was Allen and smiled for minutes. She knew that was the only way she was going to get through her own wedding.

Joy and Dean looked at each other as they repeated what the minister said.

"Now, it's time for the exchange of the vows and rings."

"Oh, my God, no!" Bea screamed out.

The minister ignored her. "May this fire of love kindle your passions for each other throughout all your years. May your love rise anew, an eternal flame to light the day. May you grow old together and share a happy home." The minister nodded at Joy to say her vows.

"I, Joy Hope Marshall, take thee, Allen Todd Johnson, to be my husband and before God and these witnesses, I promise to be a faithful and true wife."

"Who did she say?" Bea stopped crying and asked.

Joy noticed Dean and the minister looking at her with wide eyes and wondered what was wrong.

Gabby tapped on her shoulder and Maxine kept clearing her throat trying to get her attention. When she turned around to look at them, they were trying to tell Joy something with their eyes and facial expressions, but she couldn't make out their meaning.

Joy turned back around to face Dean. "Go ahead, Dean," Joy whispered. "Your turn."

"Joy, let's try this again," the minister whispered.

"And this time, say *my* name and not your ex-boyfriend's," Dean whispered through clenched teeth.

Joy felt nauseous. She put her hand over her mouth to stop herself from throwing up. *Did I really say Allen's name? Of course I did. Since I was fifteen years old, I had practiced saying my vows to Allen and no one else.*

"Do you need a minute, Joy?" the minister asked.

"No! We're ready. Right, Joy?" Dean gave Joy an evil look.

"Somebody better tell me whose name she said because I know it wasn't his," Bea asked Tyesha, Tyrese, and Juan who sat beside her looking embarrassed for Joy and ashamed of Bea at the same time.

"Right. I'm ready." Joy took a deep breath and said her vows again, this time with Dean's name.

Dean didn't skip a beat and said his vows before anyone else could interrupt them.

After they exchanged rings, the minister said, "In as much as Joy and Dean have consented in holy wedlock and have witnessed the same before God, according to the powers vested in me by the state of Maryland and being an ordained minister of the Gospel, I pronounce that you are husband and wife. In the name of the Father, the Son, and the Holy Spirit, those whom God has joined together, let no one put asunder. You may kiss the bride."

Dean took Joy in his arms and kissed her gently.

"No! I just lost my daughter!" Bea cried out.

Joy and Dean ignored her as they walked up the aisle with their wedding party following closely behind.

"Congratulations, Momma!" Gabby screamed as she hugged Joy. "I thought my wedding was full of drama but you got me beat."

Maxine approached Joy with a serious expression. "Congratulations, Joy. I hope you know that it's not a good sign when you say your vows to the man you really love while marrying a man you hardly know."

"Maxine, please don't start on me," Joy pleaded.

Before Maxine could reply, Dean interrupted them. "Excuse me, Maxine, may I have a word with my lovely wife?"

Maxine walked away without responding.

Dean escorted Joy to the end of the hall. When they were out of sight, Dean shoved Joy in an empty room.

"Hey! What's your problem?" Joy asked full of attitude.

Dean pushed Joy against the wall with anger in his eyes and nostrils flaring. "Shut the fuck up! You just embarrassed me in front of my family and friends."

Joy felt bad because she could tell how hurt he was after she said Allen's name.

Dean got so close to her face, she could feel the heat from his breath and his spit on her face. "From this second on, I never want to hear his name again. You are *my* wife now and you're having *my* child. Erase him from your thoughts. And Monday morning, you find someone to laser his name off your body. I will not fuck my wife while she has her ex-lover's name tattooed on her ass. It's a constant reminder that you fucked him. Get your act together, go to the reception, and play the perfect wife. You need to make up for the way you and your mother behaved today. Just to let you know, I will *not* tolerate anymore ignorant behavior from you or your family. You get it together before I have to do it for you," Dean commanded as he stared at Joy with the veins in his neck bulging.

The words Dean spoke to Joy and the way he looked at her had her whole body trembling from fear. This wasn't the same man she agreed to marry. She backed away from him, wondering if Bea and Maxine were right. Maybe she did rush into marrying Dean without getting to know him better. If she had seen this side of him before, there was no way she would've married him. She stared at him with frightened eyes and a feeling that she had just made the biggest mistake of her life.

Chapter 23

"Good morning, sexy. You look well rested this morning," William said as Gabby came downstairs.

"Oh, I do, huh? Well thanks for letting me sleep in today. Planning Joy's wedding and all that drama wore me out." Gabby shook her head thinking about it as she poured herself a cup of black coffee in the kitchen.

William sat at the dining room table reading the Sunday edition of the *Washington Post* and *Baltimore Sun* newspapers. He was wearing a pair of loose fitting jeans and a muscle shirt that had Gabby salivating at the mouth. It had been over a week since they had been intimate. She had put sex on the back burner while she rushed to plan Joy's shotgun wedding. Watching William made her realize how much she wanted her husband. She thought about what they could be doing while Nadia was asleep. She pulled down the paper he was reading.

"I was thinking, since Nadia is sleep, we should go upstairs and get reacquainted," Gabby said in a sexy voice.

William put the newspaper down and stood up. "I'm with you on that. Hurry up, you know she takes those cat-naps now."

They ran upstairs to Gabby's room and took off their clothes. They fell on the bed and started kissing and touching each other like teenagers exploring each other's bodies for the first time. Gabby lay on her back and spread her legs wide open. William mounted her and entered her immediately. Within minutes, William felt Gabby's body quiver as she started breathing heavily and moaning. He turned her over on her stomach and entered her ass. When Gabby started to protest, because anal sex was reserved for special occasions only, William grabbed both her hands with one of his and put his other hand on her clitoris, massaging it gently. After another few minutes, they were both shivering and screaming with pleasure.

William fell on the bed and looked at Gabby with a smile.

"Why are you looking at me like that?" she asked jokingly.

"Because I love you."

Gabby kissed William on his lips, curled up beside him on the bed, and laid her head on his chest. "I love you, too, William." And she meant it.

They grew silent as they both realized this was the first time Gabby had ever told William she loved him.

"Thank you for making me happy, William." Gabby hugged him and kissed his chest.

"I love making you happy. I thought you knew that." He kissed Gabby before he buried his head between her legs, bringing her to orgasm once again.

Three hours later, William and Gabby sat in the family room laughing at Nadia's facial expressions while she played with her toys and tried to flip herself over on the floor. When the doorbell rang, they looked at each other wondering if the other was expecting guests. William left to answer the door.

When Gabby heard Phyllis's and Sam's voices, her smile disappeared and she became angry. Phyllis always tried to do things to make Gabby look bad or put doubts in her mind about her husband. She wondered what trouble Phyllis was bringing her way today.

"Yeah, William, I know you read the Sunday paper so I thought you would've seen it by now. When I didn't hear from you, I decided to come over and check on you. Momma and Daddy are waiting to hear from me before they come over."

"What's going on, William?" Gabby asked.

William didn't answer. He had his face down reading

something in the newspaper.

Phyllis put her hands on her hips and gritted on Gabby. "You got a nerve to ask what's going on. It's you, as usual. Your face is plastered all over the sports section of the *Baltimore Sun* as the reason Rayshawn Robinson is playing poorly this season." Phyllis sighed. "Huh, you leave a trail of destruction from Bowie to Baltimore, destroying everybody in your path."

Gabby tried to remain calm, but when she heard Rayshawn's name, sweat started rolling down her back and her pulse increased. She snatched William's copy of the *Baltimore Sun* off the dining room table and quickly turned to the sports section. When she saw a clear picture of her sitting with Rayshawn at the restaurant that day she met him, she gasped.

William, Sam, and Phyllis looked at her like they were waiting for an explanation.

William was trying to remain cool, but Gabby could tell he was upset. His light complexion turned pale and he had the newspaper balled up in his hand. "You never told me you knew him, Gabby. Where was Nadia when you were off having lunch with him? Was I at work?"

"You weren't at work that day; you were home and Nadia was with you," Gabby said as she tried to think of a way to get out of this mess. She wanted to kill Phyllis because William would never have read it if it wasn't for her nosey butt.

"That doesn't explain why you were having a romantic lunch with the Baltimore Ravens' world-famous quarterback while your husband and daughter were home," Phyllis interjected.

William started reading the article again. He was trying to remember the date and what happened that day so he could get to the bottom of this.

"William, can we talk in private? This is a private matter between a husband and wife," Gabby said calmly.

"Hell no! So you can tell him more lies! I don't think so!" Phyllis screamed with both her fists buried deep in her hips.

Nadia started crying from Phyllis's loud voice. William stopped reading the paper and picked Nadia up to console her.

"Phyllis, can you not scream in our home. Our daughter is

not used to it." Gabby gave Phyllis an evil look.

"That article says customers at the restaurant heard you and Rayshawn arguing over a child." She pointed at Nadia. "Is she the child you were arguing over?"

Gabby ran to Phyllis and smacked her hand down. "Don't point at my child that way. You can come after me all you want, but leave my daughter alone. I'm going to tell you just like I told Rayshawn when I had lunch with him - William Landon is her father."

Sam held Phyllis back from going after Gabby. "Gabby, we just trying to find out why y'all were arguing in public like that and why William didn't know anything about it," Sam said.

"Sam, am I married to you? No. I don't have to answer to anyone except my husband. And I would like to do that in private. Now, get out of our home."

"That's not going to happen!" Phyllis barked.

William stood up with Nadia in his arms. "Yes, it is. This is a private matter between me and my wife. Goodbye, Phyllis and Sam."

They looked at William like he had committed a crime. When they saw that he was serious, they left without saying another word.

Gabby sat down and waited for William to come back to the family room. Instead, he went in the kitchen and fixed Nadia a warm bottle before he joined Gabby again. She watched how tender and loving he was with Nadia. Everything had to be perfect for his baby girl. She married William because she knew he would make a good father for her daughter, but now, she realized, she loved William and needed him in her life.

William feeding Nadia gave her time to think about what she was going to say. He was so calm, as if nothing had changed, and that was making her nervous. She wanted him to say something before she lost it.

"Are we going to talk about this, William?"

"After I feed Nadia and put her down for her nap. I don't want her to hear this. She's not used to loud voices and you saw how upset Phyllis made her," William said.

Even though William was visibly troubled, Gabby smiled because she loved how he put Nadia first, no matter what. She watched him take her upstairs and sat patiently until he returned. She had never seen William this cold toward her before.

A few minutes later, he returned to the family room, sat beside, Gabby, and asked, "Is there something going on between you and this man that I should be worried about?"

"No, William. I used to date him, nothing serious. He called around the time Maxine was in the hospital. I told him to stop calling me because I was happily married and we had just had a baby."

"So I'm guessing he didn't stop calling so you met him at the restaurant to get him to stop." William stared at Gabby with narrow eyes.

"Yes, exactly," Gabby agreed.

"Who was the baby you were arguing about? Was it Nadia?"

"Yes. He thinks she could be his daughter and we could live together happily ever after. I told him it's not going to happen. I'm happy with you."

"I know that, Gabby, and I trust you, but if he ever contacts you again, please tell me. I don't want to find out like this again." William hugged Gabby and held her in his arms.

"Thank you for understanding, William."

Gabby lay in William's arms relaxed and content. She should let Phyllis know the next time she saw her that she was no match for Gabrielle Louise Roché-Landon. Now that she put Rayshawn in his place and he stopped calling her, she could finally relax. She smiled, closed her eyes, and started to melt into William's chest.

"Gabby, I want to take a DNA test in case Rayshawn Robinson contacts you again asking if he's Nadia's father. That way we'll put an end to all of his doubts. I don't want Nadia turning five and this guy coming around asking questions about her. I'll check into it when I go to work next week."

Gabby's muscles tightened and her eyes popped wide open because she knew that if William took a DNA test, it was going to end the perfect life she had created for her and Nadia.

Chapter 24 —————

Maxine had just finished putting the last curl in her hair when her mother knocked on her bedroom door. She took the towel from around her shoulders, unplugged her curlers, and opened her bedroom door. "Hi, Momma. I'm going to see a foreign film in Bethesda. Wanna join me?"

"Maxine, your father and I want to talk to you," Pat said in a stern tone.

"Sure. I have a few minutes before I leave. We can talk now." Maxine followed her mother, wondering what this was all about.

When they arrived downstairs, Jim was sitting in the living room reading the Saturday edition of the *Washington Post*. Pat sat beside him while Maxine stood in the doorway.

"Have a seat, Maxine," Jim ordered.

"Okay." She took a wingback chair across from them. "What's going on?" She wondered if something had happened to one of her boys while they were with Trent's mother for the weekend.

Pat took an envelope off the coffee table and gave it to Maxine. "This came for you this morning."

Maxine took the envelope from her mother and looked at it. Her hands started trembling when she saw Trent's name on the return address. She stared at the letter like it was poison and opening it would kill her.

Jim saw his daughter's reaction. "Do you want one of us to read it to you?"

"No, I'm okay." Maxine stood to leave. "Thanks for this."

"Maxine, his mother told us he's getting out on house arrest December first." Jim sighed. "If that letter is about a reconciliation, he's not welcome here."

Maxine gave her father the evil eye. *He never liked Trent.*

"First of all, six months wasn't enough punishment for what he put you through and to only do half of that and get out with an ankle monitor is absurd. It just goes to show you how screwed up the justice system is in America," Pat complained.

"Thank you for letting me know how you feel, but I need to deal with this on my own," Maxine said in a firm tone as she smiled at her parents and left for her room where she closed the door, ripped the letter out of the envelope and started reading.

Dear Maxi,

I want to start by saying I'm sorry for hurting you and our families. I take full responsibility for all the terrible things I did. You are the most loving, caring, and understanding person I know. I took advantage of your love and hurt you and that was unacceptable. I'll spend the rest of my days trying to make it up to you. I'll be serving the last three months of my sentence under house arrest while working for Legal Aid in D.C. I don't want domestic violence to continue with another generation in my family. I would like to start family counseling with you and the boys as soon as I'm released. I know they deserve better than me for a father, but the truth is, I am their father. It is my responsibility to show them how real men act and behave. I know it's bold of me to ask this, but please consider it. I will accept whatever decision you think is best. I still love you deeply.

Trent

Maxine read the letter three more times before she put on her shoe boots, grabbed her coat and purse, and left the house. Trent's letter had her so angry, she felt like she could spit fire. *How dare he ask them to go to family counseling when she hadn't heard a single word from him since he got arrested? Did he think he was just going to walk back into their lives like nothing happened? I don't think so.*

She was fed up with men. Trent's abuse and Kevin's lies

made her lose all trust in the opposite sex. She finally got Kevin off her mind and now here came Trent with his drama. She was going to put an end to this before he got any ideas of them having a happy family reunion.

She took a detour from the movie theater and headed straight to Trent's half-way house. Since he reached out to her, she was going to return the favor and let him know exactly how she felt. She should've done this three months ago when he got arrested. Thirty minutes later, Maxine walked in the half-way house with her stomach churning and signed in at the front desk. While the guard checked her purse, she thought about how much her life had changed since she last saw Trent. She was a different person now and wondered how he would react to her new attitude. Then she quickly pushed the thought from her mind because the new Maxine didn't give a fuck how Trent felt.

The guard's deep voice reminded Maxine where she was. "Ma'am, I need you to go through the metal detector, then a guard will escort you to the visitors' room."

"Okay. Thank you." Maxine smiled politely although she was fuming inside.

She followed a tall female guard down a flight of steps and down a long, wide hallway with lights so bright Maxine had to squint to avoid a headache. She entered a large room with round tables and chairs and vending machines lined against the walls.

"You can have a seat. His counseling session ends in ten minutes," the guard said.

"Thanks." Maxine sat at a table in the back corner, took Trent's letter out of her purse, and put it on the table.

About fifteen minutes later, Trent entered the room laughing and talking with a male guard. When he saw Maxine, he stopped and stared at her for a few minutes or so before he joined her.

"Hi, Maxi. This is a surprise," Trent said nervously.

"It's a surprise to me because I wasn't planning on ever seeing you again until I got this letter." She pushed it across the table toward him.

Trent wiped his face with both hands. "I understand, Maxi. You have every right to be angry with me. But..."

"Oh, you're giving me permission to be angry." Maxine shook her head. "I can't believe you."

He reached across the table to touch her hands. "I'm trying to right my wrongs, Maxi. I'm sorry."

Maxine pulled her hands back. "It's too late for that, Trent. You ruined everything. Our love, our marriage, and even our children are broken because of you and I'll never forgive you for it," Maxine screamed.

Both guards gave her a warning look.

Trent looked at Maxine's cold expression. Her eyes shot daggers at him. It was the first time in the eight years he'd known her that he ever witnessed her this angry and out of control. He knew all the pain he caused had turned her into this person. "I'm sorry." He could barely breathe as the tears streamed down his face.

"Yeah, I know you are." Maxine stood up. "I'll allow the boys to go to counseling with you, but I'm not interested. When you're released and settled, you can have the boys every other weekend if they're comfortable with seeing you."

Trent wiped his face and shook his head. "I understand. Thank you."

"And I'll give your mother the key to the storage unit because I don't want any of the crap in there. You can have it all. It's a sad reminder of the life I used to have with you and I'm ready to move on. Good bye, Trent." Maxine left the room with the female guard.

The male guard walked over to Trent and touched him on his shoulder. "You alright, man?"

Trent wiped the tears from his eyes before he turned around to face the guard. "No, I'm not alright. I had it all, a beautiful, smart wife, two healthy sons, and family and friends who loved me. I lost it all because I tried to be somebody I'm not. I know better now, but I'll never be able to show my wife because she's finished with me and I have nobody to blame for that but myself."

Chapter 25

"Bea, it's me again." Joy sighed. "It's four o'clock on Friday, the 23rd and I'm walking into my doctor's office for my first sonogram. I know you're still not speaking to me, but I would love to have my mother by my side when I see my baby for the first time. I love you. I hope to see you there." Joy hung up the phone and wiped the tears from her eyes.

"You don't need your mother there. You have your husband and that's all you need," Dean said with an arrogant smirk.

Joy looked at her husband of two weeks and wondered how she'd tolerated him this long. The more time she spent with Dean, the more she realized she didn't like anything about him. He called her three or four times a day at work interrupting her classroom, which pissed off her principal. When she finished her evening classes twice a week, he was waiting for her when she stepped out of the building and questioned her with attitude if he saw her talking to any male classmates.

By far, the worst part of being married to Dean was the sex. Every night, after she fell asleep, he would come to bed smelling like he bathed in a bottle of vodka and expect her to endure his attempt at trying to have sex. To this day, he hadn't made it past the two-minute mark before he started ejaculating. For the past week, Joy had been ignoring his request for sex, but that didn't stop him. She woke up one night when she heard a strange sound. She caught him jerking off to Internet porn right in their bedroom. He didn't last longer than two minutes doing that either.

Joy walked into her doctor's office with Dean by her side and checked in with the receptionist. She glanced around the lobby praying that Bea was there, but she wasn't. Bea hadn't talked to her since she married Dean. Joy tried to act as if it wasn't affecting her, but it was. She always thought her mother would be by her side for every visit during her first pregnancy. Joy sat beside Dean, laid her head back, and closed her eyes for a few minutes.

"Wake up before they call your name and you miss it," Gabby said standing in front of Joy.

Joy opened her eyes and smiled. "What are you doing here?"

Maxine sat beside Joy. "We came to support you. We know it's hard not having Bea here so we decided to come in her place."

"Thank you, but I still miss her." Joy covered her face to hold back her tears.

Gabby pointed at Dean to move over to an empty seat so she could sit beside Joy, but he looked her up and down with a frown and refused to move.

"Listen, you two don't need to be here. I'm all she needs," Dean stated.

"No, Dean. I want them to stay, please," Joy begged as she wiped her face.

Dean gave Gabby and Maxine an evil look and turned his head.

The nurse called Joy's name. She wiped her face with tissues Maxine gave her and stood up. Dean started to follow Joy, then stopped in front of Gabby and Maxine.

"Don't think about trying to come back there," Dean snapped. "As a matter of fact, won't you just leave. We don't need you here."

Gabby flipped the pages of a magazine she picked up. Without looking up, she said, "Get over yourself, Dean. We're here for Joy, not you, and we're not going anywhere until she tells us to leave?"

Maxine looked up at Dean. "Dean, we're not trying to come between you and Joy. We're just here as her friends to give her some support."

Dean frowned, then walked in the back without saying another word.

Maxine and Gabby looked at each other and started laughing.

Joy was partially dressed lying on the exam table when Dean entered the room with a scowl on his face. She ignored him.

The doctor came in with a folder in his hands. "Good afternoon, I'm Dr. Fields. I see your primary doctor confirmed your pregnancy and you're a new patient with us. Welcome," he said without looking up from the chart.

"Thank you." Joy looked at Dean to make him speak to the doctor.

"Do you have a female doctor in this practice?" Dean asked.

Dr. Fields looked at Dean and then at Joy with narrowed eyes.

"I'm comfortable with Dr. Fields. He delivered Gabby's daughter and she highly recommends him." Joy looked at Dean with pinched lips and an evil glare.

"I thought you looked familiar." Dr. Fields walked in front of Joy and put her feet in the stirrups.

"Oh, yeah. I was one of Gabrielle Roché's birth coaches." Joy smiled as she remembered how Dr. Fields tried to hit on her after Nadia was born. She couldn't believe that was just five months ago and how much had changed. If Dean knew, he would pick her up, carry her out, and never return.

"Of course." Dr. Fields smiled at Joy. "I remember you. I never forget a pretty face."

Dean cleared his throat and looked at Dr. Field hatefully. "Yeah, that's why I married her."

"Well, congratulations to you both," Dr. Fields said as he put on a mask and a pair of gloves and started examining Joy.

After Dr. Fields completed his exam, he looked at Joy's chart again and then at Joy with a concerned look on his face.

"Joy, I'm going to have one of our technicians come in and do a sonogram now, then we can talk in my office."

"What's wrong? Is something wrong with the baby?" Joy took her feet out of the stirrups and sat up. "I can tell something's wrong."

Dean stepped closer to Joy and looked at the doctor. "Should we be concerned?"

"No. Nothing's wrong. The blood work your primary doctor did looks great. I'm just a little concerned about the size of your uterus."

"I told her she was gaining weight too fast," Dean complained.

"It seems that as soon as I took the pregnancy test, my stomach expanded." Joy looked at Dr. Field's for a response.

"A sonogram will confirm what I suspect. We'll talk in my office after..."

"Oh, my God! Is it Down Syndrome or is my baby autistic? It doesn't matter..."

"Hell if it doesn't! We're not having a retarded child! If something is wrong with it, we need to know," Dean screamed.

Dr. Fields put his hands up to calm the couple down. "Wait a minute please, you're jumping to conclusions. I suspect that Joy is either further along than she thinks or is pregnant with twins."

"Twins!" Dean gave Dr. Fields a fist bump. "Doc, I made twins?"

Joy was stunned silent. *Twins? How was that possible? Dean was barely in me long enough to make one, how did he pull off twins? Shit, I'll never get rid of his ass with twins.* She rolled her eyes at Dean who was doing some kind of happy dance. She needed to have this sonogram now to see what the hell was going on.

Five minutes later, the technician rolled the probe over Joy's stomach as she watched the screen trying to make out the different shapes. Nothing made sense to her.

"What do you see?" Joy asked.

"Give me a minute." He pressed down hard on Joy's stomach and she flinched.

"Be careful, man. I don't want you to hurt my twins," Dean snapped.

What about me asshole? Joy thought and rolled her eyes again at Dean.

"Okay, I can see better now. Let me get a few images for Dr. Fields and he'll talk to you in his office."

"Can you tell me anything?" Joy prodded.

"I can tell you when you conceived, since you're clearly in your second trimester," the tech said.

"No, that's not right. I got pregnant the beginning of September. A little over a month ago," Joy explained.

"Based on the size of the fetuses, you're sixteen weeks," the tech explained.

"Go get the doctor! You don't know what the hell you're doing! Tell the doctor to get in here now!" Dean yelled at the technician the same way he did to Joy after they got married.

The technician quickly left the room to summon Dr. Fields.

Joy gave Dean a supportive look to let him know he was right for getting upset. If these people didn't know what they were doing, she was going to find another doctor as soon as possible.

Dr. Fields rushed back in the room. "What's the problem?"

"Your technician is the problem. He's incompetent. We need you to do the sonogram and tell us what you see." Dean's nostrils were flaring.

Joy nodded in agreement. "Yes, please."

"Okay." Dr. Fields picked up the probe and started pressing into Joy's abdomen. "Well, you're definitely having twins. Based on their size, you conceived either the end of June or the beginning of July. So you're into your second trimester, about sixteen weeks."

"How? I just missed my period this month," Joy asked in shock.

"It's normal for some women to get their periods during their first trimester, especially with twins." Dr. Fields explained.

"I had a sonogram before, but it only showed one heartbeat," Joy explained.

"It was probably too early to see both, but you're definitely sixteen weeks pregnant with twins," Dr. Fields said.

Joy looked at Dean with sorrowful eyes and Dean glared
at Joy angrily as they realized they didn't know each other sixteen
weeks ago.

Dean stomped out of the exam room. When he got to the
lobby where Gabby and Maxine were sitting, he kicked a few
chairs over before he snatched the door open and stormed out of
the office.

Gabby and Maxine ran in the back and found Joy. She was
lying on her side on the exam table in tears with Dr. Fields trying
to console her.

"What's wrong? Did you lose the baby?" Gabby asked.

"It'll be okay, Joy. I know it's hard, but we'll help you
through this," Maxine promised.

Joy finally sat up and wiped her face. "I'm having twins!"
Joy cried.

"Twins? Is that why your chicken husband ran out of here
like that? If he can't handle twins, then good riddance," Gabby
snapped.

"That's right," Maxine agreed. "Give him some time to let
it sink it. He'll be back."

Joy tried to explain, but she couldn't talk. Dr. Fields laid
her back on the exam table and put a cold compress on her forehead and around her neck, then stepped out of the room. After a
few minutes, Joy felt better and propped herself up on her elbow
to look at Maxine and Gabby.

"I'm sixteen weeks pregnant so I got pregnant before I met
Dean, which means I'm pregnant with Allen's twins. What in the
hell am I going to do?" Joy cried out.

Gabby and Maxine gasped as they stared at Joy with their
mouths and eyes wide open.

Chapter 26

"He's trying to ruin my life and I need to know what you're doing about it," Gabby yelled into the phone.

Gabby's attorney, Jim Conman, was all too familiar with her drama. He'd been her attorney since she found out she was pregnant by Rayshawn. He negotiated her child support payments and acted as a liaison between their respective lawyers. Jim knew in the back of his mind that Gabby set Rayshawn up by getting pregnant, but he was her lawyer and hired to represent her, not be her moral compass. He got a decent monthly fee to keep his mouth shut and keep his client in check so he was always available to Gabby whenever she called.

Jim sighed deeply because he knew Gabby wasn't going to be happy with what he had to tell her. "I talked to Mr. Robinson's attorneys late Friday evening."

"Why? What did they want? And why didn't you tell me?" Gabby sat at her dining room table, bit her bottom lip, and started shaking her legs.

"I planned to tell you Monday morning when I returned to the office. Mr. Robinson's wife is filing for divorce. After the article came out, he told her about his affair with you and about Nadia. Now that it's public, he's more determined than ever to see his daughter," Jim explained.

Gabby slapped the dining room table with her open hand. "I want you to handle this. He will *not* meet my daughter. She has a father. This will confuse her and ruin my life. I don't want him anywhere near us. He should just continue to make a monthly deposit in my account and stay out of our lives. Do you hear me?"

"Yes, I hear you. I'll contact his attorneys first thing tomorrow morning and let them know how you feel. There is a good chance that he'll sue you for visitation. As her biological father, he has rights, too. He has the DNA test and proof of paying child support since shortly after Nadia was conceived. Just prepare yourself and your family for a fight."

"He's so selfish! Why won't he put his daughter's needs before his own. Contact him as soon as you can and let him know that I'm not willing to budge on this. Let him know that he'll hurt his daughter if she ever found out he was her father. She is a stable and happy child. I don't want to disrupt her life." Gabby clenched her teeth and sighed. "But first, I need you to make him stop calling me. My husband is getting suspicious again."

"Have you ever thought about telling your husband the truth?"

Gabby thought about how much William loved Nadia and his history with depression and knew that telling him the truth would be devastating. "No, that's not an option."

"Ummm, okay. Well, I'll contact Mr. Robinson's attorneys and I'll call you as soon as I hear back from them."

"Make sure you call my cell phone number," Gabby pressed. She didn't want to risk him calling her home number and William finding out.

"Okay and I'll try my best to make this work in your favor, Gabby."

"Jim, don't try your best. Do your best!" Gabby snapped before she pushed the End Call button.

Gabby sat at the dining room table thinking about Rayshawn and how much she hated him. Now that his wife was filing for divorce, he had nothing to lose. No matter what his situation was with his wife, she refused to let him meet Nadia. It would confuse her. William was the only father Nadia ever knew and she adored him. Gabby was determined to do whatever it took to stay one step ahead of Rayshawn and keep her family together.

At exactly 6:00 P.M., William arrived at his parents' house for Sunday dinner. He enjoyed it when his family got together and wished they could do it more often. Gabby decided not to attend because Nadia was running a fever, but she sent a strawberry shortcake from her favorite French bakery, Desserts by Gerard in Oxon Hill.

William's mother opened the door without her usual perky greeting. Instead, she looked gloomy, as if she were going to break down crying. William assumed she was tired from cooking dinner and made a mental note to spend more time with her. He hugged and kissed her before he joined the rest of the family in the dining room.

William walked in and stopped dead in his tracks. His temperature started rising and his heart kicked his chest when he saw Rayshawn Robinson sitting with his family at the table.

"What the hell is going on here?" William asked Phyllis in an angry tone.

Phyllis cleared her throat. "Since you wouldn't listen to me, I invited Rayshawn to dinner so you can hear the truth." Phyllis stared at William with pleading eyes.

The blood drained from William's face and he was paralyzed with anger because he knew Rayshawn was trying to make a claim on his daughter. He stared at the famous quarterback and thought he was bold to come to his parents' house with his accusations. William could tell by the way his family was avoiding eye contact with him that they were all in this together.

"What are you doing here?" William asked in an angry tone.

"I want to see my daughter," Rayshawn answered calmly.

"She's not your daughter, man!" William yelled and turned to leave, but Phyllis stopped him.

"Gabby..." Rayshawn started speaking.

Phyllis put her hand up to silence him. "William, I need you to be strong. Rayshawn has some shocking information to tell you about your wife and daughter." She sat William down and nodded at Rayshawn for him to continue.

"Gabby got pregnant by me after I signed a multimillion

dollar contract. As soon as Nadia was born, a DNA test was done. Here are the results." Rayshawn pulled a piece of paper out of his pocket and handed it to William.

William refused to take the paper, but he glanced at it. "Nadia is my daughter. Gabby told me she was mine when she found out she was pregnant." He looked around the room at his family.

"I think she told you that because she wanted a father for our daughter and I wasn't available." Rayshawn sighed and shook his head. "I didn't want my wife to know that I fucked up and fathered another child, but since the article came out, I told her the truth and now she wants a divorce."

"This is bullshit and I still don't believe you! Gabby told me she broke up with you and you're having a hard time letting go." William gave Rayshawn an evil look.

"Fuck that shit! I let that lying bitch go a long time ago. I been paying child support since Gabby told me she was pregnant. I paid her five thousand dollars a month before Nadia was born. After she was born, I started paying her ten thousand dollars a month. When she requested an increase, I gave it to her without a single complaint because I didn't want my wife to find out."

"What? Gabby doesn't have that kind of money. She's financially dependent on me since she's home with Nadia every day." William looked at his family and shook his head. "He's lying."

"Every month, I deposit fifteen thousand dollars in her account and pay her lawyer's fees. But the truth is out now and I want to get to know my daughter," Rayshawn demanded.

William waved Rayshawn off with his hands. "Yeah, right!"

"Ask to see her bank account balance. The whore is probably saving the money I give her every month and living off you." Rayshawn stood up and laughed. "That bitch is something else."

William stood up and got in Rayshawn's face. "Don't talk about my wife like that. I'll take my own DNA test. And I won't believe anything you say until I have my results. I know she's my daughter. She looks just like me, man."

William didn't want to say anything, but he had already taken Nadia for a DNA test a couple of weeks ago after the article came out. He wanted to be prepared for Rayshawn if he ever showed up. He was too busy with work to go back to get the results, but now he was going to have to make time.

"No matter what, William, we'll help you through this." Phyllis promised as she hugged her brother.

William ignored her.

"I hear you, man," Rayshawn said calmly. "You do your test. Whatever it takes to make you see the truth. I'm taking Gabby's ass to court for visitation as soon as possible. I know my rights as her father."

William looked at his family and said, "I can't believe you. You've been after my wife since you met her. So what she wanted her wedding her way. So what she's not kissing your asses to be a part of this family. You didn't have to hunt down an old, scorned boyfriend to come between us. I'm through with all of you."

"You got it wrong, William. He's telling the truth; *she's* lying," Phyllis explained.

"Listen, man," Rayshawn intervened. "Don't let Gabby come between you and your family. Her lies hurt us all. I just want Nadia to know I'm her father and that a day doesn't go by that I don't think about her. I want her to know me. I'm sure we can work something out."

Rayshawn held out his hand for William to shake, but William ignored him and walked out the house. He was unable to process what was happening. He wanted to get his DNA test results as soon as possible. Tomorrow, he'd be able to prove to everybody, once and for all, that Nadia was indeed his daughter. He decided not to tell Gabby about Rayshawn showing up at his family's dinner. No need to get her upset over a bitter ex-boyfriend.

Chapter 27 ——————

Joy used her key to let herself in her mother's house. Since Bea still refused to answer her calls or return her messages, she decided to pay her mother a visit. She needed to tell Bea what was happening with her whether she wanted to hear it or not. Although Joy complained about Bea's controlling ways, she loved her mother and missed their daily phone calls to each other. Bea was sitting in the living room watching "60 Minutes" when Joy walked in the house.

"What are you doing here, Joy?" Bea snapped.

"I went to the doctor Friday and found out I'm actually four months pregnant with twins and they're not Dean's." Joy stood still, waiting for Bea to explode or collapse from her announcement.

"What? Twins?" She narrowed her eyes. "What do you mean, they're not Dean's? Whose are they? Oh, Lord Joy! Do you know who the father is?"

Joy laughed at Bea's reaction as she sat on the couch. "Of course I do! I've only slept with two men in my life."

Bea rolled her eyes. "I'm guessing the man in Atlanta is the other man. Does he know?"

Joy hesitated because she knew what she was getting ready to tell Bea was going to change their lives forever.

"Well, don't stop talking now," Bea barked.

Joy sat beside Bea and spent the next thirty minutes

telling her mother about her ten-year relationship with Allen Johnson and how much she loved him. She described the day he proposed and how it ended because Joy didn't want to leave Bea alone. Finally, she told Bea about her doctor's appointment, Dean's reaction and how he left her.

Bea looked at her daughter, noticeably perturbed. She stood up and walked around the living room several times, her chest heaving up and down.

"Damn! Why didn't you tell me about you and Allen?" Bea looked hurt.

"Because you always said, 'Don't end up with anybody like those Johnson boys and stay away from Allen Johnson. I don't like the way he looks at you,'" Joy said in a perfect imitation of Bea's voice and facial expression.

"That's because he got arrested for breaking that boy's jaw when he was younger. I just thought he was going to be in and out of jail like his brothers." Bea sighed. "He ended up turning his life around."

Joy stood up. "Stop it, Bea! He's nothing like his brothers. He got arrested because of me."

"What? What did you do?" Bea screamed.

"You had to work late one night and didn't want me to be home alone so you told me to go to Mrs. Johnson's duplex. When I got off the bus, one of the older guys in the projects started following me. He squeezed my breasts and smacked my butt."

Bea's eyes popped out of her head. "He did what? I would've killed his ass myself and buried him under the goddamn jail. Why didn't you tell me?"

Joy took a deep breath. "I was so scared, I dropped my book bag and ran to Mrs. Johnson's house shaking and crying. Allen calmed me down and made me tell him what happened. Later that evening, after you picked me up, he found the boy and beat him up. He was just protecting me. That's the only reason he got locked up," Joy explained.

"Oh, Jesus! You should've told me that, Joy!" Bea was in tears.

Joy jumped up. "I couldn't! You bad-mouthed him so

much about turning out like his brothers, but he's a good man."
Joy closed her eyes. "I'm the one who's a screw-up. He put up
with me hiding him from you all those years. I shouldn't have
done that."

"You're right, but I was to blame for some of that, too."
Bea realized her controlling behavior and demands on her daughter had led her to marry a man she clearly didn't love. Juan and
Tyesha had pointed out some of the mistakes she made as a
mother, too.

"It doesn't matter now. Whatever I had with Allen is
over." Joy sat back down. "I called him yesterday morning in
China to tell him about *our* twins, but his girlfriend was in the
background talking so I changed my mind." Joy swallowed hard.
"I decided not to complicate his life anymore so I'm going to
raise the twins on my own."

"Absolutely not! You didn't make them by yourself and
you're not going to raise them by yourself!" Bea walked around
the living room shaking her head and waving her arms. "It was
hard on me with just one child and your father was in your life.
Imagine having two the same age, with no help from their father.
Uh-uh, that ain't gonna happen."

"There you go! I thought we could talk openly without
you trying to run my life again. This is my decision! Can you
please support me and stay out of this?"

Bea looked at Joy's angry face and caved. "Okay. Of
course, honey. I'll support your decision and respect your choice."
Bea hugged Joy and kissed her forehead.

"Thanks for understanding. I feel better now that I talked
it over with you. I need to get home and get ready for work tomorrow." Joy walked with Bea to the front door.

"What's going on with you and Dean?" Bea asked.

"By the time I got home from the doctor's office, he had
packed his stuff and left. I haven't heard from him since. I'm
going to call a lawyer tomorrow to start my divorce."

"I work with a good divorce attorney. They call her the
Barracuda. I'll have her call you," Bea said.

"Thanks." Joy hugged and kissed Bea before she walked

out the door.

"Call me when you get home so I'll know you're safe," Bea instructed.

Joy nodded and waved bye to her mother.

Bea watched Joy drive away then went back in her living room, picked up her cordless phone, and started punching in numbers.

"Tyesha, this is very important. I need you to come to my house now and bring Allen's phone number with you. I need to talk to him as soon as possible."

Bea hung up and thought about everything Joy had just told her. She knew she heard Joy say Allen's name when she got married, but Tyesha, Tyrese, and Juan denied it and she believed them. Now that she knew the truth, there was no way she was going to let her daughter be a single parent to Allen Johnson's twins. She was going to make sure of that herself. Bea could see how much Joy still loved Allen. She smiled the entire time she discussed their relationship and was in tears when she talked about how it ended. That's what Bea wanted for her daughter when she got married, real love, not a shotgun wedding. *Any man willing to go to jail to protect my daughter is all right with me,* Bea thought. She was determined to make things right between Joy and Allen.

Chapter 28

William lifted Nadia out of her crib and sat in the rocking chair in the corner of her room. He stared at her as she slept peacefully in his arms. He loved his daughter more than anything in this world and would do whatever it took to protect her. He planned to be the first person at the DNA testing center this morning to get his results and prove Rayshawn and his family wrong.

William held Nadia's warm face to his and kissed her cheek before he laid her back in her crib. He smiled as he watched her open her eyes, twist her body into her favorite sleeping position, and then go back to sleep. Gabby entered the nursery and startled him.

"Good morning. How is she?" Gabby asked before she covered her mouth to yawn.

"She's still warm. What time is her doctor's appointment?" William's eyes were on Nadia.

"Eleven." Gabby looked William up and down. "Why are you dressed for work?"

William turned around to face Gabby. "I have to go to the office for a while."

Gabby crossed her arms over her chest and looked at William suspiciously. "You never miss Nadia's doctor's appointments, especially when she's sick."

William gave Gabby a cold stare. "Well, there's a first time for everything." He walked past Gabby to his room.

She watched William with raised eyebrows because he never got smart with her. Since he returned from his parents' house last night, he's been distant. After he checked on Nadia, he went to his room and locked the door. Something he never did before. Gabby wondered if something happened at his parents' house, but didn't ask because he seemed as if he needed to be alone and she was dealing with a sick child. She wished he would cut his ties with his family because they caused him more pain than anything else. After spending time with her in-laws, she understood why William was on antidepressants when he was younger.

William took his wallet off the dresser and left the house without saying anything else to Gabby. He knew he was wrong for treating her the way he did, but he couldn't help it. He was upset with her for letting things get this out of control with Rayshawn. She should've told him the truth about their relationship and how Rayshawn thought Nadia was his daughter before the *Baltimore Sun* article came out. He planned to talk to her about it later when he returned home.

Thirty minutes later, William arrived at the DNA testing center just as they were turning on the lights and opening the front door. When he walked in, a chubby, white receptionist with red cheeks greeted him with a smile. "Good Monday morning! How may I help you?"

William swallowed hard and said, "Yeah, um, I took a DNA test a couple of weeks ago with my daughter and I need to know the results."

"What's your name, sir?"

"William Landon." His heart was beating so fast, he thought she could hear it.

"I need to see your ID." She smiled.

William took out his wallet and gave her his driver's license.

She took his ID, sat it on her desk, and stood up to look in a file cabinet behind her desk. "Landon, Landon. Oh, here it is. One of our technicians will have to meet with you to explain the results. Have a seat and I'll call someone." She picked up the phone and started pushing buttons.

William sat in the first row of chairs across from the receptionist's desk and tapped his feet nervously as he waited. After a few minutes, he started shifting in his seat and having doubts about getting the test results. Just as he stood to leave, an older white man in a white lab coat came from the back.

"Mr. Landon, you can follow me," he said.

William hesitated and then followed the man to the back.

The technician pointed at a chair in front of his desk. "Have a seat, sir." He pulled the results out of a long white envelope. "You wanted to know if the minor child, Nadia Rae Roché, is your biological child?"

William sat on the edge of his seat and leaned in closer to hear the technician. "Yes."

"According to this, the results state that you are not the child's biological father." The tech dropped the results on his desk and reached for his yogurt cup.

"What? Are you sure? There must be a mistake," William reasoned.

"Yes, sir, I'm sure. No mistakes were made." The tech put a spoonful of yogurt in his mouth.

"What is the percentage?" William remembered seeing a number on the test results Rayshawn tried to show him yesterday.

"Excuse me?" The tech wiped his mouth with his lab coat's sleeve.

"The other guy's test said 99.9% that he is the father. What is my percentage?"

"Oh, less than one percent. You're in the clear. There is no way this little girl is your child." The technician put the results back in the envelope and gave it to William.

William walked back to his truck in a daze. He didn't hear the receptionist call his name. He got in his truck and sat there staring in space until the receptionist knocked on the driver's side window. He turned his truck on and rolled the window down to hear what she was saying.

"Mr. Landon, I tried to catch you, but you didn't hear me." She handed William his driver's license. "You don't want to leave without this."

"Oh, yeah. Thanks." William took his license and threw it on the passenger seat.

"You're welcome. Have a good day!" She turned and walked back in the building.

William pulled out of the parking lot with tears streaming down his face. For the first time in his life, he knew what he had to do to make things right for him and his family. He knew he was the only one who could put an end to all the pain and shame Gabby caused him and his family.

William arrived home thirty minutes later and sat in the living room trying to get his thoughts together. He couldn't get Rayshawn's face out of his head. The guilt of keeping Rayshawn from his daughter was more than he could bear and he wasn't willing to share Nadia with him. He called Phyllis, got Rayshawn's phone number, and called him.

Rayshawn answered after a couple of rings. "Who this?"

"Oh, um, Rayshawn? This is William, Gabby's husband." William swallowed to get the lump out of his throat. This was the hardest thing he ever had to do, but he needed to do it.

"Get off me! I need to take this call." After a few seconds, Rayshawn said, "What's up, man? I'm just hangin' with this bitch I met at the club last weekend. Since I had better, she can wait. I guess you and Gabby heard from my attorneys, huh?"

William shook his head and frowned because for a quick second he understood why Gabby didn't want Rayshawn to be Nadia's father. "No. I haven't heard anything. What are your lawyers planning?"

"They serving her ass with papers to appear in court to give me visitation. Did you take your test yet?"

"Yeah, man. Um, I know she's your daughter, Rayshawn." Tears rolled down his face.

"Huh? What you say?" Rayshawn asked in a shocked tone.

"I know the truth now and Gabby's going to pay for hurting me like this!" William's whole body shook.

"Hold up, man. Don't do no crazy shit like kill her or

nothing like that. I just want to spend some time with my daughter once in a while so she can know who I am. I ain't trying to be a single father to a little girl, so think before you act, dude."
Rayshawn wondered if he was making the right choice, trying to see Nadia.

"Naw, I won't do anything like that." William paused. "I know you have company, so I'll be in touch."

"Yeah, let me know how she acts when my lawyers slam her ass with those papers."

"Sure. Later." William ended the call and dialed Gabby.

"Hi, William. I'm glad you called. Nadia has an ear infection. I'm at the pharmacy..."

"I know, Gabby. I know Nadia is Rayshawn Robinson's daughter."

He heard Gabby gasp.

"Why did you lie to me?"

"William, I..."

William was crying so hard, he could barely get his words out. "I don't want to hear any more of your fucking lies, bitch. You made me fall in love with this little girl and I had no right to love her. Everybody tried to warn me about you, but I didn't listen. Everybody knew except me. I'm so stupid for ever loving you."

"You are her father, William. I chose you to be her father because you're the better man." Gabby was almost in tears because she hadn't wanted William to find out like this.

"I called Rayshawn and apologized for keeping his daughter away from him. You lied to everybody and caused friction in my family. You're a selfish bitch and I hope you burn in hell for what you did to me."

"William, I'm sorry. I love you. We can get through this."

"No, we can't because I never want to see your face again. Goodbye, Gabby."

"Wait, William!"

He hung up.

Chapter 29

Gabby stood at the register at CVS Pharmacy in stunned silence. *William knows he's not Nadia's father. How did this happen?*

"Excuse me, but I said your prescription is ready," the clerk said as she looked at Gabby strangely.

"What?" Gabby forgot why she was in the store.

"Your prescription is ready." The clerk said again. "It's fifteen dollars."

Gabby took a twenty-dollar bill out of her purse, threw it on the counter, and snatched Nadia's prescription from the clerk's hand. "I have to go." Gabby pushed Nadia's stroller as fast as she could and left the store. She needed to get home to William and explain why she lied to him. A face-to-face conversation would change his mind and make him see her side.

Thirty minutes after William called Gabby, she pulled into the garage and took the sleeping Nadia out of her car seat and rushed in the house. She laid Nadia in her playpen in the family room and looked around the first floor for William.

When she didn't see him, she ran upstairs to his bedroom, but he wasn't there either. She went back downstairs and searched the basement and then the first floor again. She dumped her pocketbook in the foyer, got her cell phone and dialed William's phone. She heard it ringing in the house and followed the sound back upstairs.

She thought it was coming from his bedroom, but it wasn't. She dialed the number again and heard the phone ring in her bedroom. She pushed her door open and walked in. Her cell phone fell out of her hand onto the carpeted floor as she started screaming, "William, oh my God! What have you done?"

She fell to her knees, picked up her cell phone and dialed 911. "I need help! My husband is hanging from the ceiling fan and he's not moving!" Gabby started crying hysterically. "He's pale and his tongue is purple and hanging out of his mouth. Help me!"

"Ma'am, I need you to give me your address and help will arrive shortly."

"We're at 4071 Pine Orchard Lane, Bowie, Maryland." Gabby cried.

"Help has been dispatched to your location," the operator said. "I can stay on the line with you until they arrive."

Gabby sat on the floor with the phone to her ear and looked up at William's lifeless body hanging from the ceiling fan. He used the same rope he had purchased to tie their new beds to his truck. The chair from her vanity set was flipped over under his dangling body.

"Hello? Are you still there?" the 911 operator asked.

Gabby didn't answer as she looked closer at William's body and saw something she didn't see before. Attached to his shirt was a piece of paper. She stood up and walked closer to read the words on the paper - GABBY DID THIS TO ME!

"I'm okay. I have to go." Gabby pushed the End button on her cell phone.

She snatched the note from William's dead body and ran back downstairs to the foyer. She stuffed the note in an inside pocket in her purse and put all her belongings back inside. She put on her Bluetooth, called Joy, and walked back to the family room to check on Nadia.

"What's up, Gabby?" Joy asked.

"HE'S DEAD! WILLIAM IS DEAD!" Gabby cried.

"What?" Joy touched the Bluetooth on her right ear, thinking she heard wrong.

Gabby was crying hysterically. "He's hanging from the ceiling fan in my room!"

Joy screamed, "Oh, no, Gabby! Did you call 911?" Joy was crying but trying not to let Gabby hear her.

"YES!" Gabby sat on the sofa and gently rocked.

"I'll be there shortly." Joy was on her way to work, but jumped back on the Beltway toward Gabby's house.

Gabby sounded robotic. "I hear sirens. They're on the way. I should've tried to cut him down, but I knew it was too late. He was already dead."

Joy could hear the doorbell and someone knocking on the door, then Gabby's high heels clicking across the hardwood floor.

"Ma'am, did you call 911?" a police officer asked.

"Yes, my husband is upstairs dead. He hung himself." Gabby started crying hysterically.

The officer stepped in with paramedics behind him. "Ma'am, I'm Officer Brown. Where were you when this happened?"

"My daughter is sick." Gabby started walking to the family room where Nadia was napping.

Officer Brown followed her while the paramedics went upstairs. "Where were you?"

"I took her to the doctor, then got her prescription filled when he called me." Gabby dropped her head in her hands. "Everybody's going to blame me for this."

"Why would you say that?" Officer Brown asked, looking at her suspiciously.

"Gabby, don't answer any questions without an attorney. Stop talking until I can get in touch with your attorney," Joy screamed into her Bluetooth. She was glad Gabby gave her and Maxine her attorney's information in case something happened to her and Rayshawn tried to take Nadia.

Gabby knew Joy was right. She was upset and didn't want to say anything that would make this cop suspect she had anything to do with William's death. "I feel sick. I can't answer any questions right now. Can you give me a few minutes?" Gabby asked the officer as she lay on the couch.

"Sure." The officer knew from Gabby's make-up-stained face and nervous demeanor that she was genuinely upset. He went upstairs to check on the paramedics.

"Gabby, I'm going to call your lawyer. Don't say anything else until he gets there," Joy suggested.

"Okay." Gabby whispered in her Bluetooth before she ended the call.

Joy called Jim Conman immediately and he agreed to leave his office and meet them at Gabby's house within the hour. Next, Joy called Maxine and Bea and told them what she knew. They both decided to leave work early and join her at Gabby's.

Ten minutes later, Joy pulled onto Gabby's street. The entire block was covered with emergency vehicles so Joy had to park on the next block and walk. A rookie police officer was standing at the door as emergency personnel were walking in and out of the house.

"I need to go in, please. My friend called me about her husband. She's expecting me," Joy informed the officer as she approached the front door.

The officer looked Joy over. "I can't let you in. This is a crime scene."

Gabby screamed from inside the house. "Let her in! This is my house and I want her in here!"

Officer Brown came to the door and said, "She can come in." He knew sometimes people started talking more when people they trusted were around them.

Joy walked in and saw Gabby sitting on the couch in the family room. Gabby stood up when she saw Joy. Her hair was pulled back in a ponytail and not hanging loosely on her shoulders like she normally wore it. Streaks of eye shadow and liner had dried on her tormented face. Her eyes darted around, trying to take in every move the emergency personnel made, and her hands were shaking. The belt on her wrap dress had come loose and was hanging down to the floor.

They hugged each other. Joy whispered, "Your lawyer is on his way."

Gabby whispered back. "He blames me, Joy. He wrote a

note. I took it, but I don't want the police to see it. They might arrest me and then Rayshawn will get Nadia."

"Shh…Don't say anything else. You don't know who's listening," Joy advised.

They sat on the couch and watched Nadia sleep through all the commotion. Joy held Gabby's trembling hands in hers.

Officer Brown entered the room. "Are you up to answering my questions now that your friend is here?"

Joy looked at Officer Brown with a serious expression. "No, she's not. Her attorney is on his way."

Officer Brown frowned because he knew this wasn't one of those times when a person was going to talk because someone they trusted was there. He hoped this was nothing more than a suicide because now that his divorce was final, he was thinking about asking the sexy friend out. He looked at Joy and winked.

Joy stood up, removed her coat and rubbed her baby bump. Officer Brown grunted and gave Joy a knowing smirk before he left the room.

Thirty minutes later, Jim Conman arrived and asked to speak to Gabby alone. While they were in the family room talking, Joy took Nadia in the kitchen and gave her a bottle. Maxine arrived shortly after the baby finished eating and Officer Brown let her in but informed her that she had to stay on the first floor.

A couple of hours later, Phyllis walked up the front porch steps looking like a wild bull ready to attack. "What's going on? Did something happen to my brother?"

Sam and William's parents were a couple of feet behind Phyllis.

Phyllis rushed past the cop guarding the door and entered the house. "Where's my brother?"

The rest of William's family entered while the cop was trying to stop Phyllis.

"What happened? Will somebody tell me what happened?" Mrs. Landon asked.

Joy and Maxine followed Gabby as she carried Nadia to the front door with a blank look on her face. "William's dead. He's gone."

William's father caught his wife just before she hit the floor and helped her to a chair in the living room. Officer Brown called the paramedics inside to assist her.

Nadia started crying and screaming loudly.

Everybody looked at Gabby to quiet and console the baby.

Gabby turned around and shoved Nadia into Maxine's arms. "I can't help her. Can you take care of Nadia? I can't do it," Gabby uttered.

Maxine took Nadia to the family room away from everyone else.

The medical examiner and his two assistants came downstairs carrying a stretcher. William's body was covered with a white sheet. They tried to get the body out the door quickly without upsetting the family.

"Is that my son?" Mr. Landon didn't wait for them to answer. "I want to see my boy."

The medical examiner pulled the sheet back enough to reveal William's face.

Mr. Landon turned his head and started crying on Sam's shoulder. Phyllis dropped to her knees and wept.

Gabby walked over to William and looked at him. "Why did you do this to us, William? Why did you leave me and Nadia? You coward! You took the easy way out! A real man would've stayed here and dealt with his problems! I hate you for leaving us like this! You're a weak excuse for a man!"

"Stop it! My son was sick. He couldn't help it," Mrs. Landon said as she pushed the paramedics away.

"He left Nadia without a father," Gabby said to no one in particular.

"William wasn't her father. Rayshawn Robinson is her father and you know it," Phyllis barked.

"Who told you that?" Gabby inquired.

"He did yesterday at our family dinner. He had a DNA test to prove it," Phyllis replied.

Now Gabby knew how William found out Rayshawn was Nadia's father and why he killed himself. Phyllis was so determined to find out the truth that she didn't think about how much it would hurt William. The only person to blame for this was Phyllis.

"So you're the reason my husband killed himself. He knew Nadia wasn't his daughter, but he didn't want anybody else to know it," Gabby lied.

Joy gave Gabby a stern look. It was time for her friend to stop lying since the truth about Nadia's father was already known. She didn't want Gabby digging herself in deeper trouble by telling more lies.

Gabby ignored Joy.

"Stop it, Phyllis!" Mrs. Landon ordered. "This is your fault. The whole time you were overseas, we had peace in this family. Since you've been back and started all this confusion with William, he's been different. He lived for his girls and when you took them away from him, it broke his heart. You should've let it be like I asked you and he would still be here."

"I'm sorry, Ma, but this was Gabby's fault, not mine," Phyllis explained.

"You killed him! You did it!" Gabby screamed. She lunged at Phyllis but Officer Brown and Jim Conman held her back. "I want every one of you Landons out of my house! Get out now!"

Phyllis reached out to grab Gabby's neck, but Sam pulled her back. "You'll pay for killing my brother! When I get through with you, bitch, you won't have shit! I'll make sure of it! Starting with your daughter, I'm going to make sure Rayshawn gets custody of her so she won't turn out like you!" Phyllis screamed.

"Good luck with that!" Gabby gave Phyllis a mocking smirk.

Mr. Landon helped his wife out of the chair. Before she left the house, she looked at Gabby with tears streaming down her face. "He invited us over for dinner tonight. Now, I know he invited us over to claim his body. I want my son's body so I can give him a proper burial."

"You can have it; now get out!" Gabby shouted with little remorse.

Chapter 30

Joy poked her head in her guest bedroom to check on Gabby before she left for work. She was curled in a fetal position with the covers pulled up to her neck and snoring lightly. Joy needed to do something to get Gabby to join life again. Since William's suicide two weeks ago, Gabby had locked herself in Joy's guest bedroom and shut the world out.

She refused to see Nadia, claiming she was unable to give her daughter what she needed. Maxine stepped up and offered to take Nadia home with her for a few days to give Gabby time to get herself together. Nobody expected those few days to turn into two weeks, but Joy and Maxine had been doing what they could to help their friend. Last week, they thought if Gabby saw Nadia, it would snap her out of her grief, but instead, she had burst into tears when she saw her daughter and begged Maxine to get Nadia out of her sight. It broke Joy's heart and had Maxine and Nadia in tears. They couldn't understand why Gabby didn't want to see her daughter. Instead of trying to figure it out, they gave Gabby more time alone, hoping she would pull it together soon.

Joy walked into her guest bedroom, stood in front of Gabby, and stared at her wondering how she could pull her out of this depression.

Gabby opened her eyes and looked up at Joy. "What?" She growled.

"You need to get up, take a shower, and get out of this

room. It stinks in here." Joy covered her nose with her hand. "I never thought I would say this about you but, girl, you smell."

"Leave me alone!" Gabby yelled before she pulled the covers over her head and attempted to go back to sleep.

Joy decided not to spend her last few minutes home arguing with Gabby. It hadn't worked the past two weeks and she knew this morning wasn't going to be any different. She went downstairs, fixed herself an egg and turkey bacon sandwich, and left for work. Gabby was on Joy's mind her entire ride to work. She knew that guilt was eating her alive and there was nothing she could do to help her.

Later that evening, when Joy arrived home from work, Gabby was sitting in the dark in the living room. For the first time in weeks, she was dressed and her hair was brushed back in a neat ponytail. Joy dropped her work bag at the front door, joined Gabby on the living room sofa, and hugged her friend. She smiled when she smelled Gabby's favorite perfume, Arden Beauty. It was a much-needed improvement from the way she had been smelling.

"I'm so glad to see you out of that room, Gabby." Joy squeezed Gabby's hand. "I was worried about you."

"I know. I screwed up." Gabby buried her face in her hands and burst out crying.

Joy wrapped her arms around her friend. "Let it all out, girl. I know. We all make mistakes."

Gabby sat up and looked in Joy's eyes. "I did love William and he loved me and Nadia, too." She sighed. "Where did I go wrong?"

Joy gave Gabby an I-told-you-so look. "What?"

"I know. I should've never lied, but I did it because of you and Maxine," Gabby stated.

"No! You can't blame us for that. I told you after Nadia was born to call Rayshawn." Joy frowned at Gabby.

"That's not what I mean. I wanted Nadia to have two loving and supportive parents like you and Maxine do. I knew her real father couldn't give her that so I thought William was the better choice for her." Gabby pulled a tissue from the box on the coffee table and wiped her eyes.

Joy looked at Gabby with a puzzled look on her face.

"I used to watch Bea and Juan and Dr. Jim and Ms. Pat when they came to visit you and Maxine in college. They didn't just tell you how to be; they showed you and put you in the right place to be successful. When you used to talk to your parents on the phone, it sounded like you were talking to your friends, not your parents. I wanted Nadia to have that so I married William thinking he would be a good father to her. I didn't know he would take his own life when he found out the truth." Gabby shook her head despairingly.

Joy sighed. "I didn't know you felt that way."

Gabby smiled and nodded. "Now you know."

"Gabby, how do you know what kind of father Rayshawn would be if you don't give him a chance?"

Before Gabby could answer, Joy's cell phone started ringing. She saw Maxine's name on the screen and answered. "Hey, Maxine. What's up?"

"You and Gabby need to get over to Gabby's house right now!" Maxine screamed.

Joy stood up with her eyes bulging. "What's wrong, Maxine?"

"Put that back!" Maxine screamed at someone in the background. "What are you doing? Don't touch that! I'm calling the police!"

The call dropped.

Joy looked at Gabby. "Something's wrong! We need to go!"

"Is it Nadia?" Gabby felt guilty for not being a better mother to her little daughter lately.

"I don't know." Joy rushed for the front door.

Gabby jumped off the couch and followed Joy. On the way to Gabby's, they kept calling Maxine's cell phone, but it went straight to voice mail. Joy didn't know what was going on, but she could tell by the frantic tone in Maxine's voice that it was serious. They assumed Maxine walked in on a burglar since Gabby gave Maxine her house keys in case she needed to get something for Nadia. Gabby dialed 911 and had the police sent to her address.

Twenty minutes later, they pulled onto Gabby's street as two police cars drove away. They couldn't believe what they saw when they reached the house. All of Gabby's furniture and belongings were sitting on the curb in front of the house and Maxine was standing guard in front of it.

"What in the hell is going on?" Joy asked.

Gabby looked up and screamed, "That's my stuff!"

Joy parked and they jumped out the car. Gabby ran to Maxine while Joy waddled as fast as she could. Her almost-five-month twin bulge was slowing her down more and more every day.

"Maxine, who did this?" Gabby asked as she inspected her belongings.

"I don't know. The movers were almost finished when I got here to get some more clothes for Nadia," Maxine explained.

"William's family did this to us! As if I need anything else to deal with!" Gabby screamed.

Phyllis and Sam pulled up in their car. Phyllis opened the door and jumped out of the car while Sam was trying to park. "You've been evicted, bitch! Bulk trash removal will be here tomorrow to pick up all this shit if you don't have it off my property by tomorrow morning." Phyllis held up a Home Depot bag. "I'm changing the locks, too!"

"Your property? You don't own this house. It was William's and now it's mine and Nadia's," Gabby replied.

Phyllis tried to get close to Gabby, but Sam ran up and pulled her back. She dug her fists in her hips and gave Gabby a hateful stare. "You don't own this house. I do!" Phyllis laughed out loud. "William was renting this house from me until I returned from Germany. He planned to buy it, but never got around to doing it. My rental contract was with William and not you. My lawyer said you had no right to be in my house so adios, bitch."

"What!" Gabby was stunned.

"You heard me. I guess William lied just like you. And, I feel sorry for that little girl of yours. Having you as a mother is a curse she'll have to live with, but after William's funeral, we'll testify on Rayshawn's behalf so he can raise his daughter and not you," Phyllis barked.

Anger shot through Gabby's body. *When did Rayshawn ask them to testify for him? Why did they think they had the right to plan my husband's funeral?* William's parents had been leaving her messages for the past two weeks trying to get her to sign a document to release his body to them. Now she was glad she didn't respond to those messages because she was never going to give them William's body.

Joy walked to Gabby's side. "Bea called a few of Allen's brothers to come over with their trucks to help us. We can store your things in my basement and you can stay with me as long as you want."

Gabby looked at Joy and smiled. "Thanks."

Sam snapped at Phyllis. "Get the paper signed so we can get out of here."

"What paper?" Gabby asked playfully.

Phyllis tried to give Gabby a piece of paper and a pen, but she wouldn't take it.

"What do you want her to sign?" Joy asked.

Phyllis looked Joy up and down. "This is none of your business. This is between Gabby and my family."

"I'm her family. Just like you protect your family, I protect mine. She's not signing shit and if you talk to her like that again, I'll stuff that piece of paper down your goddamn throat."

Phyllis pointed at Joy's stomach. "What you should do is protect that bun in the oven and not your lying-ass friend," Phyllis barked.

"Don't waste your breathe on her, Joy." Gabby looked at Sam and smiled. "I never thought you would do this to me, Sam. I thought we had a connection."

Sam started walking in Gabby's direction, but Phyllis blocked him.

"Oh, hell no! Gabby, don't try to make my husband your next victim." Phyllis turned around and glared at Sam. "If I catch you with this bitch, I will chop your dick off and beat her to death with it."

Sam unconsciously crossed his legs and avoided further eye contact with Gabby. He knew his wife meant business and he wasn't going to risk her cutting off his manhood, no matter how beautiful Gabby was. He kept his eyes glued to Phyllis and played the supportive husband.

Gabby looked at Phyllis with a cold gaze. "No! I'm not signing anything. I'll bury my own husband! None of *you* are invited to *his* funeral! You won't know when it is, where it is, or even where his body will be buried. You want to threaten and evict me. I don't think so. You forgot who you're messing with. I run this show."

"Wait one minute. That's my..."

Gabby put her hand out to stop Phyllis from speaking. "You can have the house. Why would I want to stay in a house where weak William took his own life? Seriously? The average man would file for divorce when he found out the child he thought was his wasn't, but not William. I'm glad Landon blood doesn't run through my daughter's veins. I'll never have to worry about her being as weak as William and the rest of you Landons. Goodbye and good riddance," Gabby said and then walked away.

Phyllis tried to grab Gabby but Sam pulled her back and forced her into the car. They knew this battle was lost. There was no way Gabby would let them be a part of William's funeral. Phyllis knew she had to go to her parents' house and break their hearts again. Maybe Phyllis should've listened to them and evicted Gabby after she signed the paper releasing William's body to them. She knew her parents would never forgive her for this.

As Phyllis and Sam drove off, Allen's brothers pulled up in two pickup trucks and a car. Joy spoke and hugged each one of them as they got out of the vehicles. Although she wasn't with Allen anymore, they still loved Joy and considered her family.

Maxine approached Gabby. "Will you be alright? I need to go get Maxwell and Nadia from daycare."

"I'm fine." Gabby smiled and hugged Maxine. "Joy, come here for a minute."

When Joy joined them, Gabby leaned in and whispered,

"My attorney called me this morning and told me William left me a million-dollar life insurance policy. As soon as I get the death certificate, the insurance company will issue me a check."

Joy and Maxine stared at Gabby with shocked expressions.

Now Joy knew why Gabby was able to get herself out of bed today. She had a million reasons to get herself together. *Well, she's not living rent free off me this time.* With Rayshawn's child support payments and William's life insurance policy, Gabby could buy her and Nadia a nice home and return to work when she felt like it. Things always had a way of working out in Gabby's favor.

"What about William's service? Do you need my pastor to help you with that?" Maxine asked.

"No, I'll take care of it. I'm just going to have him cremated and then toss his ashes in the Potomac River," Gabby laughed.

"Gabby, that's not nice. What about his parents?" Joy rolled her eyes because she knew Gabby was serious.

"What about them?" Gabby sighed. "Oh, okay. I'll mail them some of his ashes before I toss the rest in the river."

Maxine frowned at Gabby. "I can't believe you. Didn't you learn anything from this situation?"

Gabby closed her eyes and thought about it. "Ummm...Yes! From now on, I'll check the mental health status of every man I date so I won't go through this again."

"After all these years, I still can't figure you out, Gabby!" Maxine sighed.

"Don't try, Maxine. At least she's back to her mean and conniving self," Joy added.

"Oh, by the way, Maxine, thank you for taking care of Nadia for me. I appreciate it, but you can bring her to me now. I'm ready to see my baby." Gabby jumped up and down excitedly.

Maxine smiled. She loved Nadia, but having a baby to take care of was taking a toll on her. "Call me when you get to Joy's and I'll bring her over."

"Okay," Gabby replied. She hugged Maxine and waved

bye to her as she left.

Gabby and Joy watched the Johnson brothers load their trucks with Gabby's things.

"Now that I'm feeling better and I've taken care of William's family, I guess it's time for me to deal with Rayshawn." Gabby pointed at Allen's brothers, then looked at Joy. "Do they provide murder-for-hire services under their list of criminal activities? That's a guaranteed way of getting Rayshawn out of my life."

Joy stared at Gabby and wondered if she was joking because, with Gabby, you never knew.

Chapter 31

Joy stood in front of Bea's bathroom mirror brushing her teeth. Either she ate too much Thanksgiving dinner or the twins didn't like what she ate. Whatever the reason, it sent her running upstairs to vomit in private. Before she found out she was pregnant, she thought morning sickness only happened in the mornings during the first trimester. *How wrong was I?* Any little thing sent her praying to the porcelain god, any time, day or night. She reached in the vanity under the sink and pulled out a bottle of Scope. She had to make sure her breath was minty fresh before she went back downstairs to the houseful of guests Bea had invited for Thanksgiving dinner.

While she was rinsing for the second time, she heard the doorbell ring, then people started cheering and talking loudly. She wondered what that was about. The house was already filled with some of Bea's co-workers, Maxine, Gabby, their children, and the entire Johnson family. Joy knew Tyesha was coming over, and maybe Tyrese, but to see most of Allen's brothers sitting in Bea's house seemed out of place. Bea associated with them, but at a distance and definitely not in her house. It made Joy notice how much her mother had changed since their disagreement over her marrying Dean last month.

Joy applied a fresh coat of lip gloss, put the Scope back under the sink, and turned off the bathroom light. On her way back downstairs, she felt a kick in her stomach. She froze in her tracks, gasped, and rubbed her huge belly. For the past month, she had been feeling little flutters inside, but this was the first time she could feel it on the outside. That one kick made her pregnancy a reality. She was actually growing two babies in her body and they were moving around inside of her.

Joy descended the stairs with a bright smile on her face. When she reached the bottom of the steps, Maxine was standing there looking excited about something.

"Girl, I need to talk to you now!" Maxine whispered as she turned Joy around to go back upstairs.

"Wait, Maxine! I just felt the twins kick for the first time." Joy giggled excitedly.

A male voice behind Joy said, "Hello, beautiful!"

She quickly turned around with her mouth and eyes wide open. Allen Johnson stood in front of her looking as sexy as ever. He was dressed in a pair of black stonewash jeans, a white button-down oxford shirt, and a gray tweed blazer. When he smiled, Joy's heart did a little shuffle. Hearing his voice and seeing him so close to her made her desire for him resurface instantly. After all these months, Allen still turned her on. She whispered, "Allen."

He pulled her close to him in a big bear hug. She felt like she was melting in his arms, falling deeper and deeper into his muscular chest as she wrapped her arms around his waist. She wanted to stay in his arms forever. The smell of his cologne and the feel of his heart beating on her cheek comforted her. He shifted his body weight so she assumed he was releasing her from his arms; instead, he pulled her closer to him and rested his chin on the top of her head. They stood their hugging each other for a few minutes until they both felt a kick from her belly.

Joy pulled away and looked at Allen. "Did you feel that?"

He smiled, touched Joy's stomach, and said, "Yes, I felt it."

Joy didn't notice everyone looking at her as she stood there, rubbing her stomach with a goofy smile on her face.

Bea made her way to Joy's side. "Are you in any pain, Joy?"

"No. Just feeling them kick makes it so real." Joy looked down at her stomach.

"Joy, it's normal. As they get bigger, you'll feel it more," Maxine explained.

"I just think they're excited to meet their daddy for the first time," Allen joked.

Joy's smile vanished. She looked at Bea with pure hatred. "Oh, Bea! What did you do? Did you call Allen when I asked you not to?"

"C'mon, you two. Let's go upstairs and talk." Bea started up the steps before Joy said anything else.

Joy looked around the room and understood why Bea invited all the Johnsons for Thanksgiving dinner. *She probably called Allen right after I told her he was the father.* Joy looked at Maxine and Gabby and shook her head before she went upstairs.

Bea closed the spare bedroom door after they walked in. "Now, Joy, before you get upset, I wanna explain something to you."

"I don't want to hear anything you have to say! You betrayed me!" Joy screamed.

"Shhh...Calm down. Your mother was just looking out for you and she's right. You shouldn't raise *our* children alone. Why didn't you tell me?" Allen moved closer to Joy.

She couldn't believe what she was hearing. The last time Joy was in Allen's presence, he didn't have anything good to say about Bea; now he was defending her. "When did you two become friends?"

"We talked things out when she called me last month," Allen explained.

"You've known since October and you're asking me why I didn't tell you!" Joy sighed and turned to leave. She couldn't take any more.

Allen pulled her back. "Wait, baby! Can we go somewhere to talk in private?"

"Allen, go talk to your girlfriend. Where is she? At the hotel or still in China? Does she know about this?" This whole scenario was making Joy more upset by the second.

"I don't have a girlfriend, Joy. And I didn't call you when Bea told me because she asked me not to, but I came home the first chance I could." Allen stared at Joy with pleading eyes.

"I called you twice and there was a woman with a British accent in the background talking to you each time." Joy stared at Allen for an explanation.

"Babe, that's my boss, Anna." Allen smiled. "Anna and her husband helped me when I arrived in China. I was a mess after losing you."

Joy gave Allen a hateful glare. "You didn't lose me, Allen, you *left* me."

"I'm sorry. I was wrong for that, but you didn't tell Bea about us and I couldn't be a secret anymore," Allen uttered.

"Uh-huh, Allen. I told her she was wrong for that," Bea interjected.

Joy shot Bea a look that told her to mind her business. Bea left the bedroom.

"Joy, it's good to see you. You're glowing." Allen twisted one of Joy's stray curls around his finger and moved closer to her. "So, we're starting a family together, huh?"

Joy nodded and used her fingertips to trace the curves on his face. Her body was craving his. Her panties were soaked from being so close to him. She wanted to make love to him right now.

As if reading her mind, he said, "I'm going to have to sneak out the back door to hide this erection you're giving me." He released Joy's curl from his finger and bit his bottom lip. "Can we go to my hotel and talk about us and our babies in private?"

Joy smiled. "Sure." She knew they needed to talk since he knew about the twins.

Joy got her coat and purse while Allen apologized to his family and promised to spend time with them tomorrow. Maxine hugged and kissed Joy and Allen repeatedly. She was happy to see them together again. Gabby, on the other hand, ignored Allen intentionally and whispered in Joy's ear, "Don't be a fool." Joy left with mixed emotions. She was happy to see Allen again, but he lived in China and she didn't want to go there. She wanted to have her children in the United States and raise them here. They said goodbye to everyone and then left, not sure where this was headed.

They sat in Allen's suite at the Renaissance in the Chinatown area of D.C. There was an uncomfortable silence between them because neither of them knew what to say. When Allen sat beside Joy on the sofa, she moved back so they weren't too close.

"What's wrong? Do I smell from being on a twenty-hour flight from Shanghai?" Allen removed his blazer and sniffed under his arms.

Joy tried not to laugh. "No, you don't smell, but we're both tired so let's talk tomorrow or Saturday." Joy stood up to leave.

"Don't go, Joy. I'm only here for a couple of days. I fly back to China early Sunday morning." Allen's eyes begged her to stay.

They looked into each other's eyes and it took Joy's breath away. She still loved him, but things were so different now. She refused to let him hurt her again by leaving her to return to China.

Allen touched her face. "Twins, huh?"

Joy nodded and smiled.

"Bea told me a little, but can you tell me how they went from being your husband's twins to mine?" He looked at her with a serious face.

Joy swallowed hard and looked down. She exhaled deeply and told Allen everything about her and Dean. He looked angry when she told him about her getting drunk and sleeping with him without protection, but he smiled when she told him that Dean walked out on her and hadn't been seen since that day at the doctor's office.

"You've been busy since I left." Allen rubbed his bald head and sighed.

"You have no right to judge me, Allen! You broke my heart when you left me," Joy cried.

"And you think I wasn't hurt? I was ready to spend the rest of my life with you. I proposed and you turned me down because of your mother," Allen spat.

Joy stood up to leave. She refused to stay here and argue with Allen about their past. She was looking forward to the future with her children. Now that he knew about them, he could decide how involved he wanted to be, but, as a couple, they were through.

Allen stood up and pulled Joy to him before she reached the front door. "I flew here to be with you and to discuss our babies."

Joy pulled away. "There is nothing to discuss now. They're due March 26th, but the doctor told me twins come early. I'll tell Bea or Tyesha to call you when they're born and we can talk then."

Allen pulled Joy closer to him. "Do you know when they were conceived? I think it was the Fourth of July, a perfect night. I'll never forget it." Allen leaned in to kiss Joy.

She turned her head. "And then you broke up with me the next day and left. Goodbye, Allen. I can't do this again." She started walking to the door.

"Come on, Joy. Don't leave me. I still love you," Allen confessed.

Joy turned back. "And what if I still love you? What does that mean? You leave for China Sunday and I'll be here."

"Can't you go back with me?" Allen pleaded.

"No! I want to have the twins here, not in a foreign country I've never been to where I don't understand the language." Joy started crying. "Coming here was a bad idea."

Allen wrapped his arms around her. "Don't cry, baby. We'll work it out."

Joy's heart skipped a beat when she felt Allen's warm breath on her face. She turned around and hugged him back. He kissed her lightly on her lips. At first, Joy started to push him away, but she missed him so much. He took his lips off hers, held her head between his hands, and looked deep in her eyes.

"I missed you, baby." He kissed her again, this time harder and with more passion.

Joy tried, but she couldn't resist him. Her body craved his, like an addiction. They started undressing each other. Allen stepped back and looked at her pregnant body. She used her hands to try to cover herself, but he moved them away.

"You're beautiful, baby," he whispered as he dropped to his knees and started kissing her five-month twin bulge.

Joy relaxed and began to enjoy Allen's attention to her body.

He stood up and asked, "Is this safe? What did your doctor say about you having sex?"

"I didn't ask, but pregnant women have sex all the time." Joy kissed Allen hard and long. She couldn't stop now if she wanted to.

They held hands and walked to the king-size bed and lay down. He turned Joy on her side and looked at her tattoo before he started kissing and tracing it over and over as if he were seeing it for the first time.

Joy lay back on the bed and Allen started kissing and sucking her breasts. He stopped for a couple of minutes to get some condoms out of his wallet. Joy looked at him questioningly because they never used condoms.

"Babe, we've been with other people. Let's use these until we're tested," Allen suggested. He had been with a few women in China, but none of them made him feel as happy and content as Joy did.

Joy nodded to show she understood and reclined back on the bed.

Allen slid the condom over his erect penis and stretched beside Joy on the bed. "Do you want me, Joy? Tell me you want me, baby."

Joy sat on top of Allen's erection and squeezed her vaginal muscles as she moved up and down his shaft. "I've always wanted you, baby." They moved together as one until Joy's body quivered from her orgasm and she writhed with pleasure. Allen kept moving inside her for a few more minutes until he moaned and released himself.

He sat up, took the condom off, and put another one on. He bent Joy over the bed and entered her vagina from the back. "Damn, baby. I missed this. Oh, you feel so good."

"I missed you too, Allen," Joy moaned.

Each time he looked down at Joy's tattoo, he moved faster and faster inside her. They sighed with pleasure as they both climaxed again. Allen fell on the bed and Joy moved beside him. They stayed in bed holding each other. Neither one spoke. They reveled in the connection they had just made with each other again.

Joy quietly got up to take a shower. After a few minutes, Allen joined her. They washed each other's bodies, dried off and fell asleep naked, wrapped in each other's arms.

The next morning, Joy woke up when she heard Allen talking to someone. She turned around and saw him standing on the other side of the suite, talking on his cell phone.

"I know and I'm sorry, but I need to do this," he whispered.

He had a frown on his face as he listened to the other person talking.

"Sure, we'll see. I'll be in touch. Thanks, Anna." Allen hung up and stared out the window.

"Allen, is everything alright?" Joy asked. She could tell by his body language that something was wrong.

He returned to the bed. "Morning, beautiful." He kissed her after he got back in the bed.

"What's wrong?" Joy propped herself up on her elbow.

Allen sighed and rubbed his forehead. "I'm not going back to China. I'm taking a six-month leave of absence."

Joy sat upright. She knew Allen loved his job in China and enjoyed the work he was doing in international finance. She didn't want to be the cause of him giving up his dream career because she was pregnant with his children.

"Don't do that, Allen. I'll make sure to keep in touch with you about the twins. I'll send pictures, we can Skype, whatever it takes to keep you informed." Joy knew how hard he had worked on that project in Shanghai.

Allen touched Joy's stomach. "Babe, I don't have the same connection to the twins that you have. I mean, I don't know. It's hard to explain. All I know is I can't go back to China without you. I don't want to lose you again. I'm *not* going to lose you again. I love you too much."

Tears started rolling down her face. "I love you, too, Allen. Thank you, baby."

He hugged and kissed Joy then smiled. "Now that I'm no longer working, we need to check out of here. I can't afford to stay in a hotel room that costs four hundred dollars a night."

Joy covered her face and burst out laughing. "Let's go home, baby."

Joy fell into Allen's arms and closed her eyes as she thought about living with him full-time. She couldn't be happier. Then her cheerfulness came to a screeching halt when she remembered that Gabby and Nadia were staying with her. Gabby and Allen never got along so she knew this happy reunion wasn't going to be as joyful as she thought.

Chapter 32 ———————

The next day, Gabby took her two large suitcases and a cosmetics' bag downstairs and sat them by the front door while Nadia was napping. She went back upstairs to Joy's spare bedroom feeling somewhat defeated. During a meeting with her lawyer the day before Thanksgiving, he advised her to do something she didn't want to do because it meant going to court and spending a lot of money on attorney fees. She thought it over and realized she needed to do what he suggested to maintain control of the situation.

Nadia started waking up in her crib so Gabby picked her up, kissed her cheeks, and changed her diaper before she took her downstairs to get ready to leave. She wondered if she was doing the right thing, then realized she had no choice.

Joy and Allen entered the house through the front door. Gabby could tell by the way they were holding hands and smiling at each other that they had probably been screwing each other's brains out since they left Bea's house yesterday.

Joy entered the living room with a concerned look on her face. "Gabby, why are your suitcases at the front door?" When she had called Gabby from the hotel and told her about Allen's decision to stay and that he was moving in with her, Gabby didn't respond, which made Joy think her friend wasn't happy about it.

"Hi, Gabby! Look, don't leave because of me," Allen pleaded.

Gabby sighed. "It's not what you think. I'm not moving out because of you."

"Then why the suitcases?" Joy asked.

Gabby looked at Joy, then Allen. "I'm running late and need to get out of here. Can you put my luggage in my truck, Allen?"

Allen knew Gabby was trying to get rid of him and wondered what she was up to now. "Yeah. Where's the key?"

She handed him the key off the coffee table but as he turned to leave, she stopped him.

"Wait, Allen." She cleared her throat. "When Joy called me earlier about your decision to take a leave of absence to be with her, I was happy for both of you."

"Thanks, Gabby." Allen half smiled because he had doubts about them all being able to live under the same roof for the next six months. Even Joy was concerned about it.

"I'm glad you two found your way back to each other. For whatever reason, you make my girl happy and she deserves that." Gabby balled her fist and pointed it toward Allen's face. "If you hurt her again, you'll have to deal with me. I already talked to one of your brothers and he said he would kill anybody I wanted if the price was right."

Joy looked at Allen because she knew he hated it when people talked about his brothers' illegal activities.

Allen held Joy in his arms. "I respect that, Gabby, but I'm not going to hurt her again. The only way you'll get me away from her is in a body bag."

Joy's body shivered and chill bumps popped up on her flesh when Allen said that. A dreadful feeling overcame her and she felt like crying. She swallowed the hard lump that formed in her throat to hold back her tears.

"Good to know," Gabby laughed and hugged Allen.

He left to put Gabby's luggage in her vehicle.

"What's up with you?" Joy looked at Gabby suspiciously.

"Nothing, girl. I'm just trying to do things differently from now on."

"Wow! I see. So, where are you and Nadia going looking

so cute?" Joy sat down on the couch because she had to pee again.

"I'm going to Baltimore so Nadia can meet her father. I called him yesterday and he invited us to the Ravens game on Sunday. I agreed to stay for a week to see how he does with my baby before I approve any visitation agreements."

Joy was speechless. She leaned back on the sofa, not sure how to respond. For the past six months, Gabby had been lying through her teeth to keep Rayshawn away from Nadia and now they were spending a week in Baltimore with him. William's suicide had changed Gabby more than Joy realized.

Allen returned, gave Gabby her keys and smiled at Nadia who was staring at him.

"Thanks, Allen. Joy, in case you're wondering, I'm staying at the Hyatt Regency at the Baltimore Harbor and *not* with Rayshawn. Unlike *you*, I don't go back to what I once had. I'll call you later." Gabby waved goodbye and closed the door behind her.

Joy cringed at Gabby's underhanded remark about her and Allen. *That bitch hasn't changed that much,* Joy thought.

Gabby and Rayshawn had agreed to meet at the Hyatt Regency's restaurant, Bistro 300, at five o'clock. She was just pulling up to the hotel at five-forty when her cell phone started ringing. She knew it was Rayshawn and ignored it. She decided to call him back after she checked in and had her luggage taken to her room.

The valet parking attendant drove Gabby's Lexus to the garage after the bell-hop removed her luggage from the back. She put Nadia in her stroller, walked into the hotel lobby, and bumped into Rayshawn who was looking at his phone and not paying attention.

"Rayshawn!" Gabby yelled because he almost fell on top of Nadia's stroller.

People in the lobby turned to look at them.

Rayshawn caught his balance and smiled when he saw Gabby. "Oh, I'm sorry! What's up, Gabby? I was just calling you." Rayshawn tried to hug and kiss Gabby but she stuck her hand out for him to shake instead.

221

He got the message, shook her hand, then bent down to look at Nadia. "So, this is Nadia, huh. Hi, Nadia. I'm your daddy, the real one." He stared at his daughter and smiled. "She's beautiful, just like you, Gabby."

"I know. Can we meet you in the restaurant in thirty minutes? I need to check in and take my things to my room," Gabby said in an annoyed tone.

Rayshawn signaled for the concierge and within seconds, the man was standing in front of Rayshawn awaiting instructions.

"I have the VIP suite reserved for the next week. Can you put her luggage in there and bring the room key to me in the restaurant?" He gave the concierge a hundred-dollar bill.

"Yes, Mr. Robinson. We'll take care of it." The concierge had the bell-hop who unloaded Gabby's luggage follow him to the front desk.

Gabby was impressed with the way Rayshawn handled that for her.

"Come on, Gabby, let's get my daughter out of this cold lobby and get her something to eat. I know she's eating table food now, right?" Rayshawn smiled at her.

Gabby looked at Rayshawn apprehensively. She had gotten used to him cursing and bad-mouthing her, so she was shocked to see this caring side of him. "Some table food, but nothing fried."

As they stepped on the elevator, Rayshawn made a funny face and started talking in a baby's voice." Of course not. Her little stomach is too fragile for that."

Gabby rolled her eyes and frowned at the ugly face Rayshawn made.

They got off the elevator on the third floor. As soon as they entered the restaurant, the hostess approached them and said, "Welcome back, Mr. Robinson. I see you found your guests." She faced Gabby. "Would you like to leave the stroller and your coats in our cloak room?"

"Yes, thank you," Gabby replied as she removed their coats and hats and gave them to the hostess along with the stroller.

After the hostess left, Gabby held Nadia in her arms and avoided eye contact with Rayshawn. He stood in front of Gabby, smiling from ear to ear while he played with Nadia. Gabby's face was pinched and tense.

The hostess returned and looked at Nadia. "Oh, my! What a beautiful baby!"

"Thank you! She's my daughter, Nadia Rae," Rayshawn bragged.

The hostess smiled and said, "Awww, she looks just like her mother. Follow me to your private table, please."

When they sat down at their table, Rayshawn held his hands out for Nadia. Gabby reluctantly let him hold her, but she kept a close eye on him. Rayshawn expressed his condolences over William's death and told Gabby how disappointed Phyllis was when he told her she didn't need to testify because they were working things out themselves. Gabby couldn't help but laugh out loud because there was nothing else Phyllis could do to hurt her.

"How are you, Gabby? You don't seem as angry as you used to be," Rayshawn said as he watched Nadia play with a spoon.

"I've changed. I'm trying to be a better person," Gabby replied.

"Did you change enough to discuss visitation and reducing my child support payments? Or do we have to drag the lawyers in this again?" Rayshawn looked at Gabby uncertainly.

Gabby sighed. "How often would you like to see her and how much child support would you like to pay?" Gabby was curious about what he expected.

"I can fly here twice a month to see her off season and I'll have to wait until the schedule comes out for each season to let you know. During the summer, I want her to go on vacation with me and my sons for two weeks. Oh, and maybe alternate Thanksgiving and Christmas every other year."

"You can visit her twice a month in Maryland, on and off season. I'll continue to be with her until she's older and more comfortable being alone with you. And I'll think about the summer vacation. It's a possibility, but don't get your hopes up. We'll never be apart on Thanksgiving or Christmas so that's a definite no."

"It's a start. What about child support?" He swallowed hard waiting for her reply.

Gabby crossed her arms over her chest and scrunched her face. "One thing at a time, Rayshawn. Let's see how you do with visitation before we discuss reducing your child support." *He must think I'm a fool to give up fifteen thousand dollars a month. I'll fight him tooth and nail in court to hold on to every penny of that money as long as I can.*

"Okay, we'll talk about it again in a couple of months. I want to reduce it, but I also want her to be taken care of. You've done a great job with her. She's healthy and looks happy."

"Thank you." Gabby gave Rayshawn a phony smile to make him think she was agreeing with him when she wasn't.

"I'll call my lawyers Monday so they can take care of it," Rayshawn said.

"Okay and I'll let my lawyer know what to expect," Gabby replied.

"Now, that we got that ugly business taken care of, let's discuss us." Rayshawn sat Nadia in the high chair between them and reached over the table for Gabby's hand. "We're both single now so why don't we rekindle things and raise our girl together."

Gabby pulled her hand back. "Rayshawn, all the money in the world won't get me back in your bed. You served your purpose and now it's time for you to move on. If that's too hard for you to understand, we can leave now and deal with this in court."

Rayshawn looked at Nadia and thought about what Gabby said. "Naw, I'm good, but if you ever get that itch down there and you need somebody to scratch it for you, call me. I'll take care of you."

Gabby glared. "No, thank you. I have a vibrator and a pulsating shower head that'll do a better job than you've ever done."

Rayshawn reluctantly gave up on any hopes of getting back with Gabby as he regarded her from across the table with a defeated look on his face.

Chapter 33 ⸻

Maxine pulled into Trent's apartment complex the second Sunday in December to pick up the boys. This was their first weekend visit with their dad since he was released on house arrest. The agreement was for him to have the boys downstairs and ready to go at exactly 6:00 P.M. It was 5:45 so she turned the volume down on her radio, laid her head back, and waited for them to come downstairs. When she opened her eyes twenty minutes later, there was no sign of Trent or her boys so she turned off the engine and went inside to his apartment on the second floor.

She knocked and waited impatiently for Trent to answer. She became concerned when she didn't hear her sons' voices. Although they were small, they were also noisy, especially when they knew somebody was at the door.

Trent opened the door and froze when he saw her. "Oh, hi, Maxi. What are you doing here?"

Maxine rushed past Trent into his apartment with her eyes bulging, searching for her sons. "What do you mean? Where are the boys? You were supposed to meet me outside with them at six o'clock."

Trent closed the door and stared at Maxine as she searched around his apartment. "I left you a message on your cell phone to pick them up at my mother's apartment. She stopped by earlier and they wanted to go home with her."

"Oh, I didn't know." Maxine forgot to turn her cell phone

back on after church. Trent was trying to clean up before Maxine saw his clothes and dirty dishes on the sofa and coffee table they used to have in their family room.

"You don't have to do that, Trent. I had a feeling it wasn't going to be tidy in here." Maxine turned around to leave.

"Since you're here, can we talk?" He cleared his throat and looked down at the floor.

Maxine looked him up and down, then rolled her eyes. "Make it quick. I need to get the boys in bed for school tomorrow."

Trent threw the clothes he was holding back on the chair and put the dirty dishes in the sink. "Sure, I understand. We can sit at the dining room table." He pulled out a chair for Maxine, then he sat across from her, intentionally keeping his distance.

"I wanted to thank you again for joining us in counseling when you saw that the boys were uncomfortable with it. I know you didn't plan to do this with us and it's not easy for you." Trent cleared his throat again and rubbed his hands together nervously.

"Actually, I think it's helping all of us, but I think three times a week is too much for the boys. We should do one session during the week and another on the weekend," Maxine suggested.

"Sure, I'll change the schedule when we go back next week," Trent agreed.

"Whatever it takes to help you and our boys have a decent relationship. I know boys need their fathers." Maxine smiled at Trent. "Oh, and I see a difference in you, too."

"Thanks. I should've gone to counseling before I screwed up and lost my family. Now I'm just trying to right my wrongs as best I can." Trent stood up, went to the refrigerator, took out two bottles of water, and gave Maxine one.

Maxine looked Trent in his eyes. "Where did we go wrong, Trent? We loved each other for so long. Did you just stop loving me? Did you hate or resent me so much that you needed to hit me? Why?"

Trent sat beside Maxine. "I'm sorry. I never stopped loving you, but I didn't know any better. I honestly didn't know how to handle all the pressure I was dealing with at work and the bills piling up at home. I was wrong for taking it out on you."

"You *were* wrong. I knew how stressed you were and I wanted to help you, but you wouldn't let me." Maxine sighed and shook her head.

Trent reached out to hold Maxine's hand, but pulled back. "I know. I was trying to live somebody else's dream life. I watched all the partners in the law firm talk about their families, homes, private schools, and luxury cars and I thought that's what I was supposed to do, too. If I had it to do over..." Trent opened his bottle of water and emptied it in two gulps.

"What would you do differently?" Maxine turned to face him.

"I would've never built that house, leased those cars, or gotten so many credit cards, and I would've communicated with you about how hard life was for me instead of taking it out on you. And, when you told me you wanted to go back to work, I would've listened and supported your decision." Trent had tears in his eyes.

"It's too late now, Trent. I made mistakes, too. I should've left with the boys and stayed with my parents the first time you hit me." Tears streamed down Maxine's face.

They grew quiet as they processed what was just said. Trent stood up to throw his empty water bottle in the recyclables. Maxine got up to leave and Trent hugged her.

He looked down at her and said, "I'm sorry for hurting you, Maxi."

He bent his head and gently put his lips on hers. She responded by sticking her tongue in his mouth the way she used to do because it always got him excited. Trent relaxed as he let their tongues explore each other's mouths again. They stood in the kitchen hugging and kissing for a few minutes until he picked her up and carried her to his bedroom. He laid her on his bed, positioned his body beside her, and pulled her close to him until there was no space between. He pulled Maxine's skirt up and stuck his fingers in her underwear, touching her moist vagina. He slid his fingers inside her, moving in and out while she moved back and forward. She started moaning from the pleasure he was giving her. He kissed her lips to quiet her. Maxine lost all control as her body shook and she soaked Trent's fingers with her juices.

Trent removed her blouse and bra before he pressed himself on top of her and started sucking her breasts. After a few minutes, he sat up, squeezed her breasts together, alternating between licking, biting, and sucking them. They were breathing heavily and moaning. He removed his jeans, then started licking and kissing Maxine's stomach and waist. When he got to her pubic area, he stuck his tongue inside her while he used his fingers to massage her clitoris. Maxine used both her hands to grab the blanket on the bed and screamed as she came in his mouth. He sat on top of her as he stuck his stiff penis between her breasts. She sucked and licked the top of his head. Within minutes, Trent grunted and cried, "I'm ready to come!" He ejaculated between her breasts as his body buckled and fell on the bed. They lay side by side, panting and speechless.

A few minutes later, Trent went to the bathroom and brought Maxine some tissue to wipe her chest. She sat up and stared at him when she noticed him avoiding eye contact with her and acting nervous.

"What's wrong, Trent?"

He sat back on the bed with tears in his eyes. "You know I want my family back, Maxi. Where do we go from here?"

Maxine moved closer to Trent and sighed. "I'm not the same person I was when we were married. I don't know if you would be attracted to the person I've become. I don't care what other people think about me now. I only care about what makes me happy. I put myself first and as long as the boys have what they need and not what they want, I'm happy."

Trent turned away from Maxine. He prayed every day to get his wife back. Now that she was here, he didn't know how to act because he was still embarrassed and ashamed for the way he treated her.

"Will you look at me, please?" Maxine turned Trent's head to face her. "I know how you feel, Trent, and I do love you, but I don't want us to rush into anything. Let's continue family counseling and maybe spend some time together with and without the boys and see how things go from there. I can't promise you we'll reconcile."

Trent looked at her with hope in his eyes. "I understand and I'll do whatever you want, Maxi. If you give me another chance, I promise I'll spend the rest of my days loving you and making you happy."

Maxine half-smiled at Trent. She knew in her heart that he would never hit her again, but the damage had already been done. Although she was willing to attend counseling because of her sons, she wasn't sure if she wanted to be with him again and she knew her family and friends weren't going to be happy about them getting back together. For now, she wasn't going to stress herself over it; instead she was going to take it one day at a time and see what happened.

Chapter 34 ———————

Joy woke up Christmas morning to breakfast in bed. Allen stood holding a plate of grits, bacon, scrambled eggs, and biscuits on a bed tray while the *Motown Christmas* CD played softly in the background.

He smiled and said, "Merry Christmas, baby!"

Her heart melted. "Merry Christmas!" She sat up in bed. "Oh, it smells so good and you know I'm hungry. Let me wash up and I'll be right back."

"Okay." Allen sat the tray on the dresser and pulled a small gift box from his pocket. He slid it under his pillow and sat in a chair until Joy came back out.

Minutes later, Joy was back in the bed smelling fresh after a quick shower and clean nightgown. She arranged her pillows behind her back, then Allen put the bed tray over her lap and sat down again.

"Where's your food?" she asked before she started eating.

"I already ate, babe. It's almost ten o'clock." Allen laughed.

"Oh!" Joy felt bad for sleeping late and missing Christmas breakfast with Allen, but she was tired from getting up all night to use the bathroom and from the twins keeping her awake with their constant kicks and moving around.

While she ate breakfast, she and Allen talked about the dinner party they planned to have tonight with a small group of their close family and friends. Allen was having it catered so they could spend their time entertaining and not worrying about cooking. Joy had the house professionally cleaned and they had put up Christmas decorations earlier in the week to make the house feel festive for their guests.

"Thanks for breakfast. It was perfect." Joy yawned. "I'm ready to go back to sleep now."

Allen removed the bed tray and sat in on the dresser. "Before you do that, look under the pillow for your Christmas gift."

Joy's eyes widened. She threw the pillows on the floor one by one until she saw a neatly wrapped jewelry box. She tore the paper off, opened the box, and took out a beautiful 18-carat gold and textured charm bracelet with three charms on it.

Allen sat on the bed and looked at it with Joy. "I hope you like it."

"I love it!" Joy looked closer at the charms.

She smiled when she saw the blue and pink baby booty charms. During her monthly checkup last week, they had an ultrasound done and found out they were having a boy and a girl. Joy touched the third charm, a set of praying hands, and looked at Allen for an explanation.

"I'm not a religious person, but the praying hands are my way of asking God to cast his angels around my family, you and the twins, and to keep you safe when I'm not around to protect you."

Allen put the charm bracelet on Joy's wrist and kissed her again.

"Oh, Allen! I love it, baby. Thank you." She stared at the bracelet and smiled.

She asked Allen to get her purse off the dresser, then took out an envelope, and gave it to him. "This is your Christmas gift." He had always wanted to go to New York on New Year's Eve to watch the ball drop so she booked a room at the Marriott Marquis in Times Square. He could watch the festivities from their room or go downstairs with the crowd and be back in the hotel before he got too cold.

Allen's eyes grew bigger as he read the travel itinerary.

"Thanks! Aw man, this is nice. I can't wait to go to New York with you," Allen exclaimed. "I wanna show you something."

He removed his shirt and showed Joy his right bicep. She covered her mouth and gasped. Allen had a tattoo of a cross that covered his whole bicep. Inside the cross vertically was her middle name, Hope, and going horizontally was her first name, Joy. The letter *O* connected both names. Her heart pounded her chest as she looked at it.

"It's beautiful, Allen. Now, I know how you felt when you saw mine." She touched it and smiled. "When did you get it? Does it still hurt?"

"My brother took me to a shop in D.C. last week. It doesn't hurt anymore, but this shit was killing me for a few days; that's why I fell asleep on the couch a couple of nights. I didn't want you to see how much pain I was in." Allen lay on his side while Joy stared at his tattoo.

She let out a sigh of relief."I thought seeing the twins during the ultrasound freaked you out and you were having doubts about becoming a father."

"No, baby. If anything, it made me want to get ready for them. Damn, we're getting ready to have a son and a daughter in one shot." Allen whistled.

"Are you happy, Allen?" Joy touched his face.

"I couldn't be happier, baby." He kissed her. "Do you think you can stay awake long enough for me to show you how happy I am?"

Joy giggled, kissed Allen on his lips, and raised her night-gown to give him easy access to her naked body. They were kissing and caressing each other's bodies when they heard footsteps coming down the hall towards the bedroom. They looked at one another with raised eyelids because they knew Gabby and Nadia had stayed with Bea last night and wasn't expected back until the dinner party tonight.

Joy froze and Allen jumped up ready to attack.

"Joy, are you up here?" a male voice called out.

Allen looked at Joy accusingly. She pulled her nightgown down and shrugged her shoulders because she didn't know who it could be. They stared at the door and waited.

Dean entered her bedroom smiling with two stuffed animals in his hands. He stared at Allen, then Joy, and frowned. "Joy, what the fuck is going on here?"

"Who are you, mother-fucker?" Allen had both fists clenched ready to attack.

Joy's worst fear was coming true right before her eyes. Her husband and the love of her life in the same room - her bedroom at that. Joy looked at their faces and knew this wasn't going to end well. She rolled out of bed and put her arms around Allen's waist to calm him down.

"Allen, this is my soon-to-be ex-husband," Joy explained.

"Allen!" Dean yelled. "What is he doing here and what is this shit about me being your soon-to-be ex-husband. We're still married so why are you laying up in our home with another man?"

"Dean, I haven't seen you in two months. When we found out the twins weren't yours, I decided to end it and thought you felt the same way since I didn't hear from you. You need to leave. Allen and I are back together." Joy was so nervous, her teeth were chattering.

"You heard what she said, now, get out!" Allen ordered.

"I'm not going anywhere! This is my fucking wife and our home." He stepped closer to Joy, but Allen stood in front of her and blocked him. "I need to talk to my wife in private. Come here, Joy."

"Not gonna happen!" Allen spat.

Joy peeked around Allen and said, "Whatever you have to say to me, you can say in front of Allen. We have no secrets."

Dean glared at her. "Okay. I was hurt when I found out the babies weren't mine. I was in bad shape, drinking, depressed, just fucked up. I got arrested for a DUI and my firm got me off, but they ordered me to go away to an in-house alcohol treatment center. I was released late last night and came here as soon as I could."

"I've already filed for legal separation, Dean." Joy prayed that would make him leave.

234

"You heard her; now get the fuck out before I toss your ass out!" Allen demanded.

Dean pointed at Allen. "Fuck you! She's my wife!" Dean looked at Joy. "I know I handled things badly, but I had time to think this out. I love you and I want to adopt the twins and raise them as my own with you." He tried to give Joy the two puppy dog stuffed animals. "See, I got these for our twins for Christmas."

Allen smacked the stuffed animals out of Dean's hands and snatched him up by the collar. "I'm their father, not you, so get your bitch ass out of here before I hurt you."

Joy covered her belly and ran in the bathroom to get away from the fight she knew was going to happen.

Dean threw a punch at Allen, but he blocked it and pushed Dean back. He fell to the floor, but bounced right back up and went head first toward Allen's stomach. Allen shoved Dean's head, causing him to fall again. Dean tried to get up again, but this time, Allen used his fist and punched Dean's face with a right uppercut and then a left hook. Dean fell down and stayed there.

Joy ran out the bathroom. "Allen, stop! That's enough, baby!" She checked his hands and looked him over. "Are you alright?"

"I'm fine." He saw the nervous look on Joy's face and pulled her close to him. "I'm okay, baby. Don't worry. I don't want you and the twins upset."

"I'm your fucking husband, bitch! You should be worried about me, not some dead beat who left you and never looked back." Dean took out his handkerchief to wipe the blood that dripped from his nose and lips.

Allen released Joy from his arms, picked Dean up by his coat collar and dragged him down the steps. "She's more my wife than yours and don't you ever let me hear you call her a bitch again or I'll kill you my damn self."

Joy followed them down the steps with her heart in her throat.

Allen pulled Dean to his feet and shoved him toward the front door. "Get out! You walked in on me getting ready to make love to my woman!"

Dean glared at Joy and refused to budge.

Allen grabbed Dean's arm and forced him to the front door.

Dean fought and kicked every step of the way, but he was no match for Allen's strength. When Allen let Dean's arm go to open the front door, he ran back in the house toward Joy.

"Is this what you really want? You want to end our marriage to be with him! I love you, Joy." Dean tried to hug her but she stepped back.

"No! This marriage is over, Dean! I love Allen," Joy proclaimed.

Allen grabbed Dean by his collar and dragged him to the front door again.

Dean yelled, "This marriage isn't over until I say it is! Legally, those children are mine because you're still my wife no matter how many times he sticks his dick in you."

Allen threw Dean out of the house, closed the front door, and bolted all the locks. He walked to Joy and wrapped his arms around her when he saw her trembling. "Calm down, baby. It's over!"

Joy jumped when she heard Dean kick the door and scream, "This ain't over, bitch! I'll be back for you!"

Joy had a terrible feeling that something bad was going to happen. She knew how persistent Dean could be and how unwilling Allen was to share her with any other man. She hoped that once Dean calmed down, he would understand and stay away, but she had a gut feeling that it wasn't going to happen that way.

Chapter 35 ─────────

Later that evening, Joy and Allen sat in the living room talking with their guests after dinner.

Allen put his arm around Joy and said, "We want to thank each of you for joining us for Christmas dinner. I know you had better places to be on this special holiday, but you chose to share it with us and for that we're grateful."

"We should all be thanking you for that wonderful meal," Juan said in his thick Puerto Rican accent and then laughed. "So how does it feel to know you're having a son and a daughter? I can't stop thinking about it and I'm just their grandpa."

"As long as they're healthy, it doesn't matter to me, Poppy," Joy said, then smiled.

Allen cleared his throat. "I love it! Most of you already know this, but my mother died when I was young, but I was fortunate to have my older siblings, especially Tyesha and her twin brother, Tyrese."

Joy put her arm around Allen when she saw him getting emotional.

"They were fifteen when I was born and the only ones still at home when she died. They stepped up and became surrogate parents to me. I'm the man I am today because of them. I owe them everything because my life could've gone in another direction." Allen bit his bottom lip to hold back his tears. "So, when I found out we were having twins, I was ecstatic, but when I found out we were having a boy and a girl, like Tyesha and Tyrese, it touched me in a way you wouldn't believe. It's like the highest compliment to the people who raised me. I hope I'm half the parent to them that you two were to me."

Tyesha and Tyrese went to Allen and Joy and hugged them. There wasn't a dry eye in the living room. Joy excused herself when she heard the doorbell.

Maxine stepped away to answer her cell phone when she saw Trent's number. The boys were spending Christmas night with him and she wanted to make sure they were okay.

Joy opened her front door and instantly regretted not looking through the peephole first. Dean was standing there with a gun pointed in her face. Although Allen had changed the locks earlier, Dean had found a way back in her house. She stepped back into the house until her back hit the wall. Dean kept the gun pointed at her while he closed and locked the door.

"What are you doing, Dean?" Joy asked as fear shot through her body.

Dean put his face close to hers and whispered, "Where is he?"

She gagged when she smelled the vodka on his breath. "Gone," Joy lied.

Dean turned his head toward the living room when he heard people laughing and talking. He grabbed her arm, pointed the gun at her and walked toward the sounds. "Be quiet," he whispered through clenched teeth.

Their laughter was interrupted by Bea's screams. "Joy! Nooooo!" She ran toward Joy, but Juan stopped her.

Everyone turned to look at Bea, then Joy. She stood at the entrance of the living room with Dean while he aimed the gun at her right temple. Tears streamed down her face as she looked at the terrified expressions on everyone's faces.

"Oh, my God, Trent! Dean has a gun pointed at Joy," Maxine cried into her phone.

"Let her go! I'm going to kill you!" Allen charged toward them, but Tyrese pulled him back.

"Maxine, get off that phone. I should shoot you for introducing me to your friend!" Dean yelled.

Maxine gasped before she hung up and sat beside Gabby who was glaring at Dean.

Trent heard Dean threaten Maxine then the line went dead. He put the boys' coats on and dropped them off at his mother's apartment. He was risking his freedom because he was still under house arrest, but he needed to get to Maxine. Since she wasn't answering her phone, he needed to try to remember where Joy lived. He had picked the boys up from Joy's house a couple of weeks ago when Maxine and the boys were visiting her. He prayed he still remembered how to get there.

Dean pointed his gun at Allen. "I came here to kill you, mother-fucker! You took everything from me! I love my wife and these children should be ours, not yours!" Dean spat.

Joy tried to turn her head because the smell of vodka coming from Dean's mouth made her nauseous. She choked back the vomit that rose up in her throat before Dean used his left hand to turn her head back around.

"What do you want, Dean?" Juan asked. "I'll give you whatever you want, just don't hurt my daughter."

Dean started pushing the barrel of the gun in Joy's temple. "I want my wife back, but I know that'll never happen. You looked at me earlier today like I didn't matter and that hurt, Joy."

"Why are you doing this, Dean? I'll go with you if that's what you want, just don't hurt anybody," Joy wept.

"No, bitch! I don't want you anymore. Now, I'd rather shoot you than fuck you!" Dean's nostrils flared and sweat ran down his face.

"It's me you want, man. Take me! Okay?" Allen pleaded.

"No, I want you to feel my pain! Didn't you say she was your wife this morning? You're going to lose your wife and children, just like I lost mine!" He removed the gun from Joy's temple and pointed it at her stomach.

Bea was screaming and crying hysterically.

"Noooo!" Joy covered her stomach with her arms and turned her back to Dean.

"Turn around, bitch!" Dean yelled as he forced Joy back

around and put the gun back to her head.

"Allen, when he shoots me, do everything you can to save our babies," Joy cried.

"No!" Allen tried to run to Joy but it took both Tyrese and Tyesha to hold him back.

"I'm tired of holding this gun. It's time to say goodbye, Joy." Dean switched the gun to his left hand and shook his right arm.

Joy quickly punched Dean in his nose with her left fist and starting striking him, fighting for her life. He blocked her punches, grabbed a handful of her long hair and pulled her close to him. He shoved the barrel of the gun in her mouth and she immediately calmed down.

Everybody started screaming and praying for Joy.

Gabby took off her Jimmy Choo shoes and threw them at Dean. "Put that gun down and fight one on one like a real man!"

Dean ducked, removed the gun from Joy's mouth, and pointed it at Gabby.

"I'm sorry I didn't love you the way you wanted, Dean," Joy said to distract him.

Dean turned the gun in Allen's direction. "It's always been about him! The first time I fucked you, I saw his name tattooed on your ass! When we got married, you actually said your vows to him while looking me in my goddamn face! But it didn't end there. When we went to the doctor's office and discovered the twins were his and not mine, that FUCKED me up! They committed my ass because of you."

"I'm sorry..." Joy's entire body trembled.

Trent rode up and down Joy's neighborhood and stopped when he saw Maxine's minivan in the driveway. He parked on the street and ran to Joy's house. He peeked in the living room window and saw everybody watching Joy and Dean, then he went to the front porch, got the house number, and called 911 on his cell phone.

Inside, Dean started waving the gun all around Joy's head. "Shut up! When I finally get it together and come back to you, I walk in on him getting ready to fuck you in our bed!" Dean hit

Joy in her head with the barrel of the gun.

She flinched from the pain and tried to rub her head, but Dean smacked her hand away.

Everybody started crying and screaming.

"That's it!" Allen broke free from Tyesha and Tyrese and ran toward Dean.

"No, Allen! Please don't!" Joy looked at Allen and put both hands on her belly.

Allen stopped in his tracks. He wanted to kill Dean, but he didn't want Joy or the twins to get hurt in the process.

Trent knew he couldn't wait for the police when he heard loud screams coming from inside the house. He went to the basement, used his coat to break the door's glass, opened the basement door, and tip-toed upstairs. He entered the kitchen and stood where everybody could see him except Dean and Joy. Trent looked around for something to hit Dean with, but feared the gun would go off and wound Joy or somebody else.

"It's going to be okay, baby! Look at me." Allen smiled to reassure her.

Joy could tell by Allen's tone that something had changed. She realized somebody else was in the house when everybody started looking past her and Dean. She was starting to feel hopeful that they could all get out of this unharmed.

Trent moved his hands up and down and pointed to the floor for everybody to get down.

"Hey, man, since you're serious about this, I want everybody to get on the floor in case bullets start flying. You only came here to hurt me and Joy so let's leave all these innocent people out of this." Allen gave Dean a convincing smile.

Bea, Juan, Gabby, Maxine, Tyesha, and Tyrese got on the floor as Allen and Trent directed them.

"Shut up, mother-fucker! I wish I had enough bullets to kill all of you, but my whore of a wife will do." Dean pressed the gun against Joy's temple.

"I wish somebody could pull Joy away from you while I whipped your ass. How does that sound, man?" Allen was looking at Dean but talking to Trent.

Trent showed Allen he understood by using his arms to show how he was going to pull Joy away from Dean while Allen attacked Dean.

"You not stupid enough to try something while I have this gun to her head," Dean teased.

"Not at all. Can I give her one last kiss before you do this?" Allen looked at Dean with pleading eyes.

"Fuck no! The only person kissing her is me." Dean lowered the gun to his side and kissed Joy on her lips.

Joy turned her head and vomited. Trent ran out of the kitchen, pulled her away from Dean, and shoved her in a corner, shielding her body with his. Seconds later, Gabby leaped from the floor and joined Allen as they ran toward Dean in an attempt to get the gun from him. As Allen, Dean and Gabby fought for control of the gun, a shot was fired. Joy turned around in time to see Dean fleeing the house. She knew something went terribly wrong when she heard everybody screaming and saw a large pool of blood on the floor. Everything went black as she sank to the floor.

To be continued in...*Where Did We Go Wrong Again?*

Visit www.MonicaMathisStowe.com for release date and details.